The SHATTERED PORTRAIT

ALSO BY ALICE QUINN

Belle Époque Mysteries

The Crumpled Letter

Rosie Maldonne's World

Queen of the Trailer Park

Queen of the Hide Out

Queen of the Masquerade

Every insane man is considered a genius, is he not? Yet if a woman considers herself one, she is declared insane!

—Gabriella Fletcher, *The Shattered Portrait*

The Lérins Isles, which to the east close the Gulf of Cannes and separate it from the Gulf of Juan, look themselves like two operatic islands placed there for the satisfaction and delight of the invalid and winter sojourners.

—Guy de Maupassant, *Afloat*

A banker is a fellow who lends you his umbrella when the sun is shining but wants it back the minute it begins to rain.

—Mark Twain

1

AN ALTERCATION

Cannes, France
January 1888

The city of Cannes sparkled, hosting an endless array of parties, galas, and concerts for the crowned heads of Europe who arrived in troves for the mild Mediterranean winters. A newcomer could never have guessed the tragedies being played out behind closed doors—tragedies caused by the recent real estate crisis that had ripped through the town and its storied fortunes. The press sometimes reported on it, but with rather couched words.

As for us at the Villa les Pavots, our vibrant and busy lifestyle was mostly sheltered from the shipwreck, for this economic downturn affected those who had tried to speculate, which was not the case for us.

My mistress, Lola, who had just entered her twenty-fifth year, often worried, however, saying that if all her paying "visitors" were to go bankrupt, we might certainly feel the effects.

But all she was really concerned about was her dear Maupassant. When would he come to Cannes? When would she see him again?

Since first meeting the famous writer Guy de Maupassant nearly four years ago, Lola had read everything she could find by the man: his chronicles, his poetry, his novellas, and every single extract of his writing that had been serialized in the newspapers.

I was a little jealous of the passion she held for his work.

I would have been thrilled had she noticed that I, the Honorable Miss Gabriella Fletcher, just like the great Maupassant, wrote too. Indeed, my first novel, *The Crumpled Letter*, had been published! But that would have served little to no purpose. Literature had nothing to do with Lola's keen interest in Maupassant's writing. I was convinced she had deep feelings for him—though she would never have admitted to them.

And I myself felt a definite attraction toward Lola. Yet these emotions were equally concealed. Although I was now approaching my fortieth birthday, I withheld my feelings as an adolescent would.

One morning, in front of the tall windows leading out onto the balcony, Rosalie had laid out a bread basket with butter and jam alongside a large coffeepot and a jug of fresh milk.

The whole house shook, for a great deal of improvements to the building were underway, and the noise made in the mornings—including deafening hammer blows and loud singing from our Italian masons—filled the entire villa, often greatly disturbing our sleep.

Anna, the young orphan whom Lola had taken under her wing four years earlier, was already sitting at the breakfast table, eating alone.

She was dressed simply but elegantly in a pale robe with a light-pink shawl. Now fifteen and entering womanhood, she had become somewhat churlish and refused to wear anything but pink. Of course, it didn't help matters that our dear friend Paul Antoine Isnard de la Motte had decreed that this hue was Anna's color. Being rather effeminate in nature, he liked to be known as the authority on Parisian fashions. He was even on familiar terms with the king of pastel-tinted muslins himself, Jacques Doucet.

As he watched me approach, Sherry, our beloved cat, jumped down from Anna's knees to come and greet me, rubbing against my ankles. I stepped over the ever-increasing pile of papers and books that were yet to find a home on our shelves and joined Anna.

Lola stepped out of her bedchamber, which adjoined the living room. She, too, was dressed and ready to take on the day. She was wearing one of her favorite "professional outfits"—a magnificent blood-red dress of high-quality silk, embroidered with purple flowers, that skimmed her thighs, complete with a massive orange bow resting on her shoulder like a monstrous butterfly.

Although the décolletage didn't plunge as much as those on some of her other pieces, she still looked to be dressed for an evening out rather than for preparing to start her daily routine.

Her minuscule waist, unrelentingly squeezed into her corset, made it difficult for her to eat breakfast. She didn't even sit down to join us.

"Maupassant is coming down from Paris," she announced with gaiety. "I'm going to meet him at the train station."

"He certainly gets around," I said. "We don't know whether he's coming or going. One minute he's in Étretat, then in Paris."

"Can I come with you, Lola? Please?" asked Anna.

"Of course! I've no doubt he'll be delighted to see you again," replied Lola. She turned to me and continued. "He doesn't appear to be at all well at the moment. Wouldn't you agree, Miss Fletcher? He is a mere shadow of the man he was back in December." She sighed before brightening once more. "You will join us, too, won't you?"

I had difficulty hiding my annoyance but agreed, letting out a small groan despite myself.

After breakfast, we set off at a quick pace down the hill from Les Pavots toward town. The air was crisp, and Lola congratulated herself on having had the foresight to wear a fur cape around her shoulders. We climbed the open staircase leading to the footbridge overlooking the station. At that moment, the train drew into the platform, its brakes emitting a piercing scream.

As the steam and smoke dissipated, we recognized the silhouette of Maupassant as he stepped down from the train. Lola waved to catch his attention.

He sported a fine top hat and a rather somber expression. His outfit was, as usual, tailor-made, and he held a silver-capped cane, which he used with a certain disdain to move folks out of his path.

He was followed by two equally well-clothed fellows, but they must have been hired help, for they remained a few paces behind him. He also had his trusted valet with him, who was occupied with unloading his master's enormous pile of trunks.

"What did I tell you, Miss Fletcher?" exclaimed Lola. "It's always such a delight to come down to the station. What sights we are always met with!" She pointed. "Look at that man there. That's the banker, Henri Cousin!"

"The man who was constructing all those new homes out on Boulevard de la Foncière?"

"That's right! I believe he's very clever, indeed. He became extremely rich selling real estate to investors to whom he'd lent the money himself."

"And how do you know all this?"

She smiled and glanced in the direction of Anna to ensure that the young girl could not overhear us. "I follow the fortunes of these men quite closely, you understand. He was the one who sold the plot of land on which my Eugène built Les Pavots."

Henri Cousin was a mature gentleman of around sixty years of age. He was thin and neat with bushy eyebrows and a severe regard partially hidden behind gold-rimmed spectacles.

"He doesn't seem particularly accommodating, does he?" I said.

Lola appeared untroubled by my impression. "When one's juggling millions, I suppose one might be a little on the austere side. He has a reputation for bringing ruin upon his contemporaries, for he is one of those men who deals with the boredom of his own life by destroying the livelihoods of others."

Out of nowhere, a man carrying a heavy basket of produce threw down his wares and rushed toward Cousin. Fists clenched, he hollered in a faltering voice, "I-I'll k-kill you, you piece of f-filth! You've absolutely r-ruined me!"

It was clear he was under the influence of liquor. Cousin held out his cane and tripped the fellow, causing him to stumble to the ground. Before two nearby police officers could intervene, Cousin struck the man twice on the back for good measure.

Not wishing to miss the next part of this exhilarating scene, we rushed down the staircase at the other side of the bridge and passed a cart belonging to the Faisan Doré—a local food and wine merchant—positioned just outside the main entrance to the station.

As we made our way under the glass roof, we noticed that the attending officers were continuing the banker's work by kicking the miscreant on the ground in his abdomen. I felt it an overreaction of the cruelest kind.

By now quite magnanimous, Cousin declared, "Leave it now, Officers. I know this man. He works for the Faisan Doré. I'm afraid he's rather fond of the odd tipple and doesn't know his own mind half the time."

"Do you intend to press charges, Monsieur Cousin?"

"Not at all. If I were to press charges against every person who feels I am to blame for his financial distress, I would spend my days doing nothing else. Poor soul. I have enough people lining up to take me to court without my adding yet more still."

Lola was so taken by the spectacle that she startled when a voice whispered in her ear, "Why, hello there, *Belle Amie*! How kind of you to welcome me. And you too, Miss Fletcher." Maupassant then turned toward Anna and placed his thumb and index finger gently on her chin. "Look at you. Even you have come!"

This patronizing gesture irritated our young friend, and she freed herself from his gentle grasp and stormed off to be by herself. It was clear we would no longer be allowed to treat her as a child.

However, Lola's face lit up as soon as she heard the writer's words. She would never admit to wanting more than friendship from Maupassant, but every time she saw him, her day certainly brightened.

"Guy, don't call me that! I have nothing in common with that monster of a character of yours," she said, pretending to sulk.

"But you do! For you have fire in your belly, my dear."

She shrugged and smiled, giving him a friendly nudge with her parasol. "Where did you come from? We were distracted by the scene here."

"Yes, I saw that. I was thankful for it, too, for it allowed me to pass through the crowds unnoticed. I have had quite enough of being greeted by throngs of admirers every time I make an appearance at this station. This fellow did me quite the favor."

"I simply adore coming down here to meet you off the train. There's always some quarrel or other to entertain!"

"Here I was thinking you came to admire the beauty of my mustache. What was it all about, in any case?"

"So many of the locals have lost everything in the real estate crisis, and Cousin has a lot to answer for. That was him reaping what he sowed, as they say." As she spotted the man with the exaggeratedly distinguished look following Maupassant, she leaned forward to speak to him. "How are you, François?"

With pinched lips, François Tassart hissed, "I'm just about managing, thank you."

The writer's valet had never taken much of a liking to Lola, whom he believed to be far too improper, particularly in her attitude toward his master.

One of his most important missions, it seemed he believed, was to protect the privacy of Maupassant, especially when his employer put pen to paper in the mornings. Lola had once dared to ignore his orders and had insisted on interrupting Maupassant during one of his writing sessions. François had never forgiven her for it. It was as if he imagined that Lola would, in some way, lead to his master's downfall. He was wrong, however, for Maupassant needed no help in this matter.

"François," said the writer, "would you be so kind as to go ahead to the Continentale Villa with my belongings, please? I won't be back for luncheon, for I will go directly to see my family following my meetings."

After everything had been sorted, we walked away slowly, listening to the catcalls of a few children as the worker from the Faisan Doré laboriously climbed up onto his cart.

As for the banker, he looked to be making his way toward an office building on the corner of Rue d'Antibes and Rue de la Vapeur.

Maupassant looked upon Lola with delight, as if breathing in her very vitality. It was true he had lost a fair amount of weight, and neither Lola nor I dared to ask after his health, fearing bad news.

With trepidation, he said, "My brother is faring rather poorly, I'm afraid. He is suffering from the most terrible convulsions. My mother has asked me to find him some sort of home where he might enjoy some respite. And on that subject . . . I was just wondering. Cousin . . . is he the banker who invested heavily in the Grand Jardin sanatorium out on the Île Sainte-Marguerite? I believe there's a certain Dr. Vidal who is in charge there. I am to meet him while I am here."

"Yes, come to think of it. There are rumors about that place . . . ," Lola said, her voice trailing off. Shaking her head, she said, "Well . . . I don't give much credence to rumors, in general."

But the sudden view of the port seemed to drive such concerns from Maupassant's mind. His face became serene, and his stride lengthened as he marched now with vigor toward the sea. Lola trotted alongside him, her arm entwined with his. She had no intention of letting go, particularly as they were attracting so much attention from passersby. The writer was very easily recognizable. This was Lola's way of proclaiming

to the world that she was intimate with the man: that well-to-do gentlemen did not fear being seen with her in broad daylight and that she
walked among some of the highest ranks of society.

We accompanied Maupassant as far as the quayside, where his boat,
the *Bel-Ami*, was docked. It was a stylish keelboat that must have been
at least thirty feet long. Standing in front of this gem of the ocean,
watching as it glistened in the morning sun, its happy owner appeared
not only to be overcome with pride but somewhat recovered in health.

2

READING ROOMS OF A SPECIAL NATURE

After bidding Maupassant farewell, we walked the length of the Allées until we reached the Rue du Bivouac.

Lola was still too early for an appointment with a client at her dear friend Madame Alexandra's reading rooms, so we headed back down to the waterfront to spend some time with her younger brother, Mario. He was supposed to be busy sealing the hull of a ship, but he was pleased to take a break and talk with us.

We looked out onto the ocean, and Lola appeared unable to draw her gaze away from the magnificence of it. After a while, we said our hurried goodbyes and moved across the dockers' yard alongside the Eglise du Bon-Voyage. I noticed that Lola glanced back to have a last look at the nearby islands as they shimmered in the now-blinding sunlight. She must have been wondering why every time her eyes were drawn to this scenery, it felt almost painful to witness its beauty.

The establishment managed by Madame Alexandra was rather particular and a concept that hadn't existed long in these parts. Born of a world of cabarets and brothels, Madame Alexandra had noted that certain clients felt bored at the ease of such debauchery. So on the first floor of her boutique was a standard bookseller's shop—perhaps with more than its share of much-talked-of and even scandalous titles, including

Nana and *Madame Bovary*. But hidden from sight and just behind the counter, a staircase led to the reading rooms on the second floor. This staircase was only made available to select clientele.

I had never ventured upstairs, but Lola has described to me the decor and ambiance.

Finely dressed ladies would take tea on an array of sumptuous chaise longues in a large lounge. From there, corridors led to secret rooms with elegant partitions between them. And most importantly as far as Lola was concerned, the cakes and biscuits were on the house. These women would meet with gentlemen who were seeking a certain kind of adventure, and the men were more than willing to compensate the ladies—for everyone needs a means of survival in this cruel world. These meetings would more often than not terminate in one of the bedchambers made conveniently available.

Nothing could be more exciting for a gentleman of good breeding than to play this game of conquests and seductions. A hesitant widow or divorcée could not be more exquisite—although none were made fools of, for this game was understood by all who participated. And it was also in this kind of place that known working girls—famous actresses in the main—might be approached by dukes and princes.

When times were hard, Lola would come here to fill her purse, and unfortunately, this occurred often. But she felt safe in the reading rooms, and she dreamed of happening upon a stable lover, a true protector. The city of Cannes, however, was far from conducive to this kind of arrangement, with those in possession of the greatest fortunes only passing through during the winter months, like swallows. However, she could be sure to encounter the same gentlemen from one year to the next.

As Lola later recounted to me, Madame Alexandra sat down with her to partake of a pot of tea while Lola awaited the arrival of her client who had, it seemed, been detained. The lounge room was almost empty. This time of the day was so rarely busy.

"I learned what happened to Eugène. My poor girl, you must be bereft."

Lola failed to understand, for her former great love, Eugène, had left her four years earlier. This could not be what Madame Alexandra was alluding to. "What are you speaking of?"

"You mean you don't know? Why, they're talking of little else in town! The de Brévilles have requested that the mayor organize a commemorative service for all the French soldiers killed in action during the conflicts in Madagascar."

"My Eugène? But he's still a boy tied to his mother's apron strings! Dead in combat? It cannot be!" Lola had a brief moment in which her heart pounded with grief at the thought of her first love having fallen. Her Eugène—the man who had so cruelly abandoned her after having promised the world.

"It is said that he died of dysentery. But he was on the battlefield, nonetheless. That much is true."

"Poor Eugène . . . The only reason he went out there was because his parents were blackmailing him to keep him away from me. Well! Perhaps they now believe it would have been preferable to allow him to have his way with Lola Deslys rather than die for the homeland. Wouldn't you agree?"

Madame Alexandra snorted. "I'm sure that's not the case at all. These people have hearts of stone. They would rather see him dead than dishonored. In any case, Mayor Gazagnaire was hesitant because, although the official reasoning behind this conflict was that we disagreed with the Madagascan government, the truth is we've been fighting the English out there. The mayor knows many of the winterers hail from across the channel, so he has had the fine idea of naming the event a 'peace ceremony.' That way, we can honor all fallen soldiers from all sides."

"That Gaza!"

"He is a clever soul. The service is set to take place in front of the music kiosk on the main square, and then people will be invited to enjoy refreshments inside the town hall. They needed to choose somewhere neutral. The hope is that they will be able to collect enough funds to assist those families who have lost a dear one. The patronesses of the event have set up a bursary."

"I absolutely must contribute something. I mean . . . it was my Eugène! He helped me get my foot on the ladder, to aim higher in life."

"Are you saying this in jest? Those women would never accept your money."

"It's good money, even if it is mine. I will find a way." Lola looked briefly over to the carriage clock on the grand mantelpiece. "My bedfellow is running rather late, is he not?"

"He? Ah, of course! I haven't yet told you. It isn't a *fellow* this time. It's a lady!"

"A woman? But I won't do that! What would ever give you that idea?"

"I was quite surprised, too, but you have nothing to lose, do you? She specifically asked for you. She is a woman of high rank but with a questionable reputation. She asked that I arrange a "group situation" for her here once, but that would be a step too far for my liking. Perhaps she will ask you about that, but I don't want it here."

A lady suddenly appeared in the corridor. She was outfitted in a white percale dress—as if she'd just come from a game of lawn tennis—and she wore a hat created by none other than Madame Camoux, the milliner who had hired Lola as a child. A thick lace veil with cream-colored polka dots partly hid her features.

She glided toward Lola, and when she was but a few steps away, Lola was surprised to recognize her. For there stood Lady Sarah Clarence, my former mistress and lover.

The woman who had shattered my heart. I had pointed her out to Lola on several occasions. But why had she asked to meet with Lola? What might she be plotting?

3

SOMETHING VENAL THIS WAY COMES

Lady Sarah gave Lola the barest of nods but refused to sit down and enjoy tea with the two women, although this was the usual custom before heading to the bedchambers.

She walked slowly but assuredly down one of the corridors and beckoned Lola to follow her. In doing this, it became clear that she knew the place well. She must have been a very frequent client, indeed, for the rabbit warren was not easy to navigate. How did she know which room to enter? Had it all been prearranged?

Lola looked back at Madame Alexandra with resignation and sighed heavily at having been ordered to follow Lady Sarah, who, she felt, had acted in an exceedingly haughty manner. The truth was, however, that she felt incredibly anxious at the mere thought of a tête-à-tête with a woman who had allowed me to suffer so. She wondered what Sarah could possibly want with her.

She understood that sapphic love was quite common among the Parisian courtesans and could even be considered fashionable. For many of these women, having a "female companion" was considered a well-earned rest. Some of the rags wrote about it quite a bit, which allowed courtesans to benefit from the free publicity. It was for this reason that they often felt no shame in displaying themselves with their lovers.

Lola was, nevertheless, determined to refuse carnal knowledge of any sort with Lady Sarah. She would not have done that to me. She would also abstain from any kind of relations where more than two participants were required. That kind of practice had never been to her tastes.

In fact, Lola has always been rather bourgeois in terms of her sensual leanings. Although she has never been successful in pursuing a monogamous loving relationship, she has always been most sincerely willing. But destiny has always decided otherwise. She isn't priggish, as a rule—she simply makes it a point of honor to choose with whom she shares a bed.

Of course, I wasn't privy to this episode until much later, when Lola would decide to confide everything to me. Despite this, I cannot be completely assured of what did or didn't occur between them that day. Nothing can guarantee that Lola revealed the entire truth. I understand her sensibilities all too well, and she is capable of sparing me if she knows it may hurt.

From what I later learned, Lady Sarah stood in front of the dressing table, lifted up her veil, and removed her Camoux hat, throwing it onto the bed. She then turned to face Lola, staring at her inquisitively.

A shiver ran down Lola's spine. She felt very ill at ease. She had seen something wild in Lady Sarah's eyes. A feline spark. So this was it. Lady Sarah was the cat, and Lola had to try her utmost not to become the mouse. This was to be a battle of wits, and she felt it keenly.

Lady Sarah approached her, her pace slow but deliberate. She pulled gently on a curl that was nestled in the nape of Lola's neck. Lola waited with bated breath.

"So, it's you?" said Lady Sarah.

Just those few words, whispered in a husky voice and with that English accent, troubled Lola greatly.

She trembled and muttered weakly, "Yes. It's me." She then added, surprised by her own response, "It's me what?"

"It's you who ravished the heart of the woman of my life," whispered Lady Sarah, leaning closer toward her, her mint-fresh breath caressing Lola's face.

Lola closed her eyes. She felt dizzy.

"What do you want from me? Why did you insist on seeing me?"

"You're quite the venal little thing, Mademoiselle . . . *Deslys*, isn't that right?"

It was almost as if she had difficulty uttering the words. She spat out her name as if it were an insult. Lola could sense the heights from which Lady Sarah looked down upon her.

However, Lola was more than practiced when it came to social humiliation. She stepped back.

"What do you want? If it's about finding out about Miss Fletcher because you miss her or you want her back, then you will fail. I don't meddle in the business of my friends. You must address her directly."

Lady Sarah laughed, but it had a false air.

"You read far too many of those romance novels, my dear. Miss Gabriella? Want her back? You must be quite out of your mind."

"Yet not a minute ago, she was the woman of your life? I believe you have lost your senses. You are desperate to know my connection to Miss Fletcher."

"You must be in the habit of thinking others enjoy the same cheap sentiments as you do."

"Oh, I see. The sentiments of ladies such as yourself are more noble than those solely inspired by love."

Now enraged, Lady Sarah screeched, "What do you know of love? You sell pleasure! What do you know of passion, of sacrifice . . . of the suffering of love? What do you know of torment and jealousy? You're far too busy finding new ways to maintain loyalty among your clients. You need them to be as faithful as dogs, I imagine."

"I am wasting my time here with you. Perhaps you only wish me to speak to Miss Fletcher of our meeting so that she suffers all the more?

So that you might mock her somehow? Is that your aim? What a waste of your money, for you will still have to pay for this room and the time spent here. Madame Alexandra will insist on that. I, however, don't want a single sou from you. I can give you no form of satisfaction. Of that, I am more than certain." Lola headed for the door. "You'll simply have to continue to torture yourself, wondering whether Miss Fletcher and I are—"

"Stop that!"

Lola gripped the door handle and added, "What is more, I will never speak of this meeting. Your wealth hasn't helped you a jot this time, has it?"

These last words appeared to hurt Lady Sarah, whose expression changed rapidly. She now looked anxious. "Pray, don't leave!"

Lola let go of the handle. "Ah! So you're going to let me in on the point of all this? I will venture to say that you're a little late in coming forward. You have waited four years before expressing yourself on the subject of Miss Fletcher. If you truly loved her, you would have reacted much quicker. So unburden yourself now. Why have you brought me here?"

Lola marched across the room and sat down on a cane chair adorned with light-brown velveteen cushions. Lady Sarah remained standing.

She spoke in such a low whisper that Lola had to ask her to repeat herself.

"I need your services," she said more loudly.

"What services? I won't engage with you in that bed. You must know that."

Lady Sarah dismissed Lola's remark with a wave of her hand.

"I'm certain it's something saucy," Lola continued, laughing nervously.

Now irritated, Lady Sarah said, "It was you who assisted Maria Alexandrovna with her little problem that time, was it not?"

Lola knew that in high society, news traveled—hushed messages whispered into eager ears. Lady Sarah was referring to a priceless earring that had belonged to the crown of England. Grand Duchess Maria Alexandrovna had lost it while sporting it in one of these very beds, and Lola had not only found it, but returned it safely. She had kept her word and not spoken of it since, nor would she speak of it to Lady Sarah now.

"I don't even know the woman. Who is she?"

Lady Sarah seemed satisfied with this response yet continued as though Lola had replied in the affirmative.

"I need the services of someone who can be discreet. Someone quite fearless, yet who knows how to hold her tongue."

"And you thought of me? Goodness! I've gone up in the world! A minute ago, I was . . . what did you say? 'Quite the venal little thing'? And now I am supposed to have all these qualities you mention?"

Lady Sarah's cheeks flushed upon hearing Lola's sarcastic tone. "And why can't a person be all those things?" Lady Sarah offered.

Lola stood, amused by this turn in the conversation. "There you are! Back to your true self. And as quick as lightning too!"

Not wanting to make another false move, Lady Sarah wrung her hands. "Allow me to explain. You must understand that this isn't easy for me."

"You mean it isn't easy to hide your disgust when it comes to little things like me? Yes, I understand how hard that must be. And we little things are overly curious, too, on top of all our other faults. I can't wait to discover what you have to tell me."

Lady Sarah picked up a bell on the dressing table and rang it. The curiosity Lola had just spoken of was now very much piqued. Light footsteps could be heard nearing. Lady Sarah opened the door and whispered something to one of Madame Alexandra's valets, who nodded, then left.

They waited for several long minutes in silence. Lola was just about to protest when, finally, the young man returned with writing materials—paper, ink, and a quill—and placed them on the dressing table.

Without thanking him, Lady Sarah escorted him back out the door, then turned, sat at the table, and set about writing a contract, which she made Lola sign. My mistress was required to write her name under a statement that said something to the effect that she was to never repeat a word of the conversation that was about to take place.

Lola signed without posing a single question, for the whole act, in her view, was quite pointless. She would speak to whom she saw fit about Lady Sarah's affairs. But perhaps this piece of paper might reassure the naive lady with her arrogant airs. It wasn't much if it meant appeasing her.

"So this means you're actually going to inform me of something? Or do you require that I spit on my hand, cross my heart, and hope to die?" asked Lola.

Lady Sarah failed to understand the joke and simply grimaced at the image of Lola spitting in her own hand.

"I'm going to give you the name of someone, and I'd like you to go see him. Well, to go to his office, at the very least. There are some papers I need you to collect."

Lola was now very interested. "You will have to tell me more. And you should know that I only accept missions that I deem fair. This means you must convince me. What do these papers have to do with you?"

Lady Sarah looked deflated. She'd certainly lost her initial haughtiness. "They're of a compromising nature." She leaned in closer, rubbing her forehead lightly with her velvet-gloved hand.

"What in the devil do you have to be ashamed of?" asked Lola.

Lady Sarah chose her words carefully, speaking slowly. "I . . . how would you say . . . I became embroiled in some sort of operation. I . . . allowed myself to be convinced by a banker named Rigal. I trusted him."

"What did you do?"

"I sold some of my personal belongings. With complete discretion, of course. I didn't wish my husband to have knowledge of it. I hoped to be advanced some money to buy some land, you understand."

"Yes. Well, everyone hopes for that," whispered Lola.

"I needed an initial sum, a deposit, in order to be accepted for the loan, so I pawned my jewelry. I thought I'd be able to buy it back. I intended to put the land on the market in the months following the loan, you see?"

"Yes, I see. You did what all the affluent people are doing these days. You're attracted by quick gains. Incredible," huffed Lola. "How very bourgeois of you."

Lady Sarah shot her a dark look. "You know nothing of my family situation or my finances, so I would request that you not judge me. Anyway, I met this Rigal fellow at a friend's soirée. He was absolutely delighted to have an English aristocrat among his clients."

"I understand. Now let me finish your little story for you. You took too long to make up your mind when it came to sell. Then the financial crash happened, and your land wasn't worth anything, was it?"

"Rigal was a charming man. He accepted a plan to postpone my payments. He hoped that land prices might return to what they once were."

"The mortgage agreement you had with him . . . Couldn't Rigal easily have taken the land from you?"

"I'm afraid Rigal simply disappeared from all good society. Bankruptcy. Blown away in the wind. It was quite the scandal. Don't you read the papers?"

"Of course, I remember! What's happening now in your case? To whom do you owe money? Where is the contract?"

"It's with another banker. Someone a lot less conciliatory."

"Ah! Cousin."

Lady Sarah blinked at Lola in surprise. "How ever did you guess?"

"Cousin picked up every last crumb. He has made an enemy of every person living in Cannes. Almost every person, anyway."

"Cousin bought all of Rigal's banking files at a very low price. He now owns all the loans. But he is a lot stricter when it comes to the repayments. More rigorous. More demanding. He made it quite clear to me that he wants every last centime owed to him."

"You have until when?"

"This week is my last chance. Rigal would have allowed me to delay, but Cousin won't even hear my arguments."

"He's a heartless rogue, I imagine. However, I can't see what's so unfair about all this. I mean, you wanted to play with more than you had, and you must know the rules of the game. What is required of you now is that you honor those rules."

"You don't know everything. And I refuse to impart it all."

"You are afraid that Cousin will ask your husband to pay. It wouldn't be that costly to you if he did so, though. You must have come with a dowry, surely? Your husband will simply have to put his hand in his pocket."

"How insufferable you are!"

"Ah, therein lies the concern! The dowry! Your husband can't possibly have spent it all, can he?"

"Far from it. He is very miserly and absolutely refuses to honor my financial engagements. He and my father know of this loan, and they won't help me. They say I have no right to spend my dowry money. He is the only one who has ever had access to it."

"But he would never allow you to go to debtors' prison, would he? You wouldn't be able to walk away from such a scandal."

"He is much more devious than you'd imagine. This is why I would be obliged to declare war on him and take him to court. I would have to sue him for the dowry to pay my debt. After all, it is my right to use my money however I may wish."

"But that goes against common law."

"And what of it? I have to start somewhere. Women want the right to vote! We should start by having a little say over what rights our husbands have over us."

"Hush now. You speak for yourself. I don't have a husband. I don't want to be lumped in the same crowd as you. I think you're a dangerous woman. I can't possibly have anything to do with this business of yours. I can't be getting involved in women's rights!"

"It would be much easier if I could get my hands on the money."

"What about your father? What does he have to say to it?"

"I believe he would work with my husband."

"You don't have any alternative?"

"I have you."

Lola felt simultaneously flattered and concerned by Lady Sarah's proposition.

"I see. If we get to the contract and make it disappear, Cousin will no longer be able to hold it against you. There'll be no need to go to court. There'll be no need to publicly oppose your husband. But why would I get involved in such a scheme with you? It's too high a risk. I don't think you understand quite how dangerous it would be for some- one in my position. And how can you guarantee you won't betray me after the fact? You may very well denounce me."

Lady Sarah laughed loudly, unable to contain herself. "What could I possibly gain from doing such a thing?"

"And what could I gain?"

"I would pay you handsomely."

"You have just admitted that you have no money."

Lady Sarah stepped over to the mirror and positioned herself close to the glass. She removed an earring.

"Here's the first half of your payment." Lady Sarah turned and extended her hand.

Lola took the earring and inspected it. It was a fine gold hoop encrusted with precious stones.

"You will have the second earring as soon as I have the contract in my hands and it is destroyed. All you need to do is break into the premises at night and find the file with my name on it. Then we'll erase all traces of there ever having been a transaction. I will be safe from my husband then."

"What can he actually do to you, though? You're the mother of his children, by my understanding."

"You don't know him." Lady Sarah returned to the bed and collapsed onto the satin sheets. "They're allies, you see. They will say I'm prone to hysteria and that I signed the contract for the loan while in such a state. They could even have me institutionalized."

"When you say 'they'—to whom are you referring, exactly?" asked Lola, her tone impatient.

"My husband and my father. I just told you."

Lola's mind raced with a rush of contradictory sentiments.

This woman who had so made me suffer, who had betrayed me so very bitterly, inspired nothing but repulsion in my friend. She has always detested boastful people who look down on others. It was evident to Lola that Sarah found pleasure in belittling those she felt were beneath her. However, running alongside these thoughts was the notion that this woman was at Lola's mercy. She had lost every ounce of dignity she'd once possessed.

Lola would have very much enjoyed refusing her, but she had just decided to donate to the cause following the war in Madagascar. The sum earned on this little expedition would certainly help. In addition to wanting to do right by the soldiers was the fact that she was reluctantly touched by Lady Sarah's dilemma. She would not have coped well in a similar position.

"Come now! Your father must be of a great comfort to you. He surely would never treat you thus."

In a barely audible voice, Lady Sarah declared, "It has happened to others before me. I looked into it. Hersilie Rouy, Marie Esquiron, Léonie Halévy—they were all rejected by their families for not bending to fit into certain roles. It's abuse, I tell you. Do you know what my husband's response was when I informed him that he had no right to put me into an asylum after he threatened me with as much?"

Lola shook her head, breathless.

"He said all he had to do was sign a slip of paper declaring me no longer of sound mind. And that was it. He could have such a paper sent to him whenever he so chose, and once I was inside the asylum, no person would be able to seek debts from me."

"I'm sure it cannot be as easy as that."

"You are sadly mistaken. All they need to do is convince a doctor of their concerns, and the task is complete. The doctor might believe in all good faith that he was acting in my better interests." Her breathing was labored, and her cheeks were now wet with tears.

"You do realize what you're asking of me, don't you? We're talking of theft here. I would be locked away for a long time if caught. And I warn you now that I would take you down with me."

"Oh, you have no heart," snapped Lady Sarah.

"On the contrary. I am all heart, and I feel your distress, but I am as wary of you as I would be a snake. You seem to have no concerns as to the danger this would entail for me. You are so angry that it has blinded you, and anger provides poor counsel. Please calm yourself. You must find out more about the laws, just as any responsible person might do."

Lady Sarah sprang to her feet and rushed toward Lola, who jolted upright in surprise. Sarah's face had returned to its normal hue, and she suddenly smiled at Lola, her harsh features softening. She looked upon her with apparent kindness and tilted her head.

Softly, she asked, "Don't you believe it is sometimes more appropriate to distance oneself from the law? Stealing the odd document here and there is hardly the worst act one might commit. In this case, I believe it to be only fair."

Lola began to sense a feeling of doubt in her bones. Lady Sarah looked too kindly, too genteel. Lola understood better now how easy it was to become ensnared in this woman's traps. Her eyes appeared to promise eternal happiness. Her mouth was so supremely voluptuous. Could anyone resist it? Lola refused to allow any other argument to weaken her own.

"I learned at school that justice is not something we seek ourselves in this great republic. Do you believe yourself to be above our laws?" asked Lola.

"Don't you?"

Lola recalled those moments in her life when she had believed that the laws of the land were not always aligned with her own notions of what was right and wrong. She remembered the time they'd seen a child being beaten half to death by his father in the street. Maupassant had reacted in haste. He'd taken the man to the police station, where he was told it wasn't against the law, that a father has every right to discipline his son. Maupassant had left the place feeling devastated and powerless. She also thought about her own experience being badly abused . . . and by a police officer, no less. She thought of the man who had taken her innocence from her when she was a child and how not a single soul had believed her.

And then she thought about her encounter four years before with the nefarious comte d'Orcel de Montejoux, a man who had no compunction eliminating those he found inconvenient. Lola had become the hand of fate while expecting nothing from the justice of men.

It was as if a floodgate opened up inside her.

"You are right," she said finally. "We must sometimes step over the law and seek justice ourselves." She nodded an agreement, inspecting the earring once more. "I accept. But I don't want you to think me a naive little strumpet. I imagine you do indeed have other sources of revenue. Clandestine and immoral sources, no doubt, but you have means. And please don't expect to get involved in the affairs of Miss Fletcher and myself. And we, in return, will not get involved in yours. *Affairs* being the operative word."

Lady Sarah blushed before again showing signs of her temper. Indignantly, she yelled, "Whom do you take yourself for? Miss Fletcher! Ha! Let us speak of your exemplary Miss Fletcher, shall we? You believe her to be beyond all reproach, is that right? You are so astute, and yet how have you not seen it? Have you not witnessed the extent to which she is capable of withholding the truth? I bet she had you believe she was out on the streets, that I chased her out of my very home? It is all lies! She betrayed me. She left me, and she stole from me on her way out the door. Fletcher is an outstanding manipulator, and you fell for her every word like the frightened little mouse you are."

Lola rose to her feet. "Don't make me regret the arrangement we have just come to. We are done now. We have an agreement, and I don't wish to hear any more words from you. I will return the contract to you, and you will give me the other earring. I then hope our paths will never cross again. Your request came at a fortunate time, for I have decided to help the families of the fallen soldiers in Madagascar. I do this in memory of my very first love."

"I beg your pardon? You are going to pledge money to the cause?"

Lady Sarah's smile was nothing but sardonic, and it injured Lola deeply.

"Why should I not?"

Lady Sarah took her time. She returned to the mirror on the dressing table and stooped over to pin her hat to her hair and pull the veil back down over her eyes. Lola felt as though Lady Sarah had grown several inches in stature by recomposing herself.

"I find you so naive, Mademoiselle Deslys," she stated.

"What is your definition of *naive*?"

Lady Sarah placed the second earring in her purse. "Have you ever donated to charitable works in the city of Cannes?"

"No, why?"

"You'll learn something new in that case. For I can assure you of one thing. Those women will not take your money." She headed for the door.

"They'll take anyone's money," replied Lola.

"I'm prepared to wager it won't be the case," stated Lady Sarah, closing the door behind her.

4

SAVING A LADY

The wind was violent, a mistral gust that had come in from the sea, making visibility perfect under the bright-blue skies. The air turned chilly, so I quickly returned home to fetch our carriage. I was now waiting for Lola in front of Madame Alexandra's. By this point, Lola had been inside for quite some time. I noted that I was drawing the attention of passersby. A female coach driver wasn't exactly the custom in this part of the world, but I was used to such reactions.

Lady Sarah suddenly stepped out onto the sidewalk, wearing one of the most magnificent hats I'd ever seen, and although she was veiled, I recognized her immediately. Her gait and the way she raised her chin before moving forward were so familiar to me.

I attempted to make myself as small as possible, lowering my body down on the seat, but Lady Sarah stopped as she reached the corner and looked up in my direction. She knew me instantly. Lola's canary-yellow landau never fails to go unnoticed.

She gave me a triumphant smirk before crossing the street and hailing a cab.

Seeing her disturbed me greatly. If there was a single place I never would have imagined running into her, it was Madame Alexandra's. The coincidence of Lady Sarah and Lola being in this establishment at the same hour affected me enormously.

When Lola finally came out to join me, her nose up in the air, humming a little tune to herself, I moved the horse forward to greet her. I had a great many questions to ask.

"I've just seen Lady Sarah," I said as Lola stepped up to the front of the carriage. "Did you meet with her? Did she proposition you? What did she want? Did she disrespect you? If that's the case, I will find her and—"

"Rest assured, Miss Fletcher," Lola said, stopping me. "Nothing happened. She would never get involved in that sort of business with the likes of me."

"Please, you have no idea what she is capable of doing if it means getting her own way. I know her well, remember."

"What would 'getting her own way' be, though?"

"Perhaps she would make me jealous? Break the bonds of our friendship? Maneuver her way into our circle?"

"What zeal you have, Miss Fletcher!" mocked Lola. "You speak as if you two separated only yesterday."

She described in the most circumspect way how her meeting with Lady Sarah had gone and the mission she'd been charged with—to steal a contract from the banker Henri Cousin.

"It's all so strange," she whispered. "This is the second time today that Cousin has entered our lives. First, at the train station, and now, Lady Sarah has asked me to have dealings with him."

"Refuse! You must. Surely this is a trap. I would be wary of that one. She's a viper at your bosom."

Lola watched me in silence as I continued to splutter.

"Are you going to accept her?"

"It is already done, Miss Fletcher. She even had me sign some sort of secrecy document."

"You've signed something? Did she keep the papers? She has you now. It's over. You're at her mercy."

"Calm yourself! We're in charge here. She needs us, and she knows that."

Our horse, Gaza, could sense my anxiety. It must have been the way I was driving. He reared up with surprising force as we neared the La Foncière crossroads. We came close to a collision.

"That's enough, Miss Fletcher. Where's that famous British stiff upper lip? Get a hold of yourself. You're frightening Gaza."

"Promise me that you won't steal that contract from Cousin."

"There's little point in my promising that, as I'm already engaged. I am deeply sorry if this upsets you, but she is paying me handsomely."

She took out of her small purse an ornate gold earring encrusted with jewels. I knew the piece well, for I had often seen them dangling from Lady Sarah's delicate ears.

"I want you to take this to the *mont-de-piété*. I need the money."

She had entrusted me with this task because she knew I had used the brokers before during more desperate times.

"But I think we should take it first to Siegl and have it valued," said Lola. "I think it would reach a pretty hefty sum. What do you think?"

"I'm sure of it," I replied bitterly. "It once belonged to Lady Sarah's mother."

"Perfect. I need cash. I want to contribute to the soldiers' memorial. I found out that poor Eugène has passed, killed in action, and I am devastated."

"I am very sorry about Eugène, but what is this? It's ridiculous to be donating money to such a thing when we have so very little ourselves. Like one of those do-gooding, pious, do-as-you-would-be-done-by ladies? You know they'll refuse your help. They'll injure your sensibilities."

"Wait and see, Miss Fletcher. Times have changed. I'm no longer someone who just has a simple gentleman admirer. I am much better protected at present."

She was not thinking straight. Not in the least. But I conceded the point, nonetheless. For who could resist Lola and her iron will?

She shuffled closer to me and planted a loud peck on my cheek.

"There you go! You see?" she declared with delight. "You will realize that I am right about this, for I am always right about such things."

Her engaging smile broke down any remaining barriers I might have had.

"I believe I have the right to stand among those ladies of class and fortune at the ceremony, and they will want me by their side. Especially when they see the amount of money I am to give!"

She didn't see me grimace at this. I could sense that her resolve would not be broken.

After we stopped to collect Anna, whom we came upon on her way back to Les Pavots, Lola continued to discuss our mission with excitement. She declared that there was no need to enter Cousin's offices in the dead of night, because that would entail too much risk. It would be far better to go during the day under some pretext and distract the fellow in order to take the document without his noticing.

Anna was very intrigued by our conspiratorial tone.

"What are we talking about?" she asked giddily. "Are you going to steal something?"

Lola snapped back at her, "Curiosity is a dreadful character fault. This is a lesson you must learn. Steal? Us? What a notion!"

Anna pulled the bow on Lola's shoulder in a teasing manner. "Please, tell me! Don't keep it to yourselves!"

As she giggled, it became difficult to stay angry with her. Lola replied, "It's just that we have to save a great lady from being locked up in an asylum. That's all!"

Of course, this response antagonized Anna further. She had learned from Lola a sense of justice, but she had no diplomacy to go alongside it. She was direct in her ways and had little understanding of compromise. Although, I suppose, this was normal for a girl her age.

"What does that mean, exactly? Why would she be put in an asylum? Who?"

"Well, there's a file, you see. A document. And if we don't manage to intercept it from a banker here in Cannes, this woman's husband and her father will declare her insane. She owes a vast sum of money, and they don't wish to pay it."

Anna didn't understand this, particularly with Lola minimizing the illegality of the plan while emphasizing how unfair the situation was for the lady.

"The banker misguided her. He is on the side of her husband, you see. It's all about who has attorneyship over the dowry. If this contract gets into the husband's hands, this woman will be finished."

Anna proclaimed her desire to help us. "I want to come with you. I think this a noble cause, and I want my part in it."

The discussion had now taken a turn that displeased me greatly.

"The two of us compromising ourselves is more than enough, thank you," I said. "It's too dangerous."

Anna, however, clapped her hands with enthusiasm. "This is a dream!" she cried. "Lola, I think you can be financially compensated for such an act! It might be an excellent means of fattening the coffers, don't you think? I heard the builders at the house say that you owed them money. How is it that this lady came to ask you for assistance? Are you friends?"

Here was this girl now meddling in affairs that were of no concern to her. Her curiosity was at a peak, and she seemed far too interested in the subject. Was nothing out of bounds?

"Your benefactress here," I said, "some time ago now, proved herself to be of great assistance in what was a very private and confidential matter to a *grande duchesse*. This means that her renown has now spread throughout good society and that she is sometimes requested to perform acts of kindness to those who find themselves in, shall we say, *delicate* situations."

Anna looked upon Lola with a keen eye, almost as if truly seeing her for the first time. I noted the disbelief on her face, mixed with admiration.

"Lola?"

"I plead guilty, Your Honor!" said Lola, smiling. "I sometimes make use of gifts bestowed upon me by Mother Nature herself to clear up certain mysteries."

"I want to help you with this. Please, I beg you! I could be of great use to you. I am as discreet as a nun. I can be as silent as the grave!"

It was impossible to hold in our laughter upon hearing her turns of phrase.

"That's quite enough," I said, attempting a firm tone. "You are still too young for this sort of business."

"But I want to go!"

"Only the queen is allowed to say, 'I want this,' or 'I want that.' Polite young women do not speak so," I said.

"But we live in a republic!" she answered, and continued on the subject with surprising fervor. "Before we go and see this banker of yours, we need to gather information. What do you know of him?"

"Only what Maupassant has told us and what I've heard around town about his role in the real estate goings-on in Cannes. He also invested heavily in a property out on one of the islands. There's a Dr. Vidal there. They constructed a sanatorium together," explained Lola.

"Perfect. Men love to talk of their achievements! It will put him off our scent and buy us some time."

Lola continued, "Yes, we will go to Cousin's office and talk about loans and this island business. While he's concentrating on these topics, I can try and make a grab for the file."

"I think this is where I should come in," said Anna. "I will be a better distraction. Who would suspect an innocent-looking thing like me? I will join you in the middle of your interview, and I will ask questions meant to confound him. I will then request a tour of the premises. Miss Fletcher can keep a watch out for our return, and you will have time to find this precious file."

Lola stared at her, her eyes gleaming with adoration.

I sighed and pushed Gaza into a trot. "How can I possibly argue against the pair of you? But this is a poor plan indeed and will surely fail. I am willing to wager on it."

"How the English like to give their money away," Lola mocked.

Their laughs rang out louder than Gaza's hooves on the roadway.

5

A Banker in a Swoon

The following day, we decided to execute our plan. Anna requested to be excused from her lessons. A message was sent ahead of us very early that morning to Cousin's bank on the corner of Rue d'Antibes and Rue de la Vapeur.

For this occasion, Lola took the surname of our housekeeper, Rosalie. *Mademoiselle Lola Rivet desires to meet with the director of the bank to discuss acquiring a loan with the intention of purchasing some land.* She noted her references and added these to the contents of the envelope. She had Maupassant; the Prince of Wales; and the Grand Duchess Maria Alexandrovna, wife of Alfred, Duke of Edinburgh, Duke of Kent, and Count of Ulster to recommend her, and they all knew her as Lola, should they be questioned. She was confident knowing that all the references cited were indeed valid: Maupassant was her friend, Bertie was her lover, and she had once done the duchess a great service.

These powerful names certainly had the desired effect, for the messenger returned within the hour with a reply. Cousin declared how honored he would be to receive us in the office that morning at eleven.

It was an ungodly hour for our household. In the midst of all the to-ing and fro-ing from the workers, the young ladies of the house had immense difficulties getting dressed and organized for our trip, and I witnessed a great many frenzied gesticulations and puffed-out cheeks. The cat made the wise decision to distance himself from such agitation and scampered outside. Rosalie called him in vain, hoping he'd finish the last few morsels of his breakfast.

Having little choice in my attire, I put on what I always wore: a black dress with a white collar and cuffs—for this is the correct outfit of any self-respecting governess. It is also what someone who has fallen from grace, as I had, might wear. Someone who was once a member of the upper class, but was, alas, no more. I ventured outside to the stable to ready the horse.

I finally had everyone aboard our carriage at exactly eleven o'clock.

"Oh, we're running so late," Lola sighed. "I cannot tolerate all that horrid hammering so early in the morning."

Lola was dressed in a cream silk Jacques Doucet gown. She must have had some difficulty in finding something so sober. Most of her clothes were bright scarlet or crimson. It boasted a high collar fastened with a cameo brooch and was enhanced with garlands of periwinkle butterflies. Her suede gloves were caramel colored and complemented the overall look perfectly. She was the picture of a virtuous and long-established member of the bourgeoisie. The tiny hat she wore perched atop her braided hair reeked of absolute class.

Anna mimicked Lola in any way she could. She wore a pale-pink dress with fine muslin layering and looked quite charming.

At a quarter past eleven, Gaza and the landau were tied up at the side of the street not far from Place du Châtaignier.

Anna stayed in the carriage while we stepped confidently into the bank, just as planned.

A clerk led us to the second floor via a grand staircase, which took us to a majestic cabinet room whose balcony overlooked the Rue d'Antibes. As I observed the hustle and bustle of the street below, I noted that we were opposite Marché-Neuf, with its fine displays showing off custom-made winter-season fashions.

As I turned to be greeted by Henri Cousin, I noticed his face appeared to match his reputation. One could glimpse, behind the golden half-moon spectacles perched on the end of his nose, an air that was at once cunning and despotic. It was as if he were devoured by an inner fire. A passion. My guess was that he was obsessed with a woman. But then again, it might simply have been an infatuation with money. Or a desire to destroy others.

After giving us a rather sharp glance, he asked us to take a seat on the two armchairs facing his large, ministerial desk.

I pulled my seat slightly back to indicate the hierarchical order more clearly, for I was just the companion in this little pairing. If there had been any doubt as to my role, my plain black-and-white clothing should have been a sign. I most definitely looked as though I was in service.

Lola took the lead from the outset, and I noted how much progress she had made of late. She now knew how to perfectly infiltrate the world of the well heeled.

She began by discussing the merits of investing in cultural heritage, throwing in the odd giggle here and there so as not to scare off the banker. A woman is supposed to have great difficulty expressing herself when it comes to a subject such as finance. She should know her place. Words such as *holdings*, *capital gains*, and *liquidations* sound like curse words from pretty little mouths such as ours.

However, Henri Cousin would not allow this to dissuade him from dealing with us, particularly when he witnessed Lola explaining her situation with her usual level of good sense.

"I am convinced, monsieur, that following the real estate crisis here in Cannes, it's now or never in terms of reinvesting. Land is worth next to nothing at the moment. I should strike while the iron is hot." She laughed modestly. "I am quite financially savvy, but I know nothing of property investments. And that is why I seek your advice. What do you think to my reasoning?"

Alice Quinn

He stared at her intently. "Mademoiselle Rivet, allow me to congratulate you on your astute analysis. That is what I would call good business sense. There have been so many young people recently, men, who have inherited large sums and gone on to ruin themselves and their family name. Believe me, some of these grand families would have been far better off had they had sons of your ilk in place of the sorry excuses for men they bore. Do you have an intended, my dear? Someone who manages your dealings?"

Lola blushed slightly. Just as much as was required. She lowered her head as if ashamed and then lifted her eyes demurely, gazing at him through her lashes. She spoke in a distressed whisper. "I . . . I don't have a fiancé. Please excuse my emotions. This subject causes me a great deal of pain."

Cousin explained that he was simply obliged to ask. Lola turned to me, and I leaned in slightly, a maternal gesture of consolation.

"Poor girl," I said with compassion, throwing a disgusted look in the direction of Cousin. "This woman has had her heart broken. Her engagement ended abruptly. It was so painful for her."

But he was not duped by our act. Perhaps he had discovered more about the pair of us prior to our arrival—everyone knows bankers like to be well informed. We had thought to change Lola's family name, but there was little we could do about her address.

But Lola hadn't finished with him yet. Vexed at his disinterest in her despair, she changed tack, wanting to prove that the relations mentioned in her message were real, that she benefited from the support of great men.

She faced me and spoke gently. "You are so kind to me, my treasured friend. What on earth would I do without you? Guy supports me to a certain extent, of course, but he is so preoccupied recently. He's looking for a hospital for his brother. The fellow has become wholly incapable of late."

She looked back toward Cousin again and asked with insistence, "Guy de Maupassant? Do you know him? The writer?" She bore a reflective expression on her heart-shaped face. "I was wondering whether that home out on the island might suit his brother, Hervé."

For the first time, Cousin looked unsettled. He hadn't been expecting this. It must have been a subject that rarely came up in his bank.

"Is he looking for a place to convalesce?" he couldn't help but ask.

Lola summarized the situation of Maupassant's brother, at least what she wanted to reveal of it.

"Do you know the Grand Jardin sanatorium? It's Dr. Vidal who runs it, isn't it?"

The banker resumed his countenance and cleared his throat. Falsely jovial, he replied, "Vidal is a longtime friend of mine. I would be remiss not to recommend his home, since I helped Vidal establish himself when I introduced him to the wealthy landowners, the Tournaires, who were looking for a tenant for their large estate on Île Sainte-Marguerite. I often go over to the island to dine with the doctor. He has some true aristocrats as . . . guests. Artists too."

"So, you would recommend this establishment, would you? It must be truly painful to have to admit a member of one's family to such a place. I feel for Guy."

"Truthfully, I am very sensitive to the needs of people having to institutionalize their loved ones, for there was such a case in my own family—a delicate case, if you will. That's why I considered that Cannes might welcome such a home as Vidal's."

Lola was visibly satisfied with how he'd softened in his attitude and started talking quite freely with them. "And so, regarding my loan application?" she said, returning to the initial conversation. "Have you come to a decision?"

He coughed with embarrassment. He had not yet finished vetting her.

"Forgive my insistence, but I cannot escape my professional obligations. Might you have a father to help you manage your financial affairs?"

Lola appeared annoyed, and I observed her carefully as her little tan boot tapped the floor in frustration.

She then brandished a lace handkerchief and placed it in front of her mouth as she uttered in almost a whisper, as if holding back a sob, "I'm an orphan. My parents are dead, and I am now forced to manage alone. Admittedly, I am of age, but the struggle is oftentimes beyond my strength."

"I will not bother you any longer with such details, mademoiselle," he said suddenly. "I can agree to lend you the money, but I must impose upon you some rather tiresome and lengthy explanations. I want you to be fully aware of what you are doing. I hope you will forgive me?"

A smile that belied the severity of his features revealed a previously unseen glimmer of kindness in his expression.

Had I misjudged this man? Was he simply misunderstood? I was eager to compare my impressions of him with those Lola had formed.

There was a discreet knock at the door.

Cousin barked with irritation, "Come in!" He was clearly not too keen on being interrupted when completing business.

Anna had chosen to make her appearance and entered like a whirlwind.

"Oh, Lola, I'm so happy to find you here! I've just left Marché-Neuf. They had the most beautiful gloves, exactly my color, and I just can't resist. They've come straight from London. I want to have them delivered to the house. Can I order them?" She went on, babbling about everything and nothing.

All three of us watched her, openmouthed.

Cousin looked stunned, as though he couldn't remember himself, his position, his very language. He stood and sat down again, staring at us in turn, as if looking to us to explain Anna's unexpected appearance.

Our young friend continued her performance of the coquettish adolescent, delighted by the effect this was having on the banker.

"That ridiculous clerk out there required a signature before he let me in." She turned to Cousin. "I beg your pardon, monsieur. Please excuse the interruption. I am ever so clumsy in my manners. My entire life is a series of blunders."

Cousin was trembling, and Anna, delighted in witnessing this, was struggling to hold back her laughter. Lola, too, was stifling a giggle.

I was the only one who considered Cousin's reaction to be rather strange. How could someone be so awestruck? He did not appear to be a man who would act so.

Anna turned to me, partly to hide her smile. "Miss, please, say something. I know you do not wish for me to abuse Lola's good nature, but just once . . . It's a matter of life and death, do you understand? How could I be expected to perform in the chorus without this pair of gloves? I just can't!"

"Please, Anna, calm yourself," I said. "A pair of gloves has not the slightest influence on your voice, as far as I know."

Anna turned to Cousin. "Tell her, monsieur! Tell her of the importance a pair of gloves might have on my performance. I'm sure you're a man of good sense. Actually, forgive me, but who are you?"

When she questioned him, it was like pressing a button. He hurried to her side.

"Why . . . I am . . . I am . . ."

Lola spoke up. "Monsieur, please allow me to present to you my protégée, Anna Martin. Anna, this is the director of the bank. Monsieur Cousin."

"Your . . . p-protégée?" he stammered.

Anna looked around her as if suddenly astounded at where she found herself.

"Bank? We're in a bank? How exciting! I've never been in a bank before!"

Cousin grumbled, "Yes, my child. This is my bank, but it is only a branch. I manage this agency in Cannes during the winter. The head office is in Lyon, and we also have an establishment in Nice and another in Paris."

"That's quite thrilling!" she exclaimed.

I closed my eyes and prayed she wouldn't overdo it. A man like Cousin could not be fooled for long, even if this whole show certainly was exceeding our expectations.

"I would very much like to see how a bank works," she continued. "I know I will not understand a thing, for it is all so new to me!"

Lola put on an annoyed air. "I beg you to excuse the impetuosity of my protégée, Monsieur Cousin. She is naive and has difficulty containing herself. Anna, please, Monsieur Cousin has better things to do than show an overly curious girl around his bank."

Anna cast a reproachful look at Cousin. "Is that true, monsieur? Do you find me too curious? I am, of course. But I won't insist."

I intervened in a sharp tone. "Anna, please desist with your naughtiness. It does you no favors. Leave Monsieur Cousin alone."

But Cousin held out his arm to her in an exaggeratedly gallant fashion. "It would be an honor to show you my establishment. *Curiosity* is an ugly word for intelligence. Ladies, you are also invited to join us, of course."

But Lola pretended to be overcome by a sudden fatigue and sank into her chair. I leaned forward as if to lend her assistance.

"Go ahead without us, I beg you. I will keep company with my friend. But please do not be too long."

I then mumbled loud enough to be heard, "That child is definitely too whimsical . . ."

Cousin, quite delighted to be left alone with Anna, apologized at length before finally leaving us in the office with the door wide open to the corridor.

As soon as he had disappeared in the direction of the grand staircase, I stationed myself on the threshold of the door to keep a lookout, while Lola rushed to the huge bookshelves behind Cousin's desk and started rummaging through his records.

Each of the large portfolios was arranged in alphabetical order. She looked first through the *L* section for "Lady," then *S* for "Sarah," but it was among the *C*s for "Clarence" that she eventually found the loan agreement signed by both my former lover and Cousin.

She grabbed it, and I helped her to wedge it under the bottom of her corset.

She sat back down in the same position as when Cousin had left the room, albeit breathlessly and a little stiffer. I followed suit. She gave a stifled sigh.

"If they delay coming back, this damn document will cut off my breath!" she said.

But Cousin and Anna entered the room shortly after. A quick exchange of glances between Lola and Anna reassured the latter.

"I forgot to ask if you already have an account here," Cousin said as he looked toward Lola. Although speaking with clarity, he appeared troubled, his thoughts most certainly elsewhere.

"It's confidential, and I would rather not talk about it in front of my friends," answered Lola with feigned embarrassment.

"I have been encouraging private individuals to open accounts since 1882, particularly in special cases such as yours," said Cousin. "I am at the origin of the current banking revolution."

The word *special* vexed Lola.

"My case is not so special," she exclaimed.

"Everyone is special in their own way," said Cousin in a serious tone. "And I understand your approach here. You are a fine strategist." He chuckled. "As I always say, 'Your average Joe is richer in certain ways than Monsieur de Rothschild.'"

"Indeed!" Lola flapped.

But he continued to have eyes only for Anna. She had ceased to care about him in any way, shape, or form and was now retying a ribbon that had come undone at her waist, pulling on her gloves, studying her reflection in the mirror above the fireplace, and readjusting her hat. She wasn't one to be kept to task for long.

I thought, smiling inwardly, *The little mite could at least keep up the pretense until we get out of here. Poor Monsieur Cousin.*

He was clearly disconcerted by her sudden lack of interest. He continued conversing with Lola but could not take his gaze from Anna. "Should we open up a file in your name today . . . erm . . . for your loan?" he asked.

But Lola had also completed her mission, and she suddenly stood, which triggered the signal of departure.

Anna was already at the door, forgetting even to say goodbye, as Lola held out a hand for Cousin to kiss from behind his ornate desk. I also rose and followed closely behind.

"I think I'll reflect upon your proposal first," Lola said. "Please be so kind as to send me a summary of your offers so that I can show them to my advisors. I will get back to you as soon as possible."

As I turned to nod goodbye to him, he appeared very deep in thought.

Later, Lola explained that before taking the file to Lady Sarah, she wanted to be assured of her loyalty, because she feared reprisals. As she spoke, my thoughts kept returning to Cousin. I had a terrible feeling in the pit of my stomach.

6

A Masked Man

The mistral persisted, and the sky was blindingly bright. Paul Antoine accompanied me with his phaeton so that I could go pay Lola's contributions to the ladies who managed the war fund.

Paul Antoine Isnard de la Motte was the heir of a rich perfumer family from Grasse. His parents had once sent him to spy on us and our quaint soap-making operation, for they sought to discover our recipe for orange-blossom soaps. Since then he had become not only a fond friend, but the main client for our handmade cleansers and other toiletries.

We skirted the Hôtel de France and drove down the Chemin de Montfleuri. The ladies had created a sort of wintering colony in the spacious Baron Villa. Likely jealous of the Cercle Nautique—not to mention the other male clubs and groups within the city—they had decided they needed a place worthy of the work they did and had set their sights on this beautiful building.

In addition to the ballroom, where lavish parties were often held, events grand enough to impress even the likes of aristocrats such as Baron Lycklama, the villa housed conversation and reading lounges, a restaurant, a music room, and a study, where the patronesses kept records of all their charitable operations.

The girl assigned to keep the register of gifts was the young comtesse de Luynes. She must have had very little interest in local gossip, as she failed to even blink when I mentioned the name Lola Deslys.

I did, however, request a full receipt and that the gift be properly recorded on any official documents. I then ensured that Lola, come the main event, would be entitled to a place on the stands among the more prestigious donors.

The young comtesse, Laure was her given name, willingly granted my three requests before escorting me out of the building with a smile. Never was a chore considered with such apprehension so easily carried out.

On the way back, Paul Antoine confided to me his concerns for Lola and her desire to attend this ceremony.

"I know she's going to have the most dreadful time," he said. "I would like to avoid any form of confrontation. I will accompany her, of course. She must feel supported."

"I can't understand why you would choose to show yourself out in public with her. With Guy it's different, because he's an artist and artists can be seen with whomever they like, but you? Do you not fear compromising your reputation?"

Paul Antoine burst out laughing. "As it stands, my parents would be more than delighted to see me out in the company of any female, and there's no doubt she's every ounce the real woman."

"Is it really that bad?" I asked.

"Absolutely. She would be doing me a favor," continued Paul Antoine. "And they know she is the one who created our latest perfume. They are delighted with the product. They have great faith in it, in fact."

"As does she," I said. "Do you think there's a chance she could make some commission? Actually, you promised her she could take another tour of your workshops at La Peyrière, did you not?"

"Yes, I've been thinking about it, but my schedule is so busy. And I detest going to those places. What a bore! My father dragged me there all the time as a child. He still wants me to follow him into the business."

"Just a few weeks ago, you couldn't have cared less what your family wanted. Has something changed?"

Paul Antoine shrank into himself slightly. "My father is threatening to cut me off. I never thought he would truly go through with it. We had quite the memorable scene, you know. He said he wanted me to be treated . . . for my condition, you see? And that he had found some sort of home I would like, a place that is very well attended."

"Dr. Vidal's sanatorium."

He looked at me, aghast. "How did you guess?"

"He's the only person anyone who's anyone talks about these days."

"My family is so very tired of all the rumors about my inclination. And there was . . . an anonymous letter . . ."

"I'm certain your father is above such idle gossip."

"I don't know. I fear the worst."

We reached home and decided to take tea in the garden. Lola was nowhere to be seen. We hadn't been sitting long when Maupassant came to join us, bringing some brioches with him. He explained that it was his pleasure to pay us a visit, as it was only at Les Pavots that he ever managed to leave aside his family worries.

When Maupassant had first met Paul Antoine, he maintained a certain distance. He might have been a little prejudiced against his kind, particularly those perfumed with violet.

Yet by some miracle, the young effeminate man had one day succeeded in entering the good graces of the writer. I believe it had something to do with swimming. Paul Antoine had beaten Maupassant on both time and distance. To discover that such a mild-mannered man could be better than he was at such sporting endeavors had forced Maupassant to review his prejudices. He had even explained rather forcefully how one could be both manly and effete.

The clement temperature made it a pleasure to be outdoors. The workers had stopped with all their noise and songs and were now loading up a cart in front of the house with all their materials and equipment.

Maupassant leaned in toward me. "Has the work finished?"

"Curious," I said, watching the workers pack up. "Not to my knowledge."

I took out my box of cigarillos and invited my friends to join me in savoring one. When I was with them, I was never concerned with propriety. However, I avoided smoking in public as a general rule.

All too soon, a slight chill in the air came about as the sun started to go down, forcing us to take refuge in the living room. Sherry had already gone ahead of us and was curled up sleeping in front of the fireplace. Rosalie brought another pot of tea and fresh cups.

I spoke to them about my apprehension concerning my mistress's desire to go to the ceremony. I dreaded the scathing vexation she might well receive from the other women.

It was getting darker by the minute, and I was just about to fire up the lamps when Lola appeared in a cloud of orange-blossom scent.

"Goodness! That took longer than expected," she said.

She had a mischievous air that seemed to amuse Maupassant as she sang in a low voice about *le roi de la Côte d'Azur*. She must have been with the Prince of Wales, for he was known as the king of the French Riviera and was often described as such in the press. It was said that Mayor Gazagnaire was very flattered indeed by such reports.

She laid her purse on the pedestal table and threw her hat down on an armchair.

"We will go to the theater tomorrow night! Not to see the play, of course. How dull! We will dine there. Would you consider joining our party?" asked Paul Antoine of Lola.

"With pleasure!" she answered, taking off her gloves. "Did the workers leave early?"

"Yes," I said. "Rather odd, is it not? They left some time ago. In the middle of the afternoon, no less."

"I had a feeling they might go," she said with a sigh. "They have refused to continue until we pay them what is owed."

"I wish them the best of luck with that," joked Maupassant.

"They asked me this morning for all the arrears. But alas, there is no more cash to hand. It is not as if the sale of soaps can cover our expenses. And if Paul Antoine and his family stop buying from us, we'll be in an even bigger mess! You're our sole client, and only because you're our friend!"

"Let's not talk about my family," said Paul Antoine. "My father is harassing me to get married. He has been threatening me with the worst calamities."

"I have an idea," said Maupassant. "Why not marry our *Belle Amie*? She would be your perfect subterfuge, and then both your situations would be resolved."

This was suggested in such a tone as to make Paul Antoine laugh with gusto. After calming himself with the help of a sip of his tea, he replied that, for the moment, his father's ideas and bluster still remained but threats. "He won't really do anything. He adores me. After all, I'm his only son!"

"And if anyone wants to know what I think," added Lola, in whose direction none of us had even cast an eye, "it's simple: I do not want to be married. Is that clear? Let all who might be interested note it."

This triggered even more laughter, because nobody was likely to ask for Lola's hand in marriage—not with a past such as hers.

Maupassant protested. "Enough, enough! I understand. Mea culpa! It was food for thought, but a farce, of course."

"Your jokes are just awful. You were really scraping the bottom of the barrel," I said.

Although I knew we were all joking, I couldn't help but think that the suggestion wasn't as ridiculous as it might have first appeared. It was told with such lightness, but if they were to marry, it would afford Lola certain respectability.

My cigarillo smoke was filling the room, and Lola opened the window for a little fresh air.

As she did so, the noise of racing footsteps reached us from the street below. It was unusual for Maupassant and me to join Lola in observing what was happening outside. These things were normally of little concern to us, and they remained of little concern to Paul Antoine, who stayed inside.

But as we peered out, a young man could be seen running toward us from the direction of the Hôtel Central.

Lola cried out in a worried voice, "It's my brother, Mario! What's happening?"

When he saw all three of us up on the balcony, he shouted out, panting heavily, "It's Anna!"

He was having difficulty opening the gate, but he finally managed it and ran inside and up to the living room.

He carried on, shouting breathlessly, "Anna was attacked!"

"*Good Lord*, no! It's all my fault. The streets have become so unsafe. I shouldn't let her out on her own," I said.

"Calm down, Miss Fletcher. Cannes is a peaceful city with a very low crime rate. Ask Commissioner Valantin," retorted Maupassant.

Lola grabbed Mario by the shoulders. "But how do you know this? Where is she?"

"She came to me in tears on the Pantiero, where I was sorting out my nets. I was shaken by the whole episode, so I took her up to the Suquet to Mama's house. I thought it would be simpler, faster. It isn't far. Then I came here as quickly as I could to tell you."

"You did well," I said.

Everyone was nervous, even Rosalie, who had followed Mario up the stairs. Sherry had disappeared, frightened by all the commotion and shouting.

"For heaven's sake! Poor mite!" Rosalie lamented.

Lola grabbed a shawl and hood. "Miss Fletcher, hitch up Gaza. We will go find her. It will be faster in the carriage. I don't want her walking back alone."

Maupassant suddenly clasped his forehead and said, "I'm sorry. I . . . can . . . not . . . accompany you." He had become overwhelmed by a migraine.

"We'll drop you off at your home," I offered.

"No, it would only delay you," said Paul Antoine. "I will accompany Guy."

"Rosalie," Lola commanded anxiously, "prepare some comforting foods for the little one, and light the fireplace in her room."

"This is all very unfortunate," Maupassant said.

Paul Antoine grabbed his coat before helping Maupassant on with his.

I slipped out and was waiting for Lola and Mario in front of the gate when all four came out and crossed the garden.

Lola and Mario jumped up into the back of the carriage while Maupassant, still holding his head, stood awkwardly while being supported by Paul Antoine. They both started to descend the slope, wavering as they did so, toward Paul Antoine's vehicle, which was stationed ahead of ours.

As Gaza set out into the night, Paul Antoine turned around and cried, "See you tomorrow night at the theater, is that right?"

Lola leaned out and replied in the same tone, "I do not know, Paul Antoine! Everything depends on Anna's condition!"

When we arrived at the Suquet in front of the building where Lola's parents lived, Lola was stopped by her father, Beppo Giglio.

When Lola was a child, he had returned from the 1870 war against the Prussians with half of his leg missing, meaning it was difficult for him to make a living. Beppo had since devoted himself to alcohol, gambling, and frequenting anarchist circles. He lived on his wife's meager earnings.

Since Mario had started working, their life had improved, but not by much.

Lola did not want to be alone with him. She had come to get Anna. She knew that any conversation would turn into a dispute, but she still stopped to say hello and to exchange a few forced words while her brother went ahead into the building.

After several minutes, she turned her back on her father and headed inside and down the dark hallway.

Just then, we saw Anna coming toward us. Mario was close behind, watching over her anxiously.

They were close in age and had practically grown up together since Anna had come to stay with us four years earlier. Little by little, their childhood friendship had turned into a budding romance. This is not something we had encouraged. Anna would have made a very bad match for Mario, for she had received an education to prevent her from becoming anything like a fisherman's wife. He could have aspired to be something more than a fisherman, but there was nothing he liked better than his nocturnal outings on his fishing boat in all weather and all seasons. He was just like his anarchist father, attaching no importance to material possessions.

We immediately noticed that the girl's dress was torn and her hair a mess.

As we stepped back outside, Anna burst into tears. Beppo turned his head briefly, confirming his indifference to the world.

Lola and I rushed to her side to take her into our arms, but she moved away from Lola and grabbed hold of me. I stroked her face and wiped her tears away with my handkerchief.

"What happened to you?" Lola asked.

She stammered, "I don't . . . don't . . . know exactly. I had just left my friend Louise, and I was walking down the alley to Rue d'Antibes when I was pushed from behind. I fell. I tried to defend myself, but it was impossible because I couldn't stand or even turn my head to see my attacker. And I was so scared!"

"What did he do to you?" Lola asked anxiously. "He didn't . . . ?"

Between sobs, we learned that he had hit her repeatedly He had even ripped out handfuls of her hair.

"Did he steal anything? Your bag?"

Anna opened her bag containing two books and two notebooks before holding out her wrist and yelping, "My bracelet! The beautiful silver bracelet that you had engraved for my birthday! Look, it's not there!"

"That filthy thief!" cried Mario. "I swear I'll catch him and kill him!"

"Do not talk such nonsense," I told him as Beppo muttered unintelligible words behind me.

"You'll never be able to find him," Anna stammered. "When he fled, I managed to catch a glimpse of him, but he was masked. I would never recognize him."

Lola was now crying too. The tears were contagious. She made a gesture toward Anna, wanting to take her and enfold her, but oddly, her protégée pushed her back again, taking refuge instead in the arms of Mario, who was delighted with this unexpected turn of events.

Her gesture shocked me. I was further surprised when Lola left abruptly with a quick step and without saying a word.

Beppo reached out for her as she turned down the alleyway outside. While Anna was being comforted by Mario, I stepped over to join Lola's father and leaned in.

"I will never understand why you argue so much with your daughter, Monsieur Giglio. Everyone knows you love her so. Life is short. Is it worth it making her so unhappy?"

"It's not my fault, Fletcher. There's something she's unable to forgive herself for."

"Are you not projecting your own feelings here?"

He looked at me with a smile. "You are an astute woman under all those false airs," he said. "You are quite right, of course. But then, so am I. It dates back to the war, you see, when I lost my leg. One day, the little one came with me out to the islands. We found a special pebble on the beach—perfect, it was. It was round and smooth, all veined with red and purple. It looked like a magic egg. I gave it to her and told her that it was a dragon egg and that it brought happiness and luck to whoever possessed it."

He went silent. His voice had broken. He then plunged into a silent reverie.

I didn't know what to say. This story of his was sweet but wholly uninteresting. I reflected on the fact that Lola's father had been crushed by too many misfortunes, and that far from being able to recover, he was sinking into a sentimentality that could only drive him further down. This contrasted with his anarchist side, where he had always been most vociferous. In summary, he seemed very lost.

After a few kind words of courtesy, I left him and returned to the carriage with Mario and Anna. They both settled in the back. I watched as she clung to him, not wanting to let go. It was as if she didn't want to be alone with me. I began to understand how Lola must have felt just minutes earlier. It was something like sorrow mingled with slight irritation, as though Anna were blaming us for what had happened.

I made a detour to Dr. Buttura's house. I wanted him to examine and treat Anna before going home, but he was not there.

When we finally arrived at Les Pavots, Rosalie was waiting for us, pacing in front of the door. She raised her arms to the sky as soon as she spotted Anna and the sorry state the young girl was in. She held Anna closely before taking her into the house. They were both in tears.

Mario ran back to his boss, fearing he would lose his job.

Rosalie guided Anna to the bathroom, where she gently bathed her.

She had warmed some water on her stove and poured it into the tub. The taps were not yet in place and weren't likely to be soon, seeing as the workers had abandoned the site.

Anna was still crying, but when we insisted she tell us whether she was in any pain, she replied, "It's nothing. It doesn't hurt anywhere."

"Tomorrow," I said, "when you're feeling better, we will go report your assault to the police."

"That is out of the question!" cried Anna. "I just want to forget everything! I'm sure Lola wouldn't agree to that either. She doesn't much like the police, does she?"

"But what is all this about?" I asked.

"Where is Mademoiselle Lola, anyway?" Rosalie asked.

Anna looked even more shaken.

"She left. She had something to do," I said.

"I don't wish to see her again!" cried Anna.

Rosalie looked at me in astonishment. "What has gotten into her?" She looked then at Anna. "Whatever did she do to you?"

Anna's eyes welled with tears.

"It's probably shock," I said. "She's been like this since we went to fetch her. She seems to be very angry with Lola."

"Come now, Anna. You shouldn't be blaming Mademoiselle Lola. She has nothing to do with this. Where would we all be without her?"

Anna suddenly found the energy to get out of the tub. She snatched the large bath towel from Rosalie's hands and fled to her room, leaving wet traces in her wake. "Leave me be! I want to be alone!"

"But . . . but . . . I've prepared you a feast. I made you that soup you love!"

All Rosalie's entreaties got her were silence and a door slamming. The noise rattled the walls.

"Such a sulky girl," exclaimed Rosalie. "I do not know what's wrong with her, but there's no need for that."

"It must be shock," I repeated.

Rosalie placed some bowls on the kitchen table, and I sat down with her to enjoy the soup. She didn't ask me any questions, and I didn't much want to talk.

It was into this gloomy atmosphere that Lola appeared.

Her dress was covered in dust. She must have taken a long walk to clear her mind of the evening's emotions. As soon as she stepped through the door, she asked after Anna, noting the fleeting glance that passed between Rosalie and me.

"What? What is it?"

"She's locked herself in her room. She doesn't want to see anyone," I explained.

She smiled bitterly. "You mean she refuses to see me!" As she spoke, her irritation grew. "But what did I do to her? Why am I to blame?"

"It'll pass," said Rosalie. "She doesn't think ill of you. Isn't that right, Miss Fletcher?"

"It's probably the shock," I mumbled for the third time that evening.

7

A Dashing Baron

The house was calm the next day, but something was certainly brewing. We could feel it in the air.

On Sundays, Rosalie headed to mass early in the morning, but Lola refused to go to church, not daring to face the knowing looks of the "honest" people there. For my part, I had lost my faith at the same time I'd lost everything else: my parents, my fortune, my status, and my illusive hopes.

The atmosphere was tense. How was I to interpret the signs? Could my intuitions be trusted?

I suspected my anxiety was due to Anna's attack.

I had been up since dawn, busy doing the accounts, but I hadn't seen Anna yet. I knocked on her door and asked if she wanted anything, but the girl replied that all was well. She simply needed to rest. I decided not to push any further.

Later, after Rosalie had returned, I helped her organize the baskets of soap.

Lola, meanwhile, awoke around midday, went to the kitchen, and gulped down a huge cup of hot chocolate. She was standing in front of the stove, yet I could see she was shivering. She wore an ordinary linen nightgown, and her braided hair was in disarray.

"This whole business is just incredible. My little Anna . . . How are we really to protect those we love?" she said to nobody in particular.

Her words resonated with me strongly, though, as it so perfectly mirrored my own daily concerns and perpetual inner quest for Lola Deslys.

Meeting her had changed my life. She had saved me, and there wasn't a day that went by that I did not seek ways to protect her, to keep her safe from danger and insecurity of any kind. My pursuit was doomed to fail, however, awakening in me a terrible sense of constant helplessness.

Rosalie noticed Lola's distress.

"Don't worry, mademoiselle, she's fine," she said. "I went to see her earlier. She's not in any pain. She's being a little cheeky, that's all."

"What do you mean by 'cheeky'? She's not usually like that. She can be a bit selfish sometimes, it's true, but she's never cheeky. In fact, she's very good. Very altruistic too. Just the other day, she wanted to help us," said Lola.

"That's right, but at her age, these things can change so quickly," replied our housekeeper.

We could hear the gate opening outside, and I went to the front door to see who it was.

Paul Antoine was crossing our garden, holding out his hands toward me.

"I was just passing by, Gabriella. I wanted to make sure that Lola is indeed coming to the theater tonight. I would very much like to introduce her to a friend I met in Paris."

Standing beyond the gate was a rather dashing man sporting a fine curled mustache. He gave me an elegant bow. I returned the gesture. It was the first time that Paul Antoine had brought a friend to the house, and I wondered how close they were. Could he have been one of Paul Antione's *special* friends? I was astonished at the thought.

Paul Antoine leaned toward me with an expression of complicity and whispered, "He is in possession of quite a fortune, and I thought he might make an interesting match for Lola."

I felt a hint of jealousy as I now examined the newcomer more sharply. He was young, perhaps only just turned thirty. His figure was athletic, and he had a fine and fresh complexion. His outfit was elegant without ostentation. I looked back to our friend.

"She is not dressed to receive. I don't think she can . . ."

Lola's voice could now be heard hollering from somewhere deep within the house. "Who is it, Miss Fletcher?"

Paul Antoine spoke for me. "It's me, Lola. I came with a friend. Are you fit to be seen?"

Lola's voice came from the balcony this time. She leaned out and shouted down, "Always, for you, my dear! Come on inside. Do you want some hot chocolate? Forgive me, I have only just this instant risen from my bed." She turned her head and continued to shout. "Rosalie, could you make some more chocolate and bring up some cups, please?"

I walked in ahead of the gentlemen and up the stairs, trying to hide my annoyance. Paul Antoine and his friend followed me.

When I opened the living room door, Lola was standing there and had quickly changed into her purple lace negligee. She had lifted her heavy hair into a bun that looked carelessly arranged, but I knew it had actually been rather meticulously studied.

Her image was reflected in the three mirrors around the room, like a triptych of magnificent oil paintings. Gone were all the previous signs of gloom and anxiety. A strong smell of orange blossom permeated the room.

"Lola, my darling, let me introduce my dear friend Ferdinand. He's a baron! We met one evening at Auteuil, at the house of the incredible Dr. Blanche, at one of his famous Sunday dinners. It's quite the thing to be seen there. Very few people have the honor. We met Manet and the Dumas family as well. Can you believe it? And Castiglione! She's one of their neighbors, in fact. It was quite something. She shows herself so rarely. I actually believed her to be dead."

Paul Antoine was excited, to say the least. I couldn't believe we were having a conversation about Dr. Blanche. He was very famous, known for treating Parisians who had . . . lost their way, shall we say? What sort of oddball was Ferdinand to be associated with the doctor? A resident of Dr. Blanche, perhaps? Hopefully not!

The man winced as Paul Antoine spoke in his exaggerated fashion. He then leaned over to Lola to kiss her hand. When he raised his head again, he looked quite different. Had the touch of Lola's skin revived something in him?

He was looking at Lola, captivated.

I was reminded of one of Guy's stories that I'd read the previous year. The main character had sported a mustache similar to Ferdinand's. Guy even suggested that a man without a mustache really is no man at all. Why men make such a song and dance about a simple tuft of hair is beyond me.

However, this young man's mouth, I had to admit, was particularly attractive. He must have been quite popular among the women who enjoy that kind of thing.

Paul Antoine had actually come with bait. This was his way of ensuring Lola would be at the theater that night. He preferred when she was there, for the evenings were always much more fun.

He'd failed to receive a promise from her, but it was not for lack of trying. The young Ferdinand was not to be outdone either. The flattery coming from his fine mouth was on another level entirely as he attempted to entice Lola to join their party.

When they left, I asked, "Will you go tonight?"

But her response had not changed since the previous day. "I don't know. It depends on Anna's condition. Paul Antoine cares not a jot about her."

But Anna would not leave her room until she heard Mario's voice. He had come to take news of her. She was dressed all in pink, as usual. She picked up a basket, and they went out for a walk around the orchard next to the house, under the pretext of picking lemons. She took some bread, wine, and cheese as well for a picnic, giving us neither a hello nor a smile, just a thank-you to Rosalie when she handed Anna the food.

On her return, with the basket full of lemons, she said goodbye to Mario and promptly returned to her room, locking herself in again.

I was in the kitchen with Rosalie, enjoying more of her soup, when Lola burst in.

"Well, that's that, then. I can see that nobody needs me here," she said. "I'll go dine at the theater with Paul Antoine. Miss Fletcher, can you fetch a messenger from down the street, please, so I can let him know? But finish your soup first while I write it."

She went back upstairs, and I barely had time to finish my bowl before she was back.

Later, once the message had been sent on its way and she was dressing in her room while awaiting an answer, she asked me what I was doing with my evening.

"We are behind on the embroidery for the soap bags. We have a delivery going out tomorrow, so I'm going to see to that with Rosalie."

"Could you help me tighten my corset?" she asked.

Lola did not desire to have a personal maid, so Rosalie and I took turns playing this role, assisting her with her hair or helping her to fit her corsets.

These moments of physical closeness were enticing, and I loved to enter into such intimacy. But tonight, the atmosphere was electric, and Lola's mind was elsewhere. She did not want to give in to my touch, and she lifted her hair on her own, weaving it quickly.

The sound of a carriage could be heard pulling up outside. We leaned out of the window. The blue lantern tied to the front of the vehicle pierced the night. We watched as a young messenger boy, around ten years of age, dashed out, sprang through the gate, and galloped up to the house, brandishing a piece of paper.

Lola hurried down and took the child into the kitchen. Rosalie handed him a penny, along with a lump of cheese, two slices of bread, and a piece of cake.

"Where are you from?"

"Officially, I'm an errand boy for a journalist, but sometimes, I make extra taking messages," bragged the boy.

"You work for a journalist? Gosh! What's your name?"

"They call me Agile Basile. I've been sent with a cab for you. The driver's outside," he said with a grin.

Rosalie burst out laughing. "You don't leave your publicity up to others, do you? Do you have a family?"

"Yes, my sister, Thérésine. She knows Mademoiselle Lola."

He fled without another word.

Paul Antoine had indeed sent a carriage for Lola. The note stated that he would pick up Maupassant, that they would all meet at the table he had reserved in a private room in the theater, and that some friends would join them.

"Oh my!" Lola said. "If they're all friends of Paul Antoine, there'll be nobody to do business with. There'll be Guy, of course, but it'll be another pointless evening."

"You are forgetting the famous baron," I stated.

"Ah yes, it's true!" she exclaimed, as if annoyed for having a reason to be satisfied rather than allowed to let her foul mood roam free.

She left, cursing that her boots were pinching her feet. Her sensibilities were fluctuating at high speed. I had never seen her in such an unpleasant or changeable frame of mind.

Later, she recounted that when she arrived at the theater and entered the restaurant through the side door, all eyes turned to her. In her incandescent purple dress, crested hat, and satin gloves accented with emerald bracelets, she looked like a bush of wild roses. The conversations, interrupted for a moment by her entrance, resumed as she ascended the staircase leading to the smaller, private salons, guided by a waiter who knew her well.

She had been the darling of this theater for an entire season, but she had since exhausted her meager talent as a singer. Her fame, however, remained, thanks to the lovers of high notoriety she had managed to collect. But most importantly, the staff knew how many tips she received and how she generously shared them with others who worked there.

On entering the private room, she immediately spotted Maupassant and Paul Antoine. The other guests were two bold-looking ladies who were evidently not from the region—Parisians, no doubt—and four somber-looking men in smoking jackets. This would be a quiet night indeed. Where was the promised baron?

She sighed and questioned Paul Antoine with her eyes.

He stood and went to meet her, guiding her to a place at the table. He explained that he had been expecting more guests but that a number of his *friends* had gone to see the play downstairs and that when it finished, they would pick him up so they could move on to someplace more private. His words were accompanied with a knowing smile.

"Have I told you that Ferdinand is a poet? He will no doubt treat us to a few of his verses when he gets here!" exclaimed Paul Antoine.

Maupassant, at the other end of the table, sitting rather too closely to one of the ladies, raised a mocking eyebrow and observed Lola from the corner of his eye.

They sat for an age. Course after course was served, and Lola sulked inwardly, having to tolerate the most dire of conversations from the somber gentlemen. She blamed Paul Antoine for this and had no idea how Maupassant was withstanding the tedium.

There was a gentle knock at the door, and she turned to see the young Ferdinand enter wearing a shy smile. His attention immediately turned to Lola. His eyes caressed her up and down. She stood to greet him. He moved her chair away from the table and stepped forward to kiss her hand gently.

As soon as she was comfortably seated again, he sat in the chair to her right, and lust was evident in his attentions. *It's true. He likes me,* Lola thought. *My evening may not be lost after all.*

Grabbing a glass of champagne that Paul Antoine had placed in front of her, she raised it in the direction of the other diners. "To your good health!" she shouted out to the room.

All responded in turn, except Ferdinand, who remained silent. He was staring at her again, devouring her with his eyes. *What's happening here?* she wondered. *Is he like that with all women, or am I having a particular effect on him?*

She leaned behind the man to her left and whispered to Paul Antoine, "What does your friend do for a living?"

"He's squandering his family's money, I imagine. Like I am!"

His nervous laughter was louder than Lola would have anticipated. This was not the reply she was expecting. "What else do you know?" she asked.

"He's rich. I know that much. His parents died when he was young, and he inherited, but a greater fortune awaits him still. He has an uncle who works in finance."

She turned to Ferdinand, determined to seize what she could. Les Pavots needed a man like this on its side.

Fascinated, his eyes widened, contemplating her every feature, yet his body remained motionless.

"You didn't go see the play?" she asked, breaking the prolonged silence that had started to make her feel uncomfortable.

The door behind her opened quickly, causing the blood-red egret feather in her hair to quiver. She turned to see who had entered and abruptly froze. She knew him. Philémon Carré-Lamadon, the man who had wanted to buy her, to reduce her to doing his bidding when she had been abandoned by Eugène. The man with whom she'd had to fight to keep her house. He made his way toward the table, an arrogant smile on his face.

"What are you doing here, my sweet? I was told there was a *very* pleasant side to this place, but I had no idea that girls like you were allowed to trade here."

He bent down to kiss her hand, trying to make his remark come across as a harmless joke.

But the shame hit Lola hard. She felt as though all eyes were on her. She turned white and then blushed, finding it difficult to catch her breath. She wanted to stand, but she knew her legs wouldn't hold her weight.

The young Ferdinand, surprised by how Lola had so transformed, turned his head to observe the man who had spoken so rudely. Paul Antoine and Maupassant, deep in conversation, had neither seen nor heard a thing.

Ferdinand could perhaps not find a pertinent comeback, but he was not mistaken when recognizing the intentions in this newcomer's eyes—the contempt, the desire to hurt, the bitter greed and frustration.

He stood in a sudden movement, knocking over his chair. Everyone turned to him. He grabbed his glass of champagne and threw it in Philémon's face. "I challenge you to a duel, monsieur! On the hills of Napoule! You will be there the day after the morrow at dawn!" he cried.

Philémon looked around the room and sensed the disapproval against him. The assembly had taken up the cause of Ferdinand and his act of heroism, and so Philémon stormed out in anger.

8

A GRAY-AND-GOLD VICTORIA

Meanwhile, Rosalie and I had settled in the kitchen next to the hot stove. Sherry had decided to keep us company, huddled on a pile of old newspapers by the fire. The table had been cleared of crockery and was now strewn with lace handkerchiefs that we assembled to make pouches for our soaps, then embroidered with Lola's initials.

We made the soaps using orange blossom from our garden. Lola had a gift for anything related to toiletries: creams, ointments, perfumes.

This activity allowed us a little extra money, but it was still not enough to support the lifestyle to which we had all once been accustomed when Philémon Carré-Lamadon had been taking care of Lola.

Helping make the soaps was not a significant part of the work I did, but at least I was contributing without having to exploit the charms of my pretty mistress. My salary then came, in part, from our business activities rather than wholly from her horizontal operations, for my upbringing would not have allowed me to accept such a state of affairs without upsetting my conscience.

The conversation was rather desultory, as Rosalie explained what she was going to buy the following day at the market. I nodded along but couldn't help thinking about Anna's strange attitude. In fact, we were both concerned by her behavior since the attack and continued to listen for noises coming from her room. Rosalie was hoping to see Anna come begging for a dish of soup, which, in her eyes, would mean her return to good sense and good health. I would simply have liked to have a real discussion with the girl. I was waiting for the moment when she would come to me.

It was just then that for the second time in the evening, a carriage drew up in front of our house. The kitchen overlooked the back of the property, so I discreetly went out into the small courtyard, not wanting to be seen, and I looked from the side of the building toward the street. Rosalie was far too curious of nature and so had to follow me.

"Who is it?" muttered Rosalie, staring out toward the street. "We can't just have gentlemen showing up here without warning."

But I immediately recognized the elegant vehicle with the gray-and-gold Victoria and House of Clarence coat of arms on the side. Lady Sarah.

A fever seized me as my hands began to tremble. What was she doing here? Why compromise her reputation by coming to this house? Was it I she had come to see? Or Lola?

Rosalie noticed how troubled I looked. "Do you know this fellow?" she asked.

Without responding, I ran back inside, grabbed my cape from the coat hook in the entrance hall, and pinched my cheeks in front of the mirror as I adjusted my robe.

With impatience, I returned outside and ran across the garden, through the gate, and onto the street beyond.

I stopped only for a brief moment in front of the closed door of the carriage, which opened in a smooth motion. Sarah reached out her gloved hand to me and helped me climb into the coach. We didn't exchange a word.

I could barely breathe. There I was, sitting next to the woman who had once set my heart on fire and then broken it into a thousand pieces.

I was finally going to be able to tell her what I felt in my soul. It had been four years since I'd almost killed myself for this woman.

I opened my mouth to talk, but she leaned toward me, closing it with a passionate kiss.

The surprise forced me to freeze. Lady Sarah had thrown herself at me as if wholly starved of love. Did she still desire me, or was this yet another form of manipulation? If so, what did she want? My head was pounding. I couldn't align two coherent thoughts, as all my senses were aflame . . . and yet her kiss had almost repelled me.

I was divided between opposing impulses, both exhilarated by the desire to forget everything, to forgive everything, to believe in us again, and the fear of intense suffering, the very same fear that had driven me to the point of wanting to die. The smell of her, the feel of her skin, the taste of her lips—it all repelled me, and at the same time, I needed her.

After the initial surprise had passed, and with a violent effort, I pulled myself away from her embrace.

"Gabriella! Oh, Gabriella!" she whispered. "Here you are, at last! I've waited so long for you. So many nights spent dreaming of you, your hands on me . . ."

Her words caused only slight reluctance in me. Too slight. I felt fragile. The mere sound of her voice had triggered a trembling shock-wave within me. How could I resist this?

Lady Sarah was pushing me. She wanted me to succumb to her, to surrender. I didn't understand her motivations, but I felt the danger of her instinctively. I was proud to realize I now had a sense of survival. This was something that had developed since I'd last seen her.

When I finally spoke, my voice was hoarse, dry. "Four years. It took you four years to come here to tell me these long-awaited words."

"My darling, if I had known! At first, I was sick, you know, and then . . . when I saw you with her . . . it was beyond what strength I had left. I was consumed by jealousy, and I truly believed you had forgotten me."

"Why have you come now? Why tonight?"

"It's too much. I can't live so far apart from you like this. Without seeing you, feeling you, touching you. My heart . . ."

Her voice held such sweetness. I felt as though I were melting with happiness, ready to give up everything I had built here with Lola. It was like returning to paradise lost, as if the past four years were beginning to fade away.

I slowly abandoned myself, bending toward her, allowing myself to be caressed, wrapped in her warm arms, my tense muscles gradually relaxing. It was then that she said softly, "As soon as my file is retrieved from Cousin, we can start all over again. We can find a way to see each other, to rediscover the happiness we once shared. Did she get it?"

Her words hit like a cold shower. She wanted her contract. That's all this was.

I was all the more bitter because I had allowed her to touch upon my weakness. Was I so in need of love that a kiss was enough for me to abandon myself?

After recognizing my vulnerability, I decided to pretend I was unaware of the mission Lola had accepted, so she would have as little control over me as possible.

"But what are you talking about?" I asked, fearing I'd be unable to hold back the bitterness in my voice.

She was a great actress, and with me as her audience, it had never been too difficult for her to lie. However, she could not hide her game for long, or her annoyance. Upon hearing my answer, the exasperation showed on her face, dimly lit by the light of the carriage lantern and the gaslights outside on the street. Her tone became sour.

"Don't lie, Gaby! I know you inside and out. And besides, I saw you both enter Cousin's bank yesterday."

"So you're spying on us?"

Her anger escalated. She was clearly unable to stand the fact that I was no longer drawn in by her.

"I'm sure you have it. I saw her leave earlier. Go get it, Gaby! Don't be difficult."

Her voice now fell between seduction and insistence. But I knew her true nature. I had seen it. And I also knew the biggest battle I faced was against myself, not her.

"I don't know what you're talking about. Mademoiselle Lola went to Cousin's yesterday to take out a loan. She wants to buy some property. I always accompany her in such circumstances. You seem to know more about her motivations than I do. If, however, she has a document belonging to you, I advise you to contact her directly."

Her eyes sparkled with rage. "But what are you playing at here? Do you consider her to be loyal to you? Do you actually believe that little tramp tells you everything?"

I knew she was a treacherous piece of work and that lying was second nature to her. However, some doubt remained in my heart. What exactly had happened between them at Madame Alexandra's? Could I really count on Lola?

My silence sent Lady Sarah into a state of pure exasperation.

"Stop this little game, Gabriella," she whispered. "She wants to blackmail me, I believe, which is why she won't want to give that file back to me. That's why you must obtain it. Make haste, I beg you! In memory of our love. If you don't, I'll . . ."

"You'll what?"

"Just give it to me, and don't tell Lola. After all, she keeps secrets from you. I know some things."

"You're hitting your head against a wall, Sarah. Lola has no secrets from me. I manage her entire life, and we trust one another. We really do."

"Is that so? Did she tell you what happened between us the other day? How she shamelessly enticed me?"

"You're the one who set up the meeting, Sarah."

"Yes, to ask her for a simple favor, and she relentlessly . . . She wanted . . . Yet she knows how much I love you. I pushed her away, of course. You occupy my every thought."

I was disgusted. She had shown herself capable of using anything she could to get what she wanted. She was usually highly skilled at these games, but she had not succeeded in bringing me back to her. However, she had succeeded in creating a soupçon of doubt within me. I was now wondering if my relationship with Lola was really based on mutual trust.

"Enough, Sarah. My answer is no. I'm leaving now, and please don't try to see me alone again. It's no use. You are banished from my heart forever."

If she only knew how much it pained me to say that. I had dreamed for so long of such different words I would speak to her. She held me by the arm.

As I waited for her to let go, she said weakly, "If you don't give me that file, do you realize what could happen to me?"

At this point, there was little use pretending I didn't know what she had asked Lola to do for her.

"Yes. Fergus will have you committed so he doesn't have to use your dowry to pay off your debts."

"My life will be ruined, Gabriella. You understand that, don't you?"

"Don't fret so, Sarah. Lola is a woman of her word. She'll return your file to you."

Her gaze was pleading before it hardened. "And know that I will take you down with me. I will reveal your true nature to the world."

A shiver ran through me. In the grips of vertigo, I had the strength to say, "I'm no longer welcome anywhere. I work for Lola Deslys. So I already have nothing more to lose. Unlike you."

She dropped my arm and collapsed into herself, devastated by her failure to blackmail me. "You're abandoning me."

Then something happened I never thought possible: I felt sorry for Lady Sarah.

I resisted the urge to comfort her, knowing she would perceive it as a weakness and resume her assault on me. I had to put it out of my mind.

I left the carriage and walked back to the house, leaving her in distress.

9

A BITTER QUARREL

When Lola came home shortly before midnight, she brought with her the dashing Ferdinand and his elegant mustache. As they discreetly entered through the side door, Rosalie didn't even see them.

I was in my room at the top floor of the house, lost in thought, feeling both troubled and feverish.

I had been an accomplice to theft, and I was starting to worry about it deeply. What had happened to Anna was also causing me a dull anguish. I was worried by her reaction to it all, particularly her quarrel with Lola. But it was Lady Sarah's impromptu attack that had revealed how fragile I really was. Finally, I wondered about Lola and where her loyalty lay. Was she really hiding important things from me? Was she taking me for a fool? She lied so well to Anna about her double life, did she not?

As I became further lost in my thoughts, I heard the front door slam.

Sounds of female voices came to me, first muffled, before becoming louder and louder.

I grabbed a dressing gown and hastily slipped it on and then headed down to the living room with my candle.

Lola, in one of her most sheer outfits and with a bottle of champagne in one hand, was standing opposite Anna. Our young friend was dressed in pink and breathing heavily, as if in a blind panic.

Sherry skipped from one to the other restlessly, his tail whipping the air around him.

"Oh, there you are, Miss Fletcher. Just in time," said Lola, taking a step toward me and pointing at Anna. "Look who's just arrived back from who knows where at this hour. Can you even believe this? I caught her climbing the stairs as quiet as a little mouse. If I hadn't come out for champagne, I never would have known she'd even been out tonight."

I turned to Anna, waiting for an explanation. It was certainly slow to come.

Anna opened her mouth and then closed it. Her face was red and patchy, but it didn't appear to indicate shame. Rather, I detected indignation, as if she found Lola's accusation to be unfair.

"How long has this secrecy been going on? Whom have you been to see? You're too young to be running around gallivanting on your own!" cried Lola.

"It's not what you think," said Anna, anger in her voice.

"Is that so? Dressed up like that at this time of night, returning from who knows where . . . and it's not what we think, is it?" continued Lola. "You were sulking in your bed earlier! Nothing could convince you to leave your den of misery!"

"That's unfair!" Anna retorted, on the verge of tears. "You dare accuse me of . . . of . . . while you are the one . . ."

Sherry stretched out his legs, placing them both on the bottom of Anna's dress as if trying to comfort her.

I remained incredulous at Anna's insinuation, and Lola had obviously taken the words as an affront. She had turned white.

"I'm the one . . . ? Please go ahead, my little one! Finish your sentence!"

Anna suddenly straightened up, without paying attention to the cat. As tears ran down her cheeks, she grabbed Lola's hands. She seemed distraught. "Oh, Lola, please don't be angry! You've done so much for me, and I'm aware of that. I don't want us to be at war."

Lola lifted her arms and walked away from Anna as if she had been burned. The conversation had taken a path from which there would be no return.

"What is this, my dear?" Lola said. "You're delusional." She turned to me, trying to buy time. "What's the matter with her, huh?"

Sensing that some dreadful discussions were ensuing that would forever change our way of life, I took a couple of steps back, shying away from the topic.

"Speak up, then!" Lola shouted at Anna.

Anna looked desperate as she whispered in a tired voice, "I know everything, Lola. I've known for a couple of days."

Lola was livid and, between gritted teeth, snapped, "What's 'everything'?"

Anna lowered her head, unable to say any more. I took a deep breath, deciding to take matters into my own hands.

I sat on one of the chairs and invited them to do the same, pointing to the sofa. They sat tentatively and continued to avoid one another's gazes.

Lola's face displayed a host of emotions, a mixture of shame and anger and fear. It was a timid fear, as though she was surprised to be feeling it. How could she, a woman who had jumped so many hurdles alone, be afraid of a mere child? The very child she had welcomed into her home, saved, and raised?

I addressed Anna. "I believe all three of us are tired, and it would be better to think carefully before you speak in a reckless manner. You're too young to understand everything, but you will one day. I give you my word. For now, I ask that you trust Lola and forget anything you may have heard. And above all else, please do not disrespect her."

Rosalie's heavy steps echoed on the stairs. She must have been awakened by the commotion. She entered the living room in a disheveled nightgown and a nightcap from which her hair escaped and flowed down her back. She blew out the candle she was holding when she entered the lit room, closed the door behind her, and leaned against the wall.

Sherry clearly had the idea that Rosalie's presence was about to make everything better. He jumped into her arms, but she pushed him away as a worried frown crossed her brow.

"What's going on up here? It sounded like an earthquake. Do you want to wake up the entire street?"

The cat, irritated at having been rejected, took refuge at the top of a bookshelf so he could get a better view of the goings-on.

Despite Rosalie's intrusion, and after a brief glance at her, we continued with the drama at hand.

"No, I'm not too young!" exclaimed Anna. "I understand very well indeed. Imagine that, Miss Fletcher. I am old enough to grasp what's going on under this roof. How could you imagine you might keep it from me?"

She kneeled at Lola's feet. "Please tell me it's untrue! Tell me you're not the kind of woman who . . . who . . . Just tell me you're a virtuous woman!"

When Lola heard this, she stood abruptly and pushed Anna away. Rosalie gasped. I couldn't tell if this was due to what Anna had said or what Lola had done.

"Virtuous woman!" said Lola. "Ha! Virtuous like the one who killed my dear friend Clara Campo? Virtuous like those who starved you at the orphanage? Virtuous like my mother, who kills herself in front of her ironing board, breathing in toxic fumes? Is that what you want me to be, Anna?"

I tried to intervene once more. "Since you think you're old enough to know . . ."

But I could go no further. Everyone waited for me to continue, but no sound came out. What could I say to defend Lola? I stammered for a few seconds before Rosalie came to the fore.

"Oh, you poor little thing! You're confused and angry. What do you know of the obligations these girls have to their masters, to their landlords? Many of them are simply trying to keep a roof above their heads. Do you think women have a choice?"

These arguments gave me courage, and I felt I could support Rosalie's point.

"The distinction between virtuous women and otherwise is fragile, Anna. I know a great number of ladies of society who take lovers. We'll discuss it further when you're old enough to comprehend, because right now, your head is full of romances . . . romances written by men."

"But I read mystery novels!" Anna protested childishly. "You don't even realize how unfortunate this makes me. Lola is compromising my future! It would have been better if I'd stayed in the orphanage. At least I would have been raised with sound morals."

"If you had survived!" exclaimed Rosalie. "Have you forgotten how your friend died? Your dear Adèle?"

"Come now, Anna," I said. "Your future? What would it have been if you'd stayed there? Let's talk about that! Right now, you . . . you . . ."

But once again, words failed me, and it was Rosalie who continued. "You'd be sleeping on a straw mattress and working at the orphanage without being paid, like a slave, until you reached the age of twenty-one. And then you'd be out on the street. It would be as simple as that. Out. Hanging around, trying to find work. And what sort of job could you find without an education? You'd be a housemaid at best, washing dishes, sleeping in a storage room, fetching coal at four o'clock in the morning, and emptying bedpans. And do you think you'd keep your virtue long under such conditions? You wouldn't be able to resist the first stable lad who offered you a bite to eat. Come on, Anna! I'm ashamed of you, my girl, truly—"

But Lola sat there twisting her hands and interrupted Rosalie. "She's right, and I was wrong. Wrong to keep it all a secret. I should have either left her to her fate or told her everything from the very outset." Her voice was filled with both compassion and guilt.

As Anna started sobbing again, Rosalie approached her, taking her into her arms and rocking her gently.

"After all," continued Lola, "what was good for me is certainly not the right course for you. I took you from the orphanage for that very reason, so that you would not end up like me . . . or worse than me. But it was perhaps a mistake."

I felt sickened by this turnaround. Dryly, I asked Anna, "Where do you think your education, your piano lessons, your lovely clothes, and your luxury toiletries come from? And even your pretty thoughts and your ability to express them? Do you think it all simply fell from the sky?"

But Anna suddenly pushed Rosalie away and clambered to her feet. "Don't tire yourselves out with your explanations—I understand you're both women who have lost their way. But you, Rosalie, I forgive you. You need to keep your place here, so . . ."

We waited for her to finish.

An idea came to me suddenly, and I broke the silence. All this had not happened by chance. Who had given Anna these notions?

I asked her in a soft voice, "How is it you're talking about this tonight? Why is your mind on such matters?"

She shook her head as she sniffed and looked at us in desperation. Lola handed her a handkerchief. "You're not telling us everything, are you?" Lola said. "What happened to you, exactly? You must have been gone for hours!"

She finally admitted that she had seen Henri Cousin, the banker, and that she'd been walking the streets in a daze since. In fact, she had seen him twice since our visit to the bank two days earlier. This news left us stunned.

"Cousin? What do you mean? But why?" I asked.

"The first time was yesterday. He waited for me after class to take me for ice cream at Rumpelmayer's."

"And you went with him so easily? Have we not taught you anything about the world?" I continued in frustration.

"I wanted to learn more about that lady we saved with the file. I wanted to see if we could save anybody else."

"What does Cousin have to do with me? I barely know him," Lola clamored.

"He told me about you, Lola. He said your income did not come from annuities or even from the sale of your soaps. He said that . . . you were . . . a woman who . . . didn't live well."

"Hush now!" cried Lola. "I live very well! What else did he tell you?"

"He told me that I shouldn't be living under the same roof as you. He seemed obsessed with the idea, proclaiming that a well-bred girl should never be here and that it would damage my reputation. He said I would never make a good marriage."

Through her tears, she looked at us with a sudden mischievous gleam in her eyes and turned to me. "He doesn't know I'm not interested in marriage, though, that I want to stay an old maid like you and become an investigator!"

Her words stung a little, but Lola spoke before I managed to find a response.

"He must think so highly of himself!" Lola shouted. "The swine!"

"He also said he's going to do everything in his power to remedy my disgraceful situation."

Anna seemed to have calmed down now that she had unburdened herself of her secrets. The banker's words seemed to have done her more harm than the physical attack. I wondered if the two events could be related.

Lola's mood lightened as she laughed nervously. "Anna, you are aware, aren't you, that Cousin is only after your virtue?"

"What do you mean?"

"I mean, all he wants is for you to go to his bed," Lola said bluntly. "And by any means necessary. I'm sure the conclusion of your discussion was that you would be better off living with him? Am I right?"

Anna glanced downward.

"You must be so careful," Lola continued. "When men covet girls, they have a thousand ways of seducing them."

"You're lying," Anna whispered, looking up to meet Lola's gaze. "You're just jealous because Monsieur Cousin is interested in me and would like to secure my future. He doesn't want compensation of any kind. He's a good man."

She rushed out of the living room and into her bedchamber, slamming the door for the second time that evening. Lola reiterated loudly that she didn't want her to see this man again.

"I will do as I see fit," Anna replied in the same tone through the door. "You have no rights over me. You're not my mother!"

Frustrated, Lola turned and shook her fist at me. I couldn't believe it.

Rosalie looked on sorrowfully as Lola ventured, "How is it that she slipped out right under your nose? Where were you tonight? You were supposed to be looking after her!"

"I went out," I said. "And what of it? I didn't know this house was a prison. Besides, Rosalie was here, and Anna was in bed when I left. Come on, Mademoiselle Lola, you can't blame me for this. It would be indecent of you."

Rosalie nodded in support.

But guilt was eating away at me. If I hadn't gone to see Lady Sarah, I could have prevented Anna's escape. I would have seen her leaving the house. I would perhaps even have followed her.

Lola, ever inquisitive, asked, "Where did you go?"

"I-I needed to get some fresh air," I stammered. "I needed a little space to think, so I went for a walk alone."

Rosalie glanced at me, realizing I had no intention of discussing the famous carriage that had come to the house. She wouldn't betray me, and she wasn't the type to interfere in anything that didn't concern her.

But Lola spotted the way we looked at one another. I noticed her bitter pout and imagined how betrayed she must have felt. By me. By Rosalie. We were her real family.

"You're lying. Both of you. You're colluding. I don't know what it's all about, but I'll find out."

Rosalie left us without further word.

Then, suddenly remembering that Ferdinand had been waiting for her in her room all this time, Lola muttered, "I have things to do."

She grabbed the bottle of champagne and returned to her room with a step that betrayed her wrath.

I slowly climbed up toward my bedchamber with the cat close on my heels.

10

FERDINAND THE HERO

Breakfast was served on the table in front of the large window. I was alone as I ate. Well, Sherry was with me, of course, but asleep on a chair rather than partaking of the feast.

I loved those moments when I could sit and listen to the sounds of the new day. They came to me like music—cockerels crowing, the bell of the Chapelle Saint-Nicolas ringing out the hour, and the squealing of the brakes as the trains entered the station nearby.

I hadn't slept well following the scene the night before, and I was worried. But my optimism, which had become a part of me upon meeting Lola, told me that everything would be fine. She would admit what lies she had told me—if what Sarah had said was true. And we were going to give my former mistress her file back so she would never have cause to harass me again. Finally, Anna would return to her senses and make peace with Lola.

The buttered toast I brought to my lips tasted delicious. The bread had been made by Rosalie, the butter came from a local dairy farmer who delivered it straight to the door, and the jam was made from cherries from the tree behind our house. This was a French breakfast fit for a king. What more could one ask for? A frisson of happiness started to permeate me.

Rosalie entered with a fresh pot of steaming coffee. The smell of it must have stirred Lola, who came out of her room in a drowsy state.

"You're up early," I said.

"I had a terrible night," she replied as she poured the fragrant beverage into one of her *de Sèvres* bowls. "I didn't sleep a wink."

After drinking almost half of the contents without coming up for air, she continued. "I'll never understand what has gotten into Anna. Honestly. She could at least give me the benefit of the doubt. Instead, she goes and trusts the first person who comes along. The more I think about it, the angrier I get."

The bell rang at the gate. Several minutes later, Rosalie knocked at the door and entered with a gentleman. Ferdinand! He greeted me with great reverence. He did not, however, lean in to greet Lola.

Before heading back downstairs, Rosalie raised her eyebrows at me and gave a sideways nod. I knew what she meant. She was letting me know that Ferdinand had simply slipped out the back of the house and come around to the front for propriety's sake.

"Dear Ferdinand!" she exclaimed. "My hero! What are you doing here at this time?"

His eyes came to life as he watched her with amusement.

"I was passing through the neighborhood. I hope it is not considered too audacious to have called upon you. I know you live here with several other women. There will be nothing inappropriate about my visit, I hope?"

"Not at all. On the contrary, I am honored! Do you know my friend Miss Fletcher? Miss Fletcher, I met with the baron last night at the theater. He saved me from quite an embarrassment when I encountered Carré-Lamadon."

"Philémon? Has he been causing trouble again?"

"It would seem so. Although I know he can't do a thing to me, whatever he says aggravates me so." Lola still harbored bitter feelings toward Philémon Carré-Lamadon, a friend of Eugène's who had tried to evict Lola from Les Pavots when she'd refused his advances.

Ferdinand approached her and touched her hair discreetly behind her back. She invited him to sit next to her, and he quickly accepted.

"This gallant young man came to my rescue! There is to be a duel tomorrow morning at Napoule."

"But that's just awful! Duels are prohibited! Someone could get killed! Now, come, you must send word out and have it stopped. We must talk to Paul Antoine and Maupassant about this. They will know what to do," I said.

"Paul Antoine Isnard de la Motte is my second," said Ferdinand in a boastful tone.

"Don't worry your pretty head about it, Miss Fletcher," said Lola. "My honor is at stake. Maupassant finds it all ridiculous and is wholly disinterested in it."

The fact was she didn't believe there would ever be a duel.

"You see here before you a brave young man. Isn't that so, my friend?" she continued.

"I'll eat him alive," said Ferdinand, laughing.

The cat jumped out of his chair and waltzed out of the living room and onto the balcony.

The young man caressed Lola, kissing her on the neck and hair.

His every action demonstrated thoughtfulness toward her, anticipating her every desire, pouring her more coffee, spreading butter on her bread, presenting her with candied fruits. It was all extremely vexing.

Of course, I didn't let my irritation show.

As for Lola—she was in heaven, smiling blissfully and looking radiant. She seemed to seek my permission with her eyes, but she was soon under his spell again. She loved nothing more than such delicate ministrations as these.

I thought well of him, despite the spectacle, and I hoped he would finally be the one who might last long enough for Lola to secure her future.

Although his simpering annoyed me, I was glad he was at least young and handsome and far better for Lola than an old, big-bellied fellow who didn't have a kind word for anyone.

Ferdinand seemed so enchanted by Lola, asking questions about her life, wanting to know every detail and expressing his admiration for her every thought.

I somehow managed to refrain from laughing, for my education has always demanded that I remain polite whatever the situation.

Lola pushed him away slightly so she could pick up her bowl, for it appeared he had wanted to take it and lift it to her mouth himself. This was too much, even for Lola. He got to his feet, perhaps a little offended, and paced up and down the room, observing everything: her bibelots, her perfumes, her books.

He didn't say so, but it was obvious he hoped to absorb everything about Lola's life. All her secrets. I even saw him discreetly pocket an old ribbon that was lying on the ground, after rubbing it softly against his cheek.

He was disconcerting, and I had forgotten the pinches of envy I sometimes felt when Lola received her visitors.

We hadn't heard the bell, but we recognized Maupassant's way of climbing the stairs, heavily and at a fast pace.

"Here's our man," said Lola, which made her new lover's ears prick up, and he stood, trembling, waiting for the door to open.

The writer stomped into the living room, out of breath, and threw a huge paper bag of warm pastries onto the table.

"I stopped by Rumpelmayer's to bring you some treats."

His voice sounded stifled, and his step was heavier than usual. I wondered whether he might have been drinking that morning, but Maupassant was not a man who drank. He must have suffered one of his painful seizures and been forced to use sedatives. I'd seen how they impaired his faculties on other occasions.

"I didn't think I'd find you up already, ladies!" he exclaimed a little too loudly, wobbling on his legs. "I have some lovely news to tell you!"

"And we might say the very same to you, Guy. What are you doing here at this hour? What about your writing session? And you are in such disarray. Your mustache is not even combed! What's going on?" demanded Lola.

"Wait until you find out!"

He only then noted the presence of Ferdinand. "Here already?" he asked the younger man in a brusque manner.

Maupassant raised an eyebrow toward Lola, who turned away from his gaze. She sometimes felt so girlishly confused in his presence. For me, this was proof that she loved him. Perhaps he was the only man she had ever loved, despite her insistence that Eugène had been her one and only true match.

She walked to the door and out to the top of the stairs. "Rosalie!" she yelled. "Could you bring up some hot chocolate? Didn't you see Maupassant arrive?"

Rosalie's voice reached us from the kitchen below. "For heaven's sake! I only have the one pair of hands! I'm coming!"

"Do you know Ferdinand, Miss Fletcher?" Maupassant said. "We met at dinner last night. Why weren't you there? Sulking again? You never come to dinner in town. Oh yes, that's right. Yesterday you had a good reason, at least, with our little Anna. How is she? Mademoiselle Lola managed only a few words. It wasn't exactly the time or the place."

I caught Lola's eye, and she replied with a nod—this was permission to speak to Maupassant in full. "Yesterday, she spent the day in bed. We still don't know who the assailant was."

Ferdinand looked deflated now that Maupassant was here. He sat next to Lola, as if to affirm his place, and tried to take her hand, but she gently shook her head.

"I appreciate your having visited this morning, my dear, but you must leave me now."

"But I feel so well by your side," said Ferdinand, almost pouting.

He didn't know yet that Lola did not like to be disobeyed. She wanted to talk in peace with Maupassant and me, and she knew that his being there bothered us both. With his continued pouting, Lola finally nodded her assent that he could stay.

I continued to recount the tale in full.

"A thief, you say. What was stolen?" asked the writer.

"A bracelet with her name on it that we gave her for her birthday."

"Was she hurt?"

"Her dress was torn, and her hair was pulled. She was so shocked! And now she feels a great deal of anger toward us, particularly Lola. She's been fighting with us, and her moods have been unpredictable. She hasn't left her room much at all."

"That's not like her. Where is she? I might just have a word. A few jokes from me, and her smile will return, I can guarantee it."

"She is still asleep! It's early!" said Lola.

Maupassant circled the room slowly, wobbling slightly. He looked as though his thoughts on what I had just told him were haunting him a great deal.

"There's just so much violence going on these days. I thought this was a safe place to live. But first this, and now Cannes's favorite banker has been found dead in his home! They say he was murdered."

"What?" Lola and I shouted simultaneously.

"You mean Cousin, don't you? Murdered?" asked Lola. "How do you know this? You didn't say anything last night."

"No one knew a thing about it last night. Well, that's not quite true. The killer knew, of course."

"How did this happen? How do you know?" Lola had a thousand questions and didn't know where to start.

"I had a front-row seat! I went with Dr. Buttura this morning. I even shook hands with Commissioner Valantin and questioned the valet, James," said Maupassant.

He continued, explaining how he had been suffering from a terrible migraine and woke up early. He went for a walk to try to ease the pain and had come across the doctor, who had been sent for to declare the banker's death. He suggested that Maupassant join him in his cab so he could administer some laudanum during the journey, believing it would provide some relief. When they arrived at the doctor's destination, they found Valantin, who had come to investigate.

As our writer friend was spilling all the details, Ferdinand stood and walked to the window. He was aggrieved because every time he went to grab Lola's hand, she pushed him away, gently but firmly.

"But how can you be so sure he was killed?" I asked.

"The blood, my dear . . ." His voice sent a shudder through my chest. "He was bathed in his own blood."

I whispered, "Cousin. Murdered . . ."

I exchanged a worried look with Lola. I knew we were thinking the same thing: Anna. The banker had followed her, and they had spoken on more than one occasion. This rapprochement was a change in his habits—in both of their habits. And suddenly the man had been slain in his own home?

Was the attack on Anna related to this tragic event somehow? Did Anna narrowly escape death too?

Neither of us took our eyes away from Maupassant, who finally sat down and leaned toward me. "I know, Miss Fletcher, it's quite shocking. I'm about to tell you everything, at least, everything I know. But what was that look between the pair of you?"

He turned to Lola, much to the great displeasure of Ferdinand, who was now seated at her side again.

"Are you keeping secrets from me?"

"No, it's just . . . We didn't tell you that . . . Anna met with Cousin."

"Oh? How is that possible?"

"Well, we went to see him a few days ago at his offices on Rue d'Antibes to ask for his advice."

"Concerning?"

"I wanted to borrow money to buy a piece of land. Well, maybe . . . I don't know if it's a good idea now."

Maupassant burst out laughing. "You always have some little venture under your cap. Women don't much care about finances as a rule, but the rules don't apply to you, do they? Good Lord, Lola, what a farce!"

Ferdinand, who until then had not taken any part in the conversation, contenting himself with begging for Lola's attention, laughed stupidly. I believe it was a reflex, a sort of solidarity that men have when laughing at women.

"Oh, you!" scolded Lola.

He immediately stopped laughing.

"Why don't you just take your cane and go home?" she spat.

Ferdinand gave Maupassant a dark look, as did I.

"And you're such a fine businessman, Maupassant, are you?" I mocked.

"Perhaps not quite a Rothschild, but let's just say that when it comes to talking to my publishers, I have a rather fine set of skills. As for Mademoiselle Lola, everyone knows she's a sieve when it comes to money. And with Cannes's current crisis regarding land and real estate, the very last thing I would do is borrow money."

Lola stood abruptly, almost knocking Ferdinand to the floor. "You're quite wrong. Cousin congratulated me on my plans."

"Of course, he did! He almost bankrupted everyone in Cannes. He must have been over the moon when he found himself another lamb to take to the slaughter."

"No. I don't think so. He said that whoever had advised me had good business sense and that it was indeed now the time to buy. I came upon the idea myself, and I believe it to be a good one."

She was so animated that she had forgotten that the imaginary loan was not the real reason that led us to Cousin's bank.

But she obviously didn't want to talk to Maupassant about Lady Sarah.

"I can make neither head nor tail of this discussion," said Maupassant. "What were we talking about again?" He looked at her quizzically before his eyes widened. "Oh yes. Of course, the murder. After I observed as much as I could, I came to tell you everything. It's incredible that I was among the first on the scene, is it not?"

"And why does that matter?" Lola asked.

"Why, because of your love for police investigations, my dear."

"Me?" shouted Lola. "You don't know me well at all!"

"What about Clara Campo? Have you already forgotten her?"

Lola looked sullen. "Not at all. But do you truly believe I tried to solve the riddle of her death for mere sport? Because I love investigations or some such nonsense? I hate death, and even more so if it's violent. So please keep to yourself any information you may have about the untimely demise of Cousin."

"I just wanted to talk you through what I saw this morning."

"I have no interest in it," she replied.

"Well, Valantin seems to have his man already."

"I don't want to know anything about it!" she insisted.

"But you know him! Valantin asked Cousin's valet, James, if his master had any enemies. I couldn't help but laugh. He had naught but enemies! Valantin demanded that I hold my tongue, but I told him about the scene we had witnessed the other day at the station, with the man from the Faisan Doré. Do you remember?"

Lola could no longer hide her curiosity. "Does the valet know the man?"

"That's what Valantin asked. James told us that the fellow had once been a wealthy wine merchant. Étienne Lecerf is his name. Just a few months ago, Lecerf was a regular at Cousin's dining table. Cousin had sold him land and lent him money to build a rental house near Boulevard de la Foncière. Like everyone else, he borrowed from the banker to speculate. And what happened to everyone else happened to him—the market collapsed, and Lecerf was ruined. He was then hired as a general drudge at the Faisan Doré."

"So that's how Valantin got his man? Good for him. It seems like the case is running smoothly. Well, my friend," she said gently to Ferdinand, taking him by the arm, "you really must go now. I have a number of things to deal with. You have no idea how busy I am. First things first, I must take my bath."

Ferdinand pretended to be indifferent to her words, but everyone could see he was affected greatly by this rejection. She accompanied him to the corridor and kissed him at length on the landing, whispering tender words in his ear. Then she came back to join us, closing the door behind him with a sigh.

"Finally," she whispered. "I thought he'd never leave!"

Maupassant gave me an amused smile as we listened to Ferdinand make his way down the stairs. Lola ran to the window to wave at him.

"He's charming, really," she said as she waved. "But I need room to breathe."

"He seems to care about you a great deal," I said in a pinched voice.

"Yes, I think so too," she said. "And I hold him in high esteem as well. According to Paul Antoine, his income is quite substantial. He hails from a family of financiers."

"Everyone has something to do with commerce or banks these days," Maupassant muttered.

He walked over to the table and looked at the various silver jugs laid out on the tray and lifted the lids, smelling the contents. "Where's Rosalie with that hot chocolate?"

"Goodness knows," said Lola. "Wasn't Valantin surprised that you knew of Cousin?"

"A little, but as I told him, who in Cannes doesn't know the fellow? He has ruined so many families. All you have to do is open a paper. Each day brings news of yet more houses and businesses for auction. I suggested to the commissioner that it might be a heart attack, with all the insulting correspondence he must receive. One of them might have been playing on his conscience. But then, there was a lot of blood."

"How Valantin must have appreciated your humor! How were they notified of the murder, exactly?" Lola asked.

"A servant found him dead in his library and ran to the police station immediately."

"Did you see the body?"

"They wouldn't let me near him, but I saw the scene through the open door. I was quite vexed not to be allowed a closer look, so I took it upon myself to ask this James man some questions. But he would not speak with me. Not at that stage. It's strange that his name is James, is it not? He has a Suquet accent. Cousin must have given it to him, thinking that an English name would make him more fashionable."

"What exactly did Cousin die of? What did Dr. Buttura say?"

"He was stabbed. Yet the murder weapon is nowhere to be found. Once the commissioner left to arrest Lecerf, James relaxed and talked more freely with me. I learned then that Cousin had given all his servants a few days' leave earlier that day."

"What a coincidence," Lola noted. "The very night he is killed."

11

THE BIRD HAS FLOWN

Lola gave me an indulgent smile. We laughed at how greedy she could sometimes be, as she served herself a second large cup of the smooth and fragrant coffee, despite it no longer being hot.

Silence then set in. Lola frowned once again. She was clearly worried. Maupassant was also sipping on some cold coffee and appeared to be deep in thought. I was forcing myself to enjoy this moment of calm before the storm. I was on tenterhooks about the very idea of Anna waking.

The sound of male voices in front of the house caught the attention of all three of us. One of the men was very angry and arguing loudly with a second, meeker-sounding gentleman. We listened to Rosalie's protests as she answered the door, and then heard hurried steps rushing up the staircase.

I was startled by the terrified howl from the cat as two uniformed police officers burst into the room. I was surprised to see there were only two. They had made such noise when they'd arrived that I'd believed there to be at least forty!

The first man greeted Maupassant in military fashion. The second officer didn't open his mouth, letting his superior do the talking. I couldn't even guess at what rank either of them was, knowing very little about police hierarchy. However, the officer standing ahead of the other, perhaps a brigadier, was looking at Lola.

Sherry was still yowling at the intruders. His tail had doubled in size. I grabbed the cat, feeling an urge to protect him, fearing a kick from one of the men, and placed him on the balcony before closing the French doors.

My young mistress looked bewildered under this man's gaze, which was rare. When the man realized I would be staying, he turned to me with a scornful look.

I understood then that it was Émile Rodot, Lola's sworn enemy— not counting Philémon Carré-Lamadon, of course. She had spoken of him on only a few occasions. He was the officer who had abused her one night at the station, taking advantage of the fact that she had been caught in a raid and that he was in a position to manipulate her. She had given in to his desire and his bidding.

Since then, she had investigated the officer and now knew his name and other aspects of his life. It was her way of regaining some control. He was a little pug of a man who knew how to abuse what power he had. And he continued to prowl around Lola.

One evening, as she was awaiting a client who was accompanying her to a private dinner at the Grand Café, she had met Rodot doing his rounds on Rue de la Vapeur. He had pinned her against a wall and threatened her with a knife while trying to force her to perform certain acts on him. She had refused and had been able to provide a few names as protection, for her position had changed, and she was no longer as vulnerable as she had once been.

Although she was excluded from society, and nothing could be done to change this, she now belonged on the periphery of the demi-monde who ruled over the working people of the city, including the police forces.

The names she had given made him stop in his tracks, but in his eyes, she understood he was intent on bringing about her ruin, that he would find a fault that would allow him to hold her once again at his mercy.

She always experienced a shiver of apprehension whenever she came across him.

This day, they were brandishing a warrant to bring in Anna Martin for questioning.

"Anna Martin?" asked Maupassant. "But she's a child! What could you possibly want with her?"

"We are not obliged to disclose elements of an investigation," said the brigadier.

"They must need her to make a statement about her assault," I said in a reassuring tone.

But no one had reported the attack, so we were left wondering how the police had learned of the sorry event.

I couldn't help but think it had something to do with Cousin's murder, since it had only just happened and Anna had been in contact with him.

"Gentlemen, this girl is under our protection," I stated. "I'll go and fetch her for you; though, of course, being a minor, she will be accompanied by one or all of us."

As I left the room, Maupassant shouted down to Rosalie to bring up two glasses and some wine. I stopped outside the door and continued to listen in on their conversation.

"Gentlemen, would you like a little tonic? I realize the day has only just begun, but we might be in need of it. What a tragedy. Poor Monsieur Cousin! Have you made any progress on that front?"

He was met with a stony silence. The drinks might indeed loosen their tongues.

I went to Anna's room and tentatively opened the door. In the dimness, I approached her bed, calling out to her softly.

"Anna, Anna . . . Wake up."

The eiderdown appeared to be unusually flat. As I got closer, I saw that the bed was empty. Anna's little head was not resting where it should have been on the pretty pink lace pillow.

I drew back the curtains and turned again to the bed. My head began to spin as I grasped the entirety of the situation. Instead of our Anna, there was blood. Blood on the floor, blood on the bed, blood on a pink dress that lay on the ground. It was the dress Anna had been wearing when she'd returned from her nocturnal outing.

The window was open slightly, and the cold air made me shiver.

I panicked. Where was Anna? She must have been kidnapped. Maybe by the same man who had attacked her. Had she been murdered too? Like Cousin? Our Anna? No! It just wasn't possible. I rubbed my forehead frantically, trying to erase the violent images from my mind.

I ran to the window, opened it wide, and leaned over the edge, trying to discern what I could . . . anything, a piece of fabric, drops of blood, prints in the grass. But the orchards and fields stretched behind our villa as far as the eye could see, dotted with a few buildings and people going about their daily business, and I spotted no suspicious movement of any kind. A farmer was pushing a wheelbarrow, and a little farther on, two young girls carrying laundry baskets chatted as they crossed the fields on their way into town.

The police! They were waiting in the living room. What would they think of this dreadful scene? Would they think Anna had run away? I had to come up with an answer before they noted my prolonged absence. We needed to stay ahead of them and the dreaded, corrupt Rodot. Protecting Anna was of utmost importance. Could I find something here that would lead us to her?

I searched the room frantically for the slightest clue. A letter? A journal, perhaps? Something that could provide some clarity to this drama. I looked under the bed and opened the large wardrobe, pulling out dresses and shawls, lifting up her books and sheet music. There was nothing out of the ordinary. Her room was untidy and disordered, but then, it always was so.

As I continued to rifle through her belongings, I heard the officers' raised voices. They seemed to be losing patience. I could feel my anxiety rising.

I walked back to the bed, appalled by the sight that my mind was refusing to accept. Did I want the police officers to see this? What would they make of all the blood? I picked up the dress, and a shiny object, a blade, fell from its folds. The noise was muffled by the rug as it hit the floor. I leaned over and grabbed it.

It was a letter opener, and it was stained red.

The blood was dry and had formed a dark, almost black crust. I read the initials H. C. engraved in the metal, just before Rodot opened the door.

And there I was with the letter opener in one hand and the dress in the other. This sight clearly angered him, as he yelled, "So? The bird has flown!"

He charged toward me, tearing the objects from my hands. I didn't cling to them. I didn't even try.

But I pushed him away and said sharply, "Please, monsieur."

I used the Ramsey tone, often employed to great effect by my father, and this made Rodot recoil. The voice of my past commanded respect.

"Madame, I would ask you to please leave the room."

I stepped out but stood in the doorway, maintaining my dignity, while he searched the scene. He followed the same path I had: the window, the wardrobe, under the bed, the small bureau. In the hallway, I encountered his colleague, who gave me the most furious look as he stormed past.

The brigadier barked at him, "She's run away! We need to tell Hippolyte to leave the carriage and come help us search the house and cellars. We should look in the outbuildings too. Let's start collecting anything with traces of blood on it. We must take it all to the boss."

Rodot then stomped out of Anna's room and pushed me out of the way. I shuffled into the living room behind him. I felt sick and could still feel a slight pain from the pressure of his hands. Maupassant rushed to my rescue. He looked shocked to see me in such a state. Lola got up hurriedly.

"What's going on?" she asked.

Rodot had opened the windows and was leaning out over the balcony. "Hippolyte, come on in. I'll meet you downstairs. We have a lot of work to do here. The bird has flown. It's her, all right. We've got her!"

He turned around and ran back to the door. But to reach it, he had to pass the three of us. We were huddled together next to the table.

Lola grabbed Rodot's arm and stuttered, "W-What . . . Whom are you talking about? What is this all about?"

He declined to answer but managed to find the time to undress her with his eyes. She, who usually never gave the lightness of her clothes a second thought, shivered and took her hand off him before crossing her arms across her chest. I was outraged to see what this rude character was giving himself permission to do. The way he observed her was appalling.

He dusted off his arm where Lola had touched him, and from a sheath on his hip, he pulled out a long knife, which he started to play with carelessly.

"Sorry? Did you ask me a question?" He smiled, mocking her.

I looked at Maupassant, but he was blind to the scene playing out before him and headed for Anna's room.

"Yes, I was quite obviously talking to you, you snipe! Don't forget that I know how you work. I know your penchants."

"Is that a threat, young lady?" The look in his eyes was beyond vicious. "Do you think a girl like you can speak like that to a police officer? You're no match for me, and you know it. I'm just biding my time, and my moment will come. You'll all end up coming for a ride in my little cage, mark my words. All I have to do now is find a reason to arrest you. Just like I did last time. Do you remember what happened last time? I certainly do. Fondly."

Lola shivered with horror as she recalled the night she had been caught in the roundup. "You won't have me a second time," said Lola with insistence.

"That's what you think," he scoffed.

Rodot ran out and down the stairs to join his colleague.

I heard Lola mutter between her teeth, "I'll get you one day. I swear it." Anxiously, she turned to me. "Tell me what's happening. Where's Anna? Fletcher, answer me!"

"She's not in her room."

"Where can she be?" Lola started whimpering loudly. "What could have happened to her? She's suffered so much already, and now you're telling me she's gone? Where?"

"I don't know. I fear the worst. Her bed . . . her dress . . . There's blood everywhere."

"What? No! Not Anna!"

"And there was a letter opener . . ."

"What letter opener?" asked Maupassant, who had just walked back in. He looked unsettled and alarmed.

"It was all tangled up in her clothing. Her dress . . . all bloodied . . . It was torn and lying on the floor. And in it there was a letter opener. It was also covered in blood."

"Anna is allowed to have a letter opener, is she not? I have one too! Who doesn't?" shouted Lola, clearly not seeing reason.

"There were initials engraved on it."

"Initials?" she asked quietly, as if she no longer wished to know.

A menacing silence hovered. The calm that precedes the storm. I continued in a whisper, "H. C."

"Henri Cousin!" Lola cried, shuddering.

"Valantin couldn't find the murder weapon," Maupassant said in a monotonous voice. "Could it possibly be that the letter opener was used to kill Cousin? But Anna has had nothing to do with that."

He must have noted our guilty expressions before adding with more than a hint of suspicion, "You said that Anna had met with Cousin. Is there more to it than that?"

"Yes. I think it's worse than that," I said.

Lola sat down slowly, using the table to steady herself. She stared at a fixed point in front of her as she spoke, no doubt numbed by the flood of shocking revelations.

"They went for ice cream, apparently. I think there was some sort of budding romance. She went out in secret and came back in the early hours."

"And what about Lecerf?" asked Maupassant.

"What Lecerf?" she said with exasperation.

"Étienne Lecerf, the fellow who works at the Faisan Doré," he explained. "This is what we need to know: Why did Valantin tell me he was going to arrest Lecerf? But now Anna is being sought, and officers are in here saying things like 'We've got her'? What is this all about?" He rushed toward the door in fury. "I'm going to clear this up with the commissioner."

We watched from the window as he scurried down the hill toward the railway tracks and the heart of the city beyond.

Lola took refuge in my arms, shaking with fear, but I felt as though I were the one who needed the most comfort.

I could not find a single word to reassure her. Along with protests from Rosalie, we could hear the racket caused by the officers as they searched through the house.

I was overwhelmed by the emotions gripping me. Brutal police officers performing an official search through the house brought back terrible memories of my parents' death.

I had thought myself capable of handling a great many things, but I could see that on the contrary, I had become vulnerable. I thought I was strong, but the sight of blood coupled with fear for a loved one reminded me of an era that I thought I'd left far behind.

But can we ever really be cured of the painful events that tear our childhoods apart?

I felt the color drain from my face. Fog invaded my mind. My limbs softened, as if I were a rag doll.

I could no longer control myself. I collapsed into Lola's arms. I should have been supporting her, and I was failing miserably.

Then I fainted.

As I slowly came to, still in a state of utter confusion, I heard rustling sounds all around me. Lola was calling out for Rosalie. I was pulled to my feet, and then someone undid my corset to help me breathe easier. I had regained consciousness by the time they had laid me down on the couch. Lola sent Rosalie to get a doctor.

The Chapelle Saint-Nicolas bell rang out the half hour. What time was it exactly? Half past what? Time had escaped me. I felt like I was losing myself.

Lola's soft hand was stroking my forehead with the most delicate of touches. She hummed a peaceful song, like a mother singing a lullaby to her child. Was she doing this for me or for her?

I opened my eyes. Her face was partially turned away as she looked toward the windows. If she had been looking at me, I wouldn't have dared to say what I said next, though eventually, I would have felt too guilty keeping it to myself.

"Lady Sarah came last night," I said in a broken voice.

She continued to look the other way. "Oh? So it was her? What did she want with you?"

"She threatened to ruin my reputation if I didn't give her that file."

"She has some good spies working for her if she knows we already have that contract. And she has far more to fear than you. Ruin your reputation, indeed!"

"You're sadly mistaken, mademoiselle. She's stronger than I. Underneath this hard exterior I put on for show, I know I wouldn't survive a scandal. I am weak. I cannot face the eyes of others upon me. I cannot. It's just . . ."

She gave me time to compose myself, but the floodgates inside me opened. She still didn't look at me.

"I've already experienced it. I've been alone and known the hostility of people. I was seventeen years old. I could never relive such a situation. I don't have it in me."

She didn't question me further. She simply continued brushing my forehead with her delicate hand. But the words started spilling from my mouth. I couldn't hold them back.

"That day, I came home from my riding class, bubbling with joy as I always was . . . Gosh, I was so carefree." My chin began to shake, and my voice faltered as I ventured further into telling the tale. "As I entered the library to collect a book, I noticed that the door to my father's study was open. It was unusual, and so I walked over to close it. I knew he didn't like to be disturbed. The curtains were drawn, but in the darkness, I saw a slight movement."

I held my breath. This was beyond what little strength I had. My eyes were wide open now, reliving the drama of the very moment my whole life had changed forever. I felt suffocated.

Lola continued for me, as if she had been there herself. She held my hand. "The movement . . . His feet . . . ," she whispered. "He'd . . ."

I felt able to speak again. "Yes, he'd hanged himself. It took me a few minutes to understand the picture before me. The chair overturned on the large varnished wooden surface of his desk. The rope hanging from the beam above. And at the end of the rope, my father's body . . ."

She squeezed my hand, and I felt her compassion.

"I was dragged away from the scene. I must have lost consciousness. And this morning . . . the letter opener, Anna's disappearance, the police in our house . . . It must have brought it all back to me. I thought I'd forgotten that part of my past."

"Nothing is ever truly forgotten," Lola whispered, her eyes cast downward. "We bury it, and we cover it up, but we don't forget." She shook her head as if to clear her thoughts, then looked at me. "But why? Why did your father . . . ?"

I pulled myself away from her caress, slowly stood, and walked over to the table to take a few sips of water before moving back toward her and sitting up straight in one of the armchairs, feeling a little more at ease.

"It's a commonplace-enough tale. He'd left a letter, of course. He'd been gambling. Large sums of money. Little by little, he squandered his . . . our . . . fortune. He spent my mother's dowry, and that's when he knew he would have to declare himself bankrupt. Rather than do so, he chose to take his own life."

The sound of an arriving train could be heard in the distance.

"What happened to your mother?" Lola asked.

"She left the Isle of Man and took refuge in Rochester, where she had spent a few happy months as a child. I followed her. She took on menial tasks—sewing and the like—and I gave singing lessons. The shock of what she'd suffered caused her to die of grief a year later. I then found a position with a wealthy family as a governess."

"And that's how you later met Lady Sarah?"

"Yes. And now you know everything there is to know, mademoiselle."

My smile was bitter. I had regained my composure, and it was now becoming difficult for me to withstand her gaze, after revealing so much. I felt so ashamed.

Lola could see how shaken I was but continued to watch me. What would happen? Would I have the courage to resist Lady Sarah? Was I still under her control?

Her voice pierced the silence. "Don't concern yourself with Lady Sarah. I will deal with her. I know something that will keep her from ever harming you. She knows that. The most she can do is threaten you. She must believe you won't breathe a word of it to me. She doesn't know that we don't keep secrets from one another."

As she spoke these words, I felt myself blushing violently.

She went on, as if thinking out loud, "I wonder if Lady Sarah murdered Cousin?"

I couldn't hold back a nervous laugh. "You don't really believe that, do you?"

"Why should it not be her? She has the motive: the threat of bankruptcy, of being ruined."

"But she is not the only one in Cannes to have such fears."

"Yes, but she's a more likely suspect than the others. She risks being locked up in an asylum for life."

She was right, but something prevented me from agreeing with her. Was it a remnant of loyalty to Lady Sarah? Did I feel that Lola wasn't telling me everything, that a lie was hidden behind her words?

"You should rest now, Miss Fletcher. The doctor will be here soon. I'm going to look for Anna in town. She's in great danger, and she doesn't even know it. Suspected of murder! What could be worse? I must find her before they do. It's possible she ran away. I just hope she wasn't kidnapped, or . . ." Her voice trailed off. The alternative was unthinkable.

"Where will you look for her?"

"I'll start at the orphanage. She knows that place like the back of her hand."

"But that's where she spent the worst years of her life. Why would she go there?"

"That's true. I'll go up to the Suquet, then, and tell my family to keep an eye out for her."

"I will come and find you at your mother's. Wait for me there. Rosalie and I will meet you as soon as the doctor leaves."

I had already started to make my way toward the stairs leading to my room.

Sherry, who had managed to get back inside, was waiting for me on my quilt. He looked uneasy.

I lay down and drifted off. My slumber was full of nightmares. I witnessed the murder of the banker as if I were in the same room but invisible. But I couldn't make out the identity of the murderer. The image of the dead man was the same as that of my father. Ghostly objects swirled in my mind. Papers were being burned. The bloody letter opener appeared. And in the hands of the banker lay Anna's missing bracelet.

I jumped up with a start, trying to catch my breath. What was I to make of this terrifying image? Could it be a clue that would lead us to Anna?

12

SUSPECTED

As Maupassant told us later, it took him less than ten minutes to reach the police station in the center of Cannes, where he was taken straight to Valantin.

"What is this charade?" Maupassant demanded. "How could you have agreed to have a young girl hunted down in such a shameful way? A warrant? Like a criminal? You're not serious, surely?"

"I'm always serious," replied Valantin, offended. He wouldn't be spoken to like this, particularly on his own territory.

"But this is insane! Come, now!"

"A man like you, so very used to logic and reason, will quickly come to understand my point of view."

"But I thought you'd found your killer? That Lecerf fellow?"

"I have since found more solid evidence, monsieur. Do you think I would have acted without good reason?"

"How can you talk so? She's gone. This child may have been kidnapped or even killed!"

"Kidnapped? Killed? And what would be the motive, for God's sake?"

"For the same reason she was assaulted in the street."

"Assaulted? Really?" Valantin tapped his mustache.

"This is a crying shame. You have nothing to blame this girl for, and yet you send your officers after her as if she were a danger to the public. While Lecerf, the actual murderer, is still at large?"

"Forget about Lecerf. The banker and the girl have been seen together. They were even seen at Rumpelmayer's. Certainly, Cousin had a third party accompany them, a fellow who worked in his offices, so as not to compromise her reputation—or his, I might add—but what about in private, huh? I think he had his eye on the girl and may have been planning to ask her to be his mistress. This is often the case when men start to age. They succumb to a sudden passion that can drive them mad. He fell for the girl, and she must have been taken in by him."

"Monsieur, hold your words. They are insulting to Anna. She would never have been in the company of a man who made inappropriate advances toward her."

Valantin appeared to enjoy what Maupassant had just said, as if the two men were sharing a joke.

"Come on, my friend! I know you've known this girl for several years now, that you've seen her grow up, but you and I both know who raised her."

Maupassant looked at the commissioner with contempt. He had always found duels to be ridiculous, but he was starting to understand the attraction. He would have liked nothing more than to cross swords with the fat fool, though he would settle for hitting him hard in the face. He wasn't all bad at boxing. But he still needed information from Valantin.

"You have nothing conclusive against her. Admit it."

"Listen. I shouldn't tell you this, but there are a number of leads that take us straight to the young woman. First of all, a girl fitting her description was seen prowling around his villa yesterday evening."

"But so many of these girls look alike! This is ridiculous!"

"Listen, would you? She went to his house last night. He had managed to draw her there under some sort of pretext. But he was rushing her. Faced with reality, she became scared and stabbed him. She was defending her virtue, you see?"

Maupassant sighed. There was a knock at the door, and Valantin excused himself and left the room, giving Maupassant time to think. Soon after, the commissioner returned with a satisfied smirk on his lips.

"It's all just guesswork," Maupassant said quickly. "I know Anna, and she's not the type to become violent. She has benefited from a very good education, whatever you may think."

"A farmer's daughter raised by a wanton woman and an old maid? Stop playing the innocent. You were at their house this morning and saw with your own eyes what my men found. I've just spoken with Rodot about it."

"Are you calling me a liar?"

"No. You are just a man who is loyal to his friends. But please. The letter opener? The initials? The blood? This is the murder weapon we've been looking for, hidden in that house of ill repute. And it wasn't even my men who found it, but your friend Miss Fletcher! What can you say to that?"

Maupassant could think of no counterargument.

It was incomprehensible, indeed. But then he cried out triumphantly, "If this were in a novel, it would be the indisputable proof that someone was trying to blame the girl! Think about it. What sort of assassin would leave the murder weapon in her own room instead of disposing of it somewhere?"

Valantin laughed. "You and your novels. I always forget you're a writer. Someone is trying to pin the murder on this girl, is that it? And you ask what sort of assassin would be so careless? I'll tell you. Someone of the weaker sex, that is, one who lacks logic. One who is young, who has no experience or maturity. You can't even begin to imagine how stupid murderers really are. Real life is nothing like in those books of yours."

Maupassant's migraine had come back with a vengeance, and he bowed his head, feeling almost crushed by the pain.

"And here's one more thing I shouldn't be telling you," continued Valantin. "There's more evidence. We have found clues at Cousin's house that provide undeniable proof of the presence of the girl. It's obvious she was the last one to see him alive. I can't tell you what the clues are, but believe me, they're incriminating." Valantin leaned toward Maupassant and whispered, "Between us, this disappearance of hers looks more like an escape, doesn't it? In my book, this is the greatest proof of the girl's guilt. And there was a letter too."

"A letter?"

"Don't tell me you haven't heard about the letter. You know there's only one rule when it comes to solving a murder, don't you?"

"What is that?"

"Who benefits from the crime?"

"But that's exactly what I'm saying," Maupassant protested. "How would Anna benefit from Cousin's death?"

"I don't know the answer to that yet."

"Ah! You see!"

"But . . . wait just a minute . . ." Valantin sat down and started shuffling papers on his desk.

"What are you saying? Tell me, Valantin!"

Valantin studied his notes. "The letter suggests the existence of a will drawn up in favor of a young girl. The reasons are not mentioned, nor is the girl's name, but it isn't the first time some old libidinous man has suddenly forgotten his family." Valantin looked up at Maupassant.

Maupassant stood without a word and left the room, feeling overwhelmed by what the commissioner had just said. He was feeling at the end of his tether, his head throbbing, but he still had to meet the famous Dr. Vidal to discuss his brother. He was very much looking forward to returning to the peace and quiet of his home.

13

A Lone Man

On his way to the docks, where he had an appointment to meet with the doctor, Maupassant came across a distraught Lola, no longer knowing where to turn in her search for Anna.

He told her about his discussion with Valantin. This seemed to make her nervous. So it was official. Anna was wanted for murder.

Not wanting to leave her friend alone, she insisted on accompanying him to his appointment with Vidal, knowing how difficult this might well be for him.

They approached a small café terrace in front of the docks. The place didn't look like much, but it was known as a place where people from all walks of life socialized.

This could mean stevedores drinking alongside regular sailors as well as rich ship owners and yachtsmen betting on regattas. Everyone shared the same passion, and every conversation concerned one of the same themes: the weather, the quality of sails, the best spots to anchor along the coast, or the latest victors of the Cercle Nautique race.

A lone man with a sober expression was sitting at a table with a jar of beer in hand. Seemingly lost in his thoughts, he didn't look up when they approached.

"Dr. Fortuné Vidal?" asked the writer, his voice suddenly more tense.

Maupassant asked so few questions, and Vidal was so taciturn that Lola was forced to guide the conversation. All responses were given laconically. The doctor was clearly under pressure and deeply depressed.

"There's no need to ask the good doctor all these questions," Maupassant intervened. "His reputation precedes him. You worked with Dr. Blanche, didn't you?"

"Yes, indeed. I was his assistant for many years. But this is about your brother, isn't it, monsieur? Let's talk of him."

"Yes. Last summer, he suffered a violent sunstroke, and since then, he has quite lost his mind. He is so cruel to his wife, almost strangling her on one occasion. My mother is in a state of disarray, but she minimizes the situation as best she can."

"Has his family situation changed of late?" Vidal asked.

"Yes, he is recently the father of a baby daughter."

"And what are your expectations in terms of what I can do, monsieur?"

"I'm looking for a place where he can stay. Not a prison, though, you understand. But somewhere he might rest, where he would be cared for with kindness . . . and even cured?"

"I can't promise anything, monsieur, but patients are well treated in my sanatorium. Cousin, the banker, was the cofounder and financier of my company, and he would have acted as my moral guarantor, if you'd needed one. But he has just passed, you see? Most tragically, in fact."

Maupassant frowned. He stood without warning and shook hands with Fortuné Vidal. "Monsieur, I will let you know the date of my next visit, and I will come directly to see you with my own boat. Can you send me the cost of board and care in writing to the Continentale Villa?"

The bereaved man stood and bowed, taking off his hat. But what little energy he had disappeared quickly, and he sat back down, staring into his drink with dull eyes, while Maupassant and Lola walked quickly out toward the pier.

"I'm no doctor," Maupassant said, "but I can give you a full diagnosis of that fellow. He is clearly afflicted with neurasthenia. I don't much believe in his ability to treat anyone. His patients need to rekindle their zest for life. How is he going to achieve that?"

"If you want my advice—"

"I didn't ask you for it, as far as I know," mocked the writer, although he was visibly upset. "Oh dear. If my mother knew of my intentions, she'd—"

"I'll give it to you, anyway," replied Lola moodily. "Stay away from that place of his."

Maupassant returned home to worry some more on the subject, while Lola headed for the Pantiero to speak with her brother.

14

The Search for Anna

Rosalie and I walked in a hurry, avoiding the debris littering the ground around the shipyard on Place du Châtaignier. The coach from Grasse was in front of the Grand Café, almost ready for departure. It was while crossing the Allées that we bumped into Lola and Mario.

"What a fortunate coincidence," declared Lola. "What did the doctor say?"

"I couldn't find one," said Rosalie. "I bought some liquor and came back as soon as I could. Miss Fletcher didn't want to stay home any longer. She's rested a little. We were going to the Suquet to find you."

"When do you think you might stop talking about me as if I weren't here? Mario, have you seen Anna? Did she come to see you?" I said.

"No," answered Lola for him. "He was at sea last night, anyway. He's been as sick as a dog since he found out Anna is missing."

"I'll come with you. We must find her," whispered Mario. "Who knows what might have happened to her? Maybe someone's trying to hurt her or even kill her. It could be happening right this instant!"

"Have you told him what the officers said?" I asked Lola. "When they shouted, 'We've got her!'"

"No! Do they suspect Anna?" cried Mario. "How absurd! That's what's known as a setup. Why not my mother, while they're at it? Maybe she did it?"

"In any case, the police are looking for her," I explained. "If she's in danger, we need to find her before they do."

Lola shivered. "Let's go see Mama. Maybe Anna took refuge with her. I've talked to Maupassant, and it seems she may have been in a lot of trouble."

But Lola's mother's astonished expression when she saw us at her door made it clear she knew nothing of Anna's current predicament. Mario was in a state of panic.

"You know what?" he said. "The other day, a banker man rented a boat to go to Île Sainte-Marguerite. Maybe it was Cousin."

"And so what?" said Lola. "We all know he went to the islands all the time. Renting boats has nothing to do with Anna and nothing to do with his death. Some man he ruined must have sought revenge, or someone tried to steal from him, or maybe it was that James fellow who Guy told us about."

"Mademoiselle Lola," I said. "You remind me of all those people who immediately accuse the servants as soon as anything happens in a house. An object of value disappears? It was the maid. A wallet was stolen? It must have been the valet. The dog died? It was the butler, for sure. A murder? The cook did it."

Lola gave me a pensive look. "Well, it had to have been someone."

"Let's split up and look for Anna," I said.

"Good idea." Rosalie approved. "Everyone can go their separate ways, and we'll have a better chance. And you," she told Mario, "go back to work, or you'll be fired."

I don't know if Mario obeyed her order. As for me, I searched every place in town. I even went for a walk along the Route de Fréjus and through the English district, despite fear of being spied by Lady Sarah.

I snooped around the Victoria Villa, the Eleonore Villa, and even the Hôtel Beau site, which had once been a Rothschild residence.

I was close to collapsing from exhaustion. My feet felt hot in my flat boots, which were usually so comfortable, and I couldn't feel my legs. As used to playing sports as I was, I had pushed my limits too far, and I didn't dare to imagine how Lola must be feeling—she who never made any voluntary physical effort and who always wore heels.

I drank at a fountain and bought an orange from a roadside seller. Despite my weariness, I couldn't give up my search.

I tried to reject the images of Anna being abused and in anguish, which haunted me at regular intervals.

As the sun set, I started on my way home and marched along the railway track. I looked down as I walked, covering my face from the suffocating soot and smoke from the occasional passing train. I noticed that my clothes and shoes would need a good cleaning, for they were covered in dust and earth.

As I entered the house, I saw that Rosalie had just arrived in a similarly disheveled state. Lola returned shortly afterward looking completely bereft.

I was sitting at the kitchen table with a chickpea pancake that Rosalie had quickly improvised. Lola joined me, and tears rolled down her face as she ate.

Before going to bed, I washed myself carefully in my room. Part of me was hoping to scrub the pain away.

I thought I'd never be able to fall asleep, but it came quickly, almost as my head hit my feather pillow. No visions came to haunt me as I thought they may, but someone else's screams woke me in the middle of the night.

It was Lola. She was caught up in one of her recurring nightmares. I scrambled downstairs as fast as I could. I knew what to do. I made her take several deep inhalations from her laudanum bottle and lay down beside her as I waited for the medicine to take effect.

As she usually did when suffering from a night terror, she was talking in a disjointed manner. She was agitated. It was as though she were struggling to defend herself from an attack. Rodot's name came up in her ramblings more than once.

I now understood that the real reason she feared Anna being arrested was because she feared the perversity of this man.

The drug started to take effect, and the threatening shadows of her memory faded away. But they were immediately replaced by thoughts that must have been troubling her since that morning.

"I'll go and see Cousin's villa tomorrow. Maybe Anna is being held there," she muttered.

She finally sank back into a peaceful sleep, overwhelmed by the liberal dose of sedative. As for me, I found it difficult to return to my slumber. I lay there, motionless, imagining the very worst of situations for Anna, that she was alone and far away from us, the people who loved her, while we were warm and safe in our home.

15

AN EXPEDITION TO COUSIN'S VILLA

Early the next morning, we headed out onto the battlefield and readied ourselves to go to Cousin's villa. Rosalie wanted us to eat some bread and drink some hot chocolate, but her efforts were in vain. We were anxious that we would not be in time to save Anna from the hands of her captors.

But a small voice inside us, still full of hope, whispered that she may simply have run away. This voice was both reassuring and disturbing. If she had gone off like that alone, then where was she? How had she survived the night? What had she eaten? Whom had she met alone out there in the cold?

We had to reach her. It was now an obsession.

I was surprised to see that Lola was dressed up as if ready for work. "I sent a messenger to make an appointment for Lady Sarah to meet with me at Madame Alexandra's. I'll go after our visit to Cousin's. I'm not sure yet if I will return her contract to her. It will all depend on her attitude. I want to see if she's playing me or if she's telling the truth. And she may have killed Cousin! She had motive enough! I'll have to see her face to face. I'll know by her eyes whether or not she's killed. You know I can always guess what is deepest in people's souls. And it may just save my Anna."

She had pulled on one of her most beautiful dresses: a pale-purple silk number with white embroidered flowers that cascaded down across her bust diagonally and ended up lost in the ruffles, folds, and ribbons along the hemline. She looked stunning.

The collar was high, and on the front of the bodice were navy-blue velvet knots forming a double row of buttons. The matching hat was small with velvet ribbons, tulle detailing, and the same embroidered flowers as on the dress. Her umbrella and gloves were both white to match the overall look.

She explained that she didn't think she'd have time to come home between all the missions scheduled for the day. Her cloak had a large inner pocket into which she slipped Lady Sarah's much-desired file.

"I don't want all this business turning against me. She is the one who had dealings with Cousin, just like Lecerf and the others. Not me."

"Yesterday in the newspaper, there was a number of land auctions announced," I stated.

"Yes, did you notice? That's all I see now. Every day there are more and more. Most of them are in some way due to Cousin's operations. His murder must have complicated things. Surely the police should be looking into all these other people."

I understood her. It was vital to demonstrate that someone compromised financially by Cousin had something to do with his demise. Lady Sarah was the perfect choice.

I wasn't dressed anywhere near as fancifully as Lola. I had put on my sports outfit. I had designed it myself and asked Daumas, the English tailor based on Rue Notre Dame, to fashion it for me. He told me he'd been trained by Henry Poole, the Prince of Wales's very own couturier. He had cut two models of it for me. The fabric was of the most luxurious, yet solid wool, inspired by the very much on-trend jackets popular with smokers. Which, as a smoker myself, was rather fortunate. I appreciated the silk lapels that went down the chest, so that the ashes of my cigarillos would slide off and not get caught in the woolen threads.

Lola followed me outside and waited as I tethered Gaza to our carriage. She then climbed into the back, and we made our way slowly but steadily to Avenue du Petit Juas.

The gate to Cousin's was wide open. Two officers were standing in front of the large porch, questioning visitors. The parade of people was unceasing, composed of acquaintances of Cousin who had come to express their condolences, indiscreet people who wanted to satisfy an unhealthy curiosity, and his financial victims who were there to take in the reality of the circumstances: their worst enemy, the one whose end they had repeatedly wished to see, was no more.

A man in a mourning suit, whom we had seen at the station, escorting the banker, stood at the top of the front steps, collecting cards and words of consolation. He didn't let everyone in. Some less-fortunate people were turned away.

Lola leaned over to me and said, "The killer is certain to be among these people. I wish there was some way we could take those cards and look through them. But it looks to be impossible. Don't park here. Let's go around to the service entrance."

I drove around the left wing of the house and dropped Lola off in front of the basement door leading to the kitchens. I tied Gaza to a cherry-tree trunk that shaded the small courtyard a little farther on and walked back to meet her. We rang the bell. After what felt like an eternity, a young girl opened up. In fact, she was probably leaving the house by chance rather than being of service to us. She carried a huge bundle of clothes in one hand and a large tapestry bag in the other. She was crying.

When she saw us, she simply let us pass without saying a word.

"Are you leaving?" asked Lola.

"I am indeed. I have little choice in the matter. There is no longer enough work, and it is the kitchen girl who has to go first, I am told, since there will be no more meals to prepare. Everything here will be sold. It's all been decided. Who are you?"

Lola metamorphosed right before my eyes, taking on the persona typical of girls from her childhood neighborhood.

"James is a cousin of mine," she lied, with a strong Suquet accent. "On my mother's side. I need to see him about a family matter."

The girl sniffed and looked at Lola from head to toe. She couldn't work her out. The accent was local, very much like her own, but the outfit belonged on a lady, and her behavior was rather commonplace, like a woman of the people.

"I've heard the tragic news," Lola continued. "Didn't the police ask you to stay and answer questions?"

"Why would they? We know who did it."

Lola started. "Is that so? It's not good to spread rumors. Who was it, then?"

"Some little wench in pink who'd been hanging around him. He wasn't interested in her, you see? There's no two ways about it. It was her, all right."

"A wench?" Lola looked a little panicked.

"That's what I think. I think she was a working girl. I saw her myself that very night. The old man gave us the day off, for once! But I was dragging my feet on purpose, you see, so I could pinch some leftovers. I wanted to take them to my mother's house. Anyway, down the street at the crossroads, I saw her walking."

I trembled at the thought of someone having witnessed Anna's nighttime escapade.

"If you want to see James, it's that way," she continued as she pointed in the direction of the corridor leading to the service rooms. We stepped inside cautiously as she left and headed down the sandy path.

Standing before a large table, a servant wearing a wide blue apron was shining men's leather shoes. He looked up as we approached. He didn't seem surprised to see us.

"Mesdames? May I help you?"

"We're here to see James."

"That's me."

"We're friends of Maupassant, the writer."

"Oh yes! I met him. He was with Valantin, the police commissioner. Excuse me if I continue to work while I'm talking to you, but I have to prepare my master's clothes for when he returns from the morgue."

"Oh? Did they take him away?" I asked.

"Yes. It was a violent death. I can't bear to think about it. Now the heir will soon be upon us, and what he'll have in store, nobody knows."

"Do you know who will inherit?" asked Lola.

"I think the gentleman had only his nephew left, but he's unwell, I believe. Then there's some letter that talks of a change to the will, so all bets are off. In any case, it makes no difference to me."

"I heard they didn't find the murder weapon. Do you know anything about it?" asked Lola.

"Yes, they found it! On a girl who'd hunted him down."

"Did you see her?"

"No, but there's a letter opener missing, and I heard they found it at her house. I wouldn't be surprised if she was the owner of the famous bracelet."

Lola gave me a worried look as I felt the color drain from my face.

"What bracelet? We've heard nothing of this," I said.

"The one I found on the floor in my master's hand."

I suddenly remembered my dream.

"What?" said Lola. "But Maupassant didn't tell us anything about that!"

"Of course he didn't. I gave it to a police officer, and he told me not to tell a soul, for the purposes of the investigation and all that. But now that matters have progressed somewhat, I don't mind telling you. It was made of silver, and there was an engraving on it."

Lola trembled as I asked with bated breath, hoping for a negative response, "Did you read what it said?"

"Yes, it was an unusual name. Spanish maybe . . . Anthea . . . Anita . . ."

Lola moved closer to the table, took a chair, and sat down, staring into the void. "Anahita," she whispered.

"Yes, that's right! How did you . . . ?"

When he saw her pallor, he didn't finish his sentence but rushed to fetch her a glass of sherry.

I guided the conversation through a range of banalities as she drank, and we hastily brought our visit to an end. We now had the information we'd been seeking. The clues were stacked heavily against our poor Anna: the letter opener, the bracelet . . . it was a lot for the child. How would we fight this?

As we climbed up into our carriage, Lola spoke as if thinking out loud. "It's not her. We can be sure of that now. She lost the bracelet when she was attacked. Or at least it was taken from her."

"That's true!"

"So she couldn't have lost it again in there, could she? Her assailant had it. We should have gone to the police and made a statement as soon as it happened. That will teach me to be so wary of them. Now it's all coming back on her. Not one of them will believe us now!"

"Yes, it's too late for that. How in the hell did that bracelet get into Cousin's hands? You know something? Just yesterday, I thought these two tales might be linked."

"Why yes, it seems evident to me! This is by Lady Sarah's hand!" exclaimed Lola. "Did she mention Anna at all when she came to see you? It was the same night of the murder. She was being driven around Cannes, wasn't she? And I imagine Lord Clarence was not at home. We need to find a witness who might have seen her in the vicinity of Cousin's house."

I answered as gently as possible, "Yes, but it wasn't Lady Sarah's bracelet in his hand, was it? And it wasn't at her house that I found the bloody letter opener."

Lola looked at me with a suspicion that I found painful. I could clearly read what she was thinking: *What if it was Fletcher who put that letter opener in Anna's room? Perhaps Lady Sarah gave it to her?*

With tears in my eyes, I jolted Gaza's reins and twice almost ran over passersby who hadn't had time to get out of my way. They shouted insults at us as we flew past.

Lola didn't say anything further. She was acting like she hadn't noticed my reckless driving.

16

CAMOUFLAGE

Farther down the road, we met with traffic and struggled to move between the hordes of people on foot and in carriages.

"What are all these people doing?" Lola snapped. "We're going to be late!"

We learned from a passerby that today was the day of the ceremony for the soldiers who had fallen in the war.

"Mademoiselle Lola, you wanted to attend so badly. Wasn't Paul Antoine to accompany you?"

"Oh, I'm no longer in the mood, Miss Fletcher. Of course, it is important for me to carve a place among those people, but today, saving Anna is what counts!"

When I felt I wasn't able to drive any farther, I stopped the carriage. We were a fair distance from Madame Alexandra's for Lola's meeting with Lady Sarah. She jumped down to the ground and forgot her good manners as she ran toward the reading rooms without saying anything, leaving me to find a suitable spot to tie up Gaza.

She was more than half an hour late. I sensed there was an atmosphere of real joy throughout the city, though the event was actually a tribute to the dead. The people of Cannes were heading toward the music kiosk in front of the town hall. We had seen the marching band pass by in ceremonial dress a little earlier.

Lola was struggling to find her way through the middle of a crowd as it headed toward Allée de la Marine.

I'd been forced to make a large detour to reach Rue du Bivouac, yet I still had trouble finding a place to park our vehicle. Finally, I managed to attach Gaza to another carriage stationed across the street from Madame Alexandra's, making sure I left a space wide enough for other drivers to use the road in both directions. I had entrusted the surveillance to a young boy who was hanging around looking for a task. It was up to him to move our horse and carriage if the owner of the other vehicle wanted to leave. He was happy enough with the deal, but it didn't stop him from negotiating another sou out of me.

I gave in because I didn't want to leave Lola alone with Lady Sarah. And I must admit that I was curious at the idea of visiting the upper strata of the reading rooms, for I had only ever seen the ground level.

As I was leaving the businessman in the making, I saw Lola almost walk into someone coming out of Madame Alexandra's. I recognized her as Lady Sarah, and I saw she was furious.

She was dressed most formally. She quickly gauged the situation, looked around, and noted there were too many people nearby for her to talk with Lola. She would cause no scene.

She didn't speak to her, but rather looked straight at me and walked with a shaky step toward the Allées. Despite her self-control, one could see how angry she was.

Lola wanted to run after Sarah, and it was my role to dissuade her. I hurried toward her.

"There would be very little point. She won't talk to you in public. Anyway, it's too late. It's too crowded now. We would never catch up with her," I explained.

"I'm sorry, Miss Fletcher. I have to see her face to face, if only for a few moments. Come on!"

Following in Lady Sarah's footsteps, we soon realized she was on her way to the ceremony. There was no way to circumnavigate the crowds. Everyone was dressed in their finest and making their way to the stands. They looked around at their fellow members of the upper classes and applauded and admired those with the prettiest outfits. The whole thing was ridiculous.

Their comments were bold, sometimes impertinent, but mostly approving. When it was our turn to approach the stands, Lola received her share of flattering remarks from those who did not recognize her. As for me, in my carefully put-together attire, I provoked either restrained laughter or nasty smirks. I was more than likely categorized as an eccentric foreigner and dismissed from the general conversation as being of little importance.

The ceremony was to be played out in two stages: the laying of wreaths, speeches, and an honorary concert by the brass band, and then the donors would go to a room made ready at the town hall, where a toast would be made in remembrance of our heroes.

Lady Sarah crossed all the barriers that had been used to cordon off the area and joined a group of men in ceremonial clothing up on the stands.

"It's now or never. You can see how my donation came in useful," said Lola.

We presented ourselves at the barriers.

I saw the young Laure de Luynes, who this time recognized me and welcomed us with a wide smile. She shook Lola's hand warmly and thanked her for her gift.

Lola looked delighted and was about to climb up to a row on the stands when the young comtesse pointed out to me the side where the English aristocracy stood and, unbeknownst to me, gently directed Lola toward another corner, where the Cannes bourgeoisie had been placed.

"You are with the thoroughbreds," she called to me with a smile.

I had already begun to walk in the direction indicated by the young socialite and could see that Lady Sarah was just ahead of me. But then I realized Lola was blocked and not allowed to follow me, so I retraced my steps back to her, for I didn't like the idea that we were to be separated.

We found other seats and sat together. Neither of us was in our designated spot. We hadn't been seated for more than a few minutes when I noticed a swirl of motion around us and some loud chattering. A lady—certainly a wealthy businesswoman of some kind—was looking at Lola, openmouthed, surrounded by babbling friends. Her fascination was something to behold. Could Lola feel the insistent stare? It seemed not. For Lola, usually so curious about everything, was sitting up with her back as straight as an arrow, refusing to take her eyes off Lady Sarah on the other side of the stands. It was her stubborn streak taking over again. Did she have an immediate sense of what was going to happen, though?

The lady continued to gawk. Of course, she had recognized this young woman dressed as a member of the bourgeoisie as the floozy who often made the front pages with her escapades. She and her sycophantic companions had probably watched Lola as she paraded herself up and down the Croisette in extravagant clothes and made suggestive poses, contrary to what the good book taught and at the risk of corrupting the young girls from respectable families who walked there.

Lola was far from being the sole woman in Cannes who worked on her back. That was a certainty. However, she was the only one who had dared to make a donation and expose herself thus in the midst of a gathering of the upper crust.

More movement. More jostling. More commotion. People were getting to their feet, walking away from us, and moving to other stands. Within a few seconds, just as the brass band started to play, it was if a desert had been created by our side.

As I turned to confer with Lola, I could see she had frozen completely and that she was no longer even looking at Lady Sarah, only at the empty space next to us. Below, where the families of the fallen soldiers were standing, I noticed a couple in their fifties, dressed from head to toe in black.

The lady's eyes were reddened with grief, whereas her husband looked slightly bored. I watched as a well-meaning gentleman leaned toward them and whispered something as he pointed up toward us. This gesture shocked me. What was it these people wanted? I looked around me. Was it, in fact, us to whom he was pointing? But there was no doubt about it. Their eyes were on Lola.

The lady turned white, opened and closed her mouth several times, before turning her head away again with contempt. The man stared hard at Lola for what seemed like an age, taking in every last detail of her.

Without moving, Lola whispered, "I know you can't place them. They're Edmond de Bréville and his wife!"

Of course! Eugène's parents! They were behind this entire tribute.

"I saw them once before, from afar," she continued, maintaining a proud air, but I knew how distraught she must have been inside. "They won't speak to me, I know. And why would I care? Besides, I'm here for Lady Sarah. Their schemes don't bother me a jot. As soon as I can move from this spot, I'll try to get closer to your Lady Sarah over there. I just have to wait for this dreadful music to finish!"

"She is not my Lady Sarah," I muttered, sulking.

"I don't understand, Miss Fletcher. I feel an intense rage, yet at the same time, a sort of dizzying grief. I'd like to hide in a corner somewhere and be left to die like a mangy dog."

My heart tightened. "You're vulnerable right now. That's why you feel such things. It's because of Anna. You're worried."

"That would be the reason if I were a good person, Miss Fletcher. I should only think of Anna and not let their contempt touch me. Why are we here? Because of the money I gave. I thought money would erase everything. How very stupid of me. Have you seen all the people here,

Miss Fletcher? Many of the men are clients of mine, you know. And not a single one greeted me."

"But come, Lola, you knew it would be like this. We knew it from the beginning. The likes of us don't belong in their world. We made our choices."

"That's not quite true. You made your choice. But still, your place is among them. That was obvious earlier, wasn't it? Even if they may not invite you to their gatherings, you remain one of them. I didn't have a choice. And when I come to a place like this, my limits are defined quite clearly."

I sensed someone hovering to our left. Our friend Paul Antoine, dressed elegantly but slightly disheveled, had made his way over to us. He sat beside Lola, gasping for breath, his top hat askew on his head.

"Sorry for the delay. After all the emotions this morning, I completely forgot my promise to accompany you to the ceremony. It was my father's fault. He's been so very annoying of late. When he found out I'd been to second a duel at dawn, he almost collapsed, I tell you."

But Lola wasn't listening. She was delighted to see him and looked around her triumphantly.

"Your presence here brings me great comfort. You are wonderful."

"However, I will not be able to attend the event that will follow. I have some friends to see in Monaco. I'm taking the train. Aren't you going to ask me what happened this morning?"

"Ask you what?"

"For heaven's sake, woman, the duel! Had you forgotten? I was Ferdinand's second versus Philémon Carré-Lamadon!"

"So that went ahead?" I exclaimed. "With this murder business and Anna, we had completely erased the event from our minds. We've been—"

"Is Philémon Carré-Lamadon dead?" Lola interrupted.

"No, nobody's dead, but—"

Lola interrupted again. "If he's still alive, then I don't wish to hear the end of the story."

Just then, as the last cymbal sounded, Monsieur de Bréville stepped forward to speak to the crowd. He was a member of Parliament and used to making speeches to large audiences. Some of the ladies present were in tears.

Mayor Gazagnaire then took his turn to address the assembly, officially closing the public ceremony. The second part of the proceedings was by private invitation. However, those who had made donations were welcome to attend the gathering at the majestic town hall.

"I have to go. Forgive me," said Paul Antoine as he kissed our hands and fled to the opposite side of the stands.

"Don't take your eyes off Lady Sarah. We can't lose her," said Lola.

But Lady Sarah was well surrounded as she made her way toward the entranceway of the town hall. I knew Lola wouldn't be admitted. Disaster was imminent.

As we approached, I could see a steady flow of ladies and gentlemen entering through the large doors, which were guarded by police officers who had, I believe, been forewarned of our presence.

Lady Sarah rushed into the building.

Just to the right of the doors, we spotted Philémon Carré-Lamadon looking at us and whispering into the ear of one of the officers.

"Look at that wretch! He's definitely alive, then!" she whispered between her teeth. "What does he want from me now?"

As we neared the entrance, one of the officers moved to one side to let me in and then stepped back to block Lola before she could follow me, holding up his hand.

Lola was completely rejected. I turned around and went back outside to stand by her side. Her humiliation was total and reinforced by the knowledge that Philémon and many others had witnessed it. The shame of being rebuffed and disgraced was running wildly through her mind, in addition to her desire to save Anna and the worry that was causing her.

She rounded on me. "But why did you come back? You have to go in and speak to Lady Sarah."

"You're the one who needs to deal with her. I don't have your intuition."

"Just go on in! You are not barred from entering. Your pity pains me."

I moved away from her, as if bitten by a snake, for she hadn't whispered this time but spoken quite loudly.

With my stomach in knots, I knew she would sink even further into public scandal if she continued to raise her voice. She was ashamed of what she was doing, I could see that much, but it seemed nothing could have stopped her. She started screaming.

She verbally attacked the officers who were blocking her path, as well as all the elegant people passing in front of her who rushed toward the promised land and despised her very presence.

The more she shouted, the more she made a fool of herself, and the more ashamed she became. Philémon didn't move from his observation post, smiling with satisfaction. He had been joined by Edmond de Bréville, and they were talking in low voices as they watched the scene unfold.

At the risk of being slapped, I approached her. I grabbed her by the arm firmly and started to pull her away, fearing she would say things that were irremediable.

She pushed my hand away to free herself from my grip when de Bréville suddenly stepped in front of us, barring the way.

17

LADY SARAH'S LOST GAZE

Edmond de Bréville took Lola by the waist and whispered something in her ear as he walked off with her. I followed them from a small distance.

His strides were long, and she had trouble keeping up with him in her little heeled boots. He led her to the fountain on the main square, where several vehicles were waiting for their owners to return from the event. In the midst of the hubbub, and far enough from the town hall to avoid everyone's attention, he must have felt he could speak safely.

As I looked around, I spotted Lady Sarah a short distance away. Had she come to find us?

De Bréville looked at me and must have wondered what my connection to Lola was, but that didn't stop him from saying what he had to say.

"Come, mademoiselle, why create such a scandal?"

"You!" shouted Lola. "You're the reason my Eugène lost his life!"

His face hardened. "You might want to question your own part in his death. If he hadn't met you, we never would have sent him to war."

Lola hiccupped as she tried to hold back her tears of indignation.

"Might I suggest you calm down?" he said. "As far as we're aware, our money had already reached you by the time Eugène left."

Lola blushed. "Do you think I want money? On the contrary! I made a donation!"

I was distracted from the scene unfolding by the one that was now taking place with Lady Sarah, and I noticed that Lola, too, even in the grips of emotion, had seen Lady Sarah and was now staring at her.

I wondered if Lady Sarah had witnessed what had happened. Her gaze met mine. She seemed both distraught and embarrassed as she quickly looked downward. Was she ashamed at having found us in such a compromising situation? No, that wasn't her style.

In fact, de Bréville giving Lola a dressing down so publicly should have made her gloat.

I then focused my attention on the two men by her side. Lord Clarence, her husband, was one of them, and there was an older man with white hair who I assumed was her father, for there was a resemblance.

"Stop being so childish," said de Bréville to Lola. "A pretty girl like you!"

His harsh expression softened. I'm sure that the smell of sweet orange blossom and musk emanating from Lola's hair must have had something to do with it. He appeared flushed as he leaned in toward her. He was too close, as far as I was concerned.

"Come on, little kitten. I understand your emotion."

Lola was now speechless. She knew the male species better than most and was resigned to what would follow. De Bréville laughed a little, just enough to make himself understood.

"I'm a de Bréville, too, after all. It seems the men in my family are not insensitive to your charms."

I could sense Lola's humiliation. She shuddered before looking around her like a drowning woman seeking help, and then closed her eyes. He interpreted this as a victory.

At the same time, Lady Sarah spun on her heel. She was attempting to head toward us when her father grabbed her, and Lord Clarence then held her by the waist. What was going on? What was she being forced to do . . . or not do?

The parallel between the two scenes struck me. While Lady Sarah was restricted by her husband and father, Lola was being kept back by an increasingly oppressive de Bréville, who now held her middle tightly with both hands.

Lady Sarah was being maneuvered away from us. Just before she turned her face, she gave me a lost look.

Lost? Lady Sarah? It wasn't possible. I must have imagined it.

Their small group was now moving toward the port.

"You're such a good little girl," said de Bréville to Lola. "Wait for a message from me. I'll let you know."

He let go of her so abruptly that she almost fell to the ground. He kissed her hand before walking back to the town hall at a brisk pace.

When she could no longer hear his footsteps, Lola opened her eyes, and I saw her transform right in front of me. She shook herself down, took a deep breath, and said to me, "Hush now! Don't pull a face like that. It's thanks to that fool that we avoided even more of a scene with those simpering idiots at that ridiculous party. I've had quite enough of it all, you know. What nonsense."

I nodded.

"But what a pity to have lost your friend!" she continued. "She saw everything. And she pitied me, that much I could tell. I have truly fallen to a low point if that woman feels my pain. Have you ever seen her be lenient?"

"Never," I replied. "She's made of steel."

"I saw compassion in her, though. It's as if I heard her whispering to me, *I told you so! You shouldn't have come here.* But I know she wants that file. And if she bears any responsibility for what's happening to Anna, I'll find out sooner or later."

"I had the impression that—"

She cut me off. "Let's go to the Pantiero and talk to Mario to see if he has any news."

"But it means having to pass in front of the entrance to the festivities again," I protested.

"So what? Do you think I would care about such a thing?" asked Lola boldly. "Look! There's Guy!"

She frowned. He had just crossed the famous threshold she had been barred from passing. He was surrounded by a group of friends and admirers, and she did not want to embarrass him by calling out.

She turned and started hastening her step, when suddenly he saw her.

"Lola!" he shouted. "Miss Fletcher! Wait for me!"

He left his friends and bustled over to join us. We were already briskly making our way toward the Pantiero.

"I've been looking for you. Where have you been? This ceremony business is in very poor taste. How sorry I am to have come. Thank God you're here. Did you see de Bréville showing off?"

Lola evaded answering and instead told him of the latest twists and turns in the story: what James had told us about the bracelet, her suspicions about Lady Sarah's possible involvement, and her desire to get to the truth. She told him nothing about de Bréville, not wanting to relive that shameful moment. Lola had an amazing ability to erase anything from her mind that could damage her determination or take something away from her vital energy.

Maupassant followed us to a mooring allocated to Pierre Gaglio, Mario's fishing master. Lola wanted to ask her brother a few questions, specifically if he had seen Anna or received any news of her.

But he wasn't at work. We spoke briefly to Gaglio, who was extremely angry and threatening to fire him.

As Maupassant and Lola pled Mario's case, I pretended to have forgotten something so that I could turn back. As a matter of fact, I was worried about Lady Sarah. The scene we had just witnessed was unusual, to say the least. It looked similar to a kidnapping.

Something was going on, but what? On my way back, I had to make my way through the crowds waiting to take boats out to the islands.

I saw the steamer *Le Cannois* on its way out to sea. She was slowly moving away from the dock, and I stood for several moments to admire her. That's when I noticed Lady Sarah on board, fully veiled, standing straight, looking dignified, but this time hemmed in by three men rather than two.

Her father and her husband were still there, but they were now joined by a slim, harsh-looking individual wearing a gray mourning suit. I would later learn that it was Dr. Vidal.

18

THE RIGHT INGREDIENTS

When I returned to the Pantiero, there was no trace of Maupassant or Lola. They hadn't waited for me. I didn't dare ask Mario's boss if he knew where they'd gone.

I was distraught by what I'd just seen. I felt lost and aimless. Worse, I didn't know how to go about tackling our problems.

I became aware that day of my total dependence on Lola. Without her to point me in the right direction, I would sink. For four years, I had been guided by her and her choices.

And what was wrong with that? Since my father's death, I had always suffered greatly. But with her, at least I felt useful. I was a faithful means of support, and I could be counted on for protection.

As I was slowly driving back to Les Pavots by myself, Maupassant was introducing Lola to a journalist friend they had just met at the Grand Café. Lola later told me the entire story.

◆　◆　◆

Sitting at a table with a small jug of absinthe that he was about to pour over a sugar cube, the journalist barely raised his head when Maupassant greeted him.

Joseph Murier was a columnist for several local publications. He also acted as a ghostwriter for many prominent members of society who wished to write their memoirs. It was said he had information on everyone who spent any length of time in Cannes, and he boasted that within an hour, he could write the obituary of anyone who might die in our good little town.

"Ah, Joseph! I've been looking for you since yesterday. I have a pressing matter to discuss," said Maupassant. "Do you know Mademoiselle Deslys?"

"Who doesn't know her?" scoffed Murier.

Although this remark could well have been taken in a different sense, Lola was delighted to be thus spoken of. She sat down and ordered a coconut sorbet.

"Why aren't you at the war party?" asked Maupassant.

"Why aren't you?" Murier replied with a complicit smile.

"The whole thing seemed rather tiresome."

"Exactly. I'm on the constant lookout for tidbits, but I need things a little more salacious than *The ladies were so finely dressed, and their kindness was only equaled by their beauty in this vibrant tribute to our valiant soldiers . . . and on, and on, and on . . .* These kinds of events are not exactly hard-hitting."

"What about Cousin? There's something to get your teeth stuck into."

"Now you're speaking my language." The journalist laughed. "Do you have any leads on that?"

Lola then jumped in and explained how she was directly involved in the case. She withheld certain pieces of information such as the theft of Lady Sarah's file, the bloody letter opener, and James's mention of the bracelet. She feared that this evidence, which still seemed somewhat irrefutable, would distort the journalist's judgment.

Murier appeared intrigued, though in his view, the theory that Anna may have killed to defend herself was ridiculous. He had known the banker personally.

"Cousin is not a ladies' man. Not like you, my dear Maupassant!" Maupassant smiled with pride, and Lola shrugged.

"He was unlikely to have been attracted to the girl," Murier continued.

"Why?" asked Lola. "Was he more effeminate in nature? If he was, I'm sure I would have known it. I recognize that kind."

Murier stared at her as Maupassant explained, "She's very close to Isnard de la Motte the younger."

"Ah, indeed, I understand! No, he wasn't inclined that way. He had some great mysterious love from which he never recovered. That's why, so I'm told, he would never marry. He was a man known for his great decency. He never had a mistress; he didn't play cards; he wouldn't bet on horses. Nothing of the kind. The man was as cold as a machine. Only one thing drove him: money. He was tough in business."

"But money is certainly at the heart of this story. Do you know how many people blame him for their ruin?" said Lola.

"I've heard, of course," said Murier.

"Valantin suspected Lecerf at first. Do you know him?" Maupassant asked.

"Yes, Lecerf, the former wine merchant. He went to work at the Faisan Doré, I believe?"

"Why do you say, 'I believe,' when you know it full well?"

Murier laughed. "A figure of speech! Valantin was on the right track. He should have known better than to have abandoned it. Lecerf threatened to kill Cousin several days ago outside the station."

"I know! We were there!" cried Maupassant.

"But that's not the main reason I suspect him. Lecerf is a terribly sore loser. He just hasn't been able to find a way to bounce back. He's always whining. And then the drinking started. He loves nothing more than drowning his sorrows, reflecting upon his failures, and blaming the whole world for them—with Cousin at the top of the list. Even before his bankruptcy, he was unreliable. He's always gambled. He's always been attracted to easy money."

"But he was rich, wasn't he?" Lola asked.

"Yes, his business was profitable. He had a clientele composed of the English for wine, the Russians for strong liquor, and the Germans for beer. And he supplied absinthe to all the clubs and cafés in the city. In other words, his business was golden, especially in a place like Cannes."

"Why would he want more money?" asked Maupassant.

"What he had came from his wife. It wasn't of his own merit. And he inherited the business when his father-in-law died. He was already complaining about the business, saying how long the working day was and so on. That he wanted to enjoy life. When he saw the fortunes made by those who first bought up some of the Foncière land, he did everything within his power to get a meeting with Cousin and to then be admitted to his inner circle and eventually to his table. He thought it would put him in a good position to find out the best tips, the best plots to buy, and so on. He wanted the inside information. He ignored all the warning signs and believed that with a single big operation, he would be secure for the rest of his life. That he could finally play the big landlord. But it was too late . . . He got a whole lot more than he'd bargained for."

"I adore you!" said Lola.

She suddenly saw in Murier the man who would exonerate Anna by handing over enough information that had thus far remained secret—and that this information would lead to Lecerf's arrest.

He looked at her with admiration. "A declaration of love! Why, I've never known the like! Let's go!"

"Where?"

"Let me take you to the newspaper archives in the basement of the Bengali Villa at Saint-Nicolas. We'll take a look through some of the old newspapers and glean some information as to exactly who Cousin bankrupted."

"But it's right next door to my house!" exclaimed Lola.

"I know," sighed the journalist. "I often pass by, and I sometimes see you there taking tea in the garden, and I think, *What a wonderful creature!*"

Lola giggled as only she knew how. She had found herself again. Maupassant, amused, stroked his mustache as he watched them. He knew he was witnessing more than simple banter. The journalist was seriously smitten with Lola. He would be unlucky there. He simply wasn't wealthy enough for her. And she was a woman who never allowed herself to be overwhelmed by her feelings.

19

THE ARCHIVES

Murier took them in through the back door and introduced them to the concierge and the archives clerk before bringing in a whole host of files on both personal and corporate bankruptcies. He also asked the clerk to bring in some tenders and a range of documents concerning store closures. He spread them across the table, explaining that he wanted to take a closer look at them and identify what had happened to people following their ruin.

"I will make piles by order of magnitude of finances lost," he told them. "Those who have lost everything, those who still have something left, and those who have managed to recover."

Lola, who could not believe the number of files piling up, gave him a dumbfounded look as he began to explain the workings of the crisis. It was known as a real estate scandal, but he stated it was important to understand that it was no such thing.

"I wouldn't call it a scandal as such, because as long as it works, everyone's happy. There have always been people who like to play with fire, who want to speculate, and they're surprised when the house of cards inevitably topples. But if they've already withdrawn from the game, they rub their hands together, right? They're a real greedy bunch, let me tell you. I have no mercy for these people. No time for it at all."

He laughed at Lola's frown.

She would later tell me that she felt strangely targeted, because even though she had never speculated in her life, she understood the process, and this potential to earn easily certainly attracted her.

"Even so, those poor people," she said. "Some of them gambled everything they had."

"You said it! They gambled, just like in roulette. I have to make this clear to you. When you gamble, you know what you're risking, don't you? The initiators here didn't plan on ruining people. They feel they did everything right. The only thing they didn't plan for was that there wouldn't be enough people to come and live in the houses they built. Between 1886 and 1887, a total of thirty-four bankruptcies were declared here. For a smaller town like Cannes, that's somewhat spectacular! Of these thirty-four, at least twenty were subject to creditor proceedings. That's where our friend Cousin comes in."

All this quickly tired Lola, but Maupassant asked for further explanations. He was looking to better understand the system to perhaps use the details in a future novel.

He learned that in the Foncière district, entrepreneurs had worked together to set up a significant real estate operation from scratch. The idea was to create a majestic boulevard linking the center of Cannes to the village of Le Cannet. This would create a whole new district, for those who lived in Cannes felt suffocated at times due to the lack of space.

The partners, on Cousin's initiative, had initially bought all the land from farmers. On either side of this magnificent and grandiose boulevard, equipped with both electricity and main drainage, splendid villas and apartment buildings as well as hotels and boarding houses would be built.

They'd started with a hotel at the entrance of the boulevard. A few meters beyond, two superb caryatids were built around a small square, which signaled what was to come farther along the road.

Cousin had been the most successful in the venture because after having acquired nearly all the plots at low cost, which stretched along the future Boulevard de la Foncière, he had been able to offer comprehensive transactions to people attracted by the project and by the lure of huge profits. This meant that, on one hand, his bank sold the land and, on the other hand, he granted loans to the very same people so they could buy the properties or have them built.

When the value of these assets collapsed due to the crisis, he was the only winner. The investors had lost everything. The banker took back his land. Everyone else was ruined.

The Rigal Bank, a company founded in Cannes in 1835, had also lent a great deal, but it could not honor its creditors when its debtors were no longer solvent. Its liquidation took some time and had only recently been completed. The owner of Rigal had gone on the run at one point, but the authorities had caught up with him.

The journalist put some of the files and papers to one side.

"We need to look at those who might still want to enact physical revenge on Cousin. I have done some separating here. I have excluded the moderates, those who have since fallen ill, those who have left the city, those who have gone on to rebuild houses elsewhere, those who were helped out by their families . . . Actually, most of them are out of the picture."

"Perhaps it's rare to continue dwelling on something like that," said Lola. "You have to move on with life. Who's left?"

"Here they are. Three possibilities, in my opinion. Their current situations are what one might call unusual."

"Who are they?"

"We have Yasmina Clément. A widow. She's the daughter of an African warlord who married into the Abdelkader family."

"An African warlord? But then, she's . . ."

"Yes. She looks like Jeanne Duval, Baudelaire's Black Venus," he said, nodding, then proceeded to tell them the whole story. "The whole family was imprisoned on Île Sainte-Marguerite in 1843."

"I remember my father talking about it!" cried Lola.

"This widow arrived on the islands at the age of fourteen. She was promised to an emir, but when they were liberated in 1847, she fled with Séverin Clément, the captain of the guard, who then left the army. They married a few years later, and as he was rather wealthy, they bought a building that they turned into a boarding house. The mirage of the Foncière project grabbed their attention, and on Cousin's advice, they sold everything they owned. It was all lost in just a few months. Clément had an accident at his home a year ago while cleaning his gun. It is believed he killed himself accidentally. Yasmina Clément now lives alone in a miserable little rented room on Rue Grande and works for a corset maker."

"It must be her," said Lola. "She has every reason to want revenge on the banker."

"Something doesn't quite fit, though," said Murier. "She's very discreet, seems not to want to make waves, and is well accepted in her neighborhood. I believe that the death of her love, Séverin, destroyed her."

Lola grimaced and muttered with spite, "Too bad. Who else is on the list?"

He set her file aside and looked at the next one. "Lecerf, whom you know—the drunk who threatened Cousin."

"Yes! I suspect him most of all," said Lola. "I'm going to track him down and force his hand."

"And then there's Vidal," he said, looking at the final file.

"Vidal?" cried Lola and Maupassant in chorus.

"That's not possible," said Maupassant. "Vidal was friends with Cousin, who was one of the donors to his sanatorium. A significant investor, in fact. Without Cousin, it would never have transpired. I don't think he had any grudges to bear."

"Very well. He lost a lot of money, and he's quite the depressive, you know, but let's put him to one side. That leaves us with Lecerf," explained Murier.

He moved the papers containing the story of Vidal's financial troubles to the edge of the table and opened the Lecerf file.

"He started drinking a lot of alcohol, but we know that . . . Oh yes . . . here's an interesting fact. His son is currently suing him for the mismanagement and squandering of his inheritance. The hearing took place at the Grasse courthouse just the other day."

"It's him! I'm certain of it!" said Lola.

"This fact doesn't constitute proof," explained Maupassant.

"Hush now! I'll go and see him, and I'll get him to confess," said Lola. "He can't have a very clear conscience." Lola then noticed something. "But you don't have Lady Sarah on your list."

As the words came out of her mouth, she regretted saying them. Murier, as good a man as he appeared to be, was above all else a journalist. She feared he would use any information she might give him maliciously.

"Clarence? Oh, really? I didn't know she had anything to do with him. Just as I didn't know she had money to spend."

Lola was biting her lips. Maupassant gave Murier a menacing look. A look that meant, *Let me warn you, my friend, if you use that information against Lady Sarah, you'll have me to deal with . . .*

But Murier had taken Lola's hand. "Don't worry. What you just said won't leave this room. I'm not a sewer rat. You can count on my silence."

Fairly suspicious in nature, Lola was now even more concerned. A young messenger boy entered the room as if from nowhere, past the concierge. He looked as though he didn't have a care in the world.

Lola recognized Basile, the young boy who'd come to her house the other day to deliver a note. He'd said he was Thérésine's brother.

He went straight to Murier. "I knew I would find you here! I've got some news for you!" he cried out in the familiar Suquet accent. "I kept it just for you. It's fresh!"

"Hello, little brat. Well, talk, then, damn it!"

"Do you have a smoke for me?"

Murier took out a cigarette from a small case in his pocket and stuck it behind the child's ear. Obviously playing to the audience, Basile said with dramatic emphasis, "They've arrested the banker's slasher. Her name is Anahita Martin."

"Where did you get this from?" asked Maupassant.

"I had a front-row seat. She was at my sister's house."

Lola stifled a scream and started hyperventilating. Maupassant panicked, believing she was going to faint.

"What's wrong with the lady?" asked the boy. "Hey! Wait! I know you. You're the Canary Lady. You've got that yellow carriage. The Giglio girl. Congratulations, ma'am! You are my sister's idol. She has only one dream: to become just like you!"

He bowed awkwardly. Lola stared at him as though not quite following what he was saying. She grabbed a sheet of paper and dipped a quill into the inkwell on the table before scribbling nervously. After writing for several minutes, she folded the letter without waiting for the ink to dry and handed it to the little one with a sou.

"Please run to Les Pavots right away. It's by the convent to the left of the Hôtel Central. It isn't far."

"I know! You're near the Mon Plaisir boarding house. I was just there the other day."

"You're a clever boy. You'll ask for Miss Fletcher and give her this note in person. Be pleasant, and maybe she'll give you one of her cigarillos. She smokes the best in Cannes."

The message contained a specific request. Lola had planned to go to Lecerf's house immediately and make him confess. This had become all the more important now that Anna was in the hands of the police. But the situation had changed.

She now needed to go see Anna at the station. And she was afraid. So she asked me to visit Lecerf as soon as possible, for someone had to talk to him.

She stated she was certain he was the culprit and that Murier had given her some enlightening evidence to this effect.

Little Basile was delighted with his task and ran off as quick as the wind.

As Lola and Maupassant went to say goodbye to Murier, he replied, "I'm coming with you. I'll be the first one there. I might get an exclusive! I can't miss out on this."

Lola's heart sank as she imagined the headlines of the following day's newspapers. Anna's story would certainly overshadow any reports on the ceremony for the soldiers.

They had no carriage between them, so they hailed a four-seater cab to take them to the station on Rue Macé.

The streets were still congested, and they had trouble making any progress through the traffic. When they reached the top of Rue Châteaudun, Lola could no longer contain herself.

"We'll walk the rest of the way," she said. "We can get there faster."

The men jumped down from the cab, and Murier settled the fare.

"Don't worry, I can put it on my expenses," he told them.

They reached the police station, all a little out of breath, and learned that Anna had been discovered on Le Suquet, near the *faïencerie*, and the police officers had taken her to a temporary cell at the town hall. They hadn't wanted to risk crossing the city to the Macé station with all the crowds out on the streets.

Lola, while fearing she might meet people who had witnessed her rejection during the memorial event, rushed there, anyway, with both Murier and Maupassant in tow.

20

In Prison

At the town hall, Maupassant, Murier, and Lola were greeted by a guard who simply answered no to their every request. Mademoiselle Deslys, as an ordinary citizen, was not allowed to see the defendant. Monsieur Murier, as a journalist, was not allowed to approach Anna either. And Monsieur de Maupassant, as a writer, could certainly not talk to her.

"And as a friend and guardian?" asked Maupassant.

The man started to lose patience.

Maupassant also turned to anger, and in a stern voice, he asked to speak to someone in charge. Attracted by the commotion, a man came out of a closed office at the end of a hallway.

A shiver ran down Lola's spine.

It was Émile Rodot.

She had feared meeting witnesses to her earlier embarrassment, but what was now transpiring was so much worse than that. He looked at them all, but particularly Lola, and said, "What's all this fuss? What are you doing here?"

Lola forgot all prudence and diplomacy. Her day had been quite busy, and she was at her wits' end.

"I can't believe this. It's almost as if you're following my every move, is it not, Brigadier? I can't take a step in this town without running into you."

The man's expression hardened even more, if that were possible.

"Shut your mouth," he said. "I'm on a case here, and it's to be expected that we'd run into each other, since the murderess is your little orphan child. I'm the one who should be suspicious seeing you everywhere I turn. What were you doing this morning at Cousin's?"

Maupassant felt that things might soon be turning sour for Lola, and so he intervened by positioning himself in front of her.

"Officer, I had the honor of meeting you at the young lady's house, remember?"

The man deigned to look at Maupassant. "Yes, I remember, monsieur. Who are you?"

"I am Guy de Maupassant. I write now, but I had the honor of serving in the Second Division Class Seventy as a lieutenant. We may have met during my army days. As for why I'm here . . . I'm a good friend of Commissioner Valantin, as well as of the girl who is imprisoned here. Would you allow us to talk to her for a few minutes, Officer? I am appealing to your heart, as a man of honor. She's still very young, and she spent the night outside. We're worried, and we want to reassure her and find out if she needs anything."

"I must follow orders. It's not my responsibility."

"On the contrary, monsieur, I think Valantin would be upset to know you refused to grant me entry."

Rodot looked shaken.

"I have an idea," said Maupassant. "Why don't you go ask him? He is likely still at the war ceremony. Mademoiselle Deslys was one of its most significant donors. It's still taking place upstairs, right? It would only take you a few minutes. We can wait."

The policeman rubbed his chin and then turned his back on them, speaking sharply to his colleague. "We can't disturb the boss now. Open the door for them."

As they followed the officer, Lola whispered, "You were a lieutenant?"

"Not at all. I was just your everyday cannon fodder. But that wouldn't have gotten us anywhere, would it?"

They found Anna sitting on a bench all alone in an empty room, which the guard opened for them.

Anna threw herself into Lola's arms, tears flowing down her face. Lola also began to sob.

"They're right, Lola," Anna said. "I was there. And I was alone with him!"

Lola made a gesture to quiet Anna. "I know you're upset, but you must think before you speak."

But Anna continued. "He told me he wanted to show me something important. He said it would change my destiny. I wasn't supposed to tell anyone until everything was registered with the notary."

"But what is this?" asked Murier, who stood apart from the group.

She looked at him mournfully before turning back to Lola. "Monsieur Cousin, peace be upon him . . . he asked me to meet him at his home at around eight o'clock. I waited until you had gone to the theater before I left. But then Miss Fletcher didn't leave with you. She and Rosalie were working downstairs. I was fretting because I didn't want to be late. Fortunately, a carriage arrived shortly afterward, and Miss Fletcher got into it. Rosalie went to bed. I slipped out quietly."

"Going out in the middle of the night like that, like a . . ." Lola turned pink and stopped talking with an abruptness very much unlike her.

"I know, Lola," said Anna softly. "That's not how you raised me. But it was all such a mystery. And I love a good mystery! I don't know what got into me. I think I felt betrayed because of what I'd found out about you. I know it was wrong of me, but perhaps I wanted to hurt you. I thought if anything happened to me, well, it'd be all your fault and you'd be punished."

"There you go. Your wish has been granted. I'm being punished, indeed! But you even more so. I'm afraid for you, Anna. If only instead of running away, you'd told us all this!"

"I panicked when I woke up. I saw the blood on my bed and on my dress. I couldn't think straight. My dress was lying on the floor, although I'd put it in the wardrobe when I went to bed. I was so scared that all I could think to do was run."

"My poor child."

Anna went on. "Earlier that evening, when I sensed that everything had gone quiet, I entered the villa. There were no servants, because Cousin had given them all time off."

"I can't believe you did this, Anna! You're very silly for going there! Didn't you understand that that man wanted you?"

"You don't understand anything about any of it. Your idea of this is so distorted. There are nice, selfless men around, you know? We just talked, that's all."

"But talked of what?"

"He had something important to tell me. I can't repeat it to you. And it's not what you think it is. It doesn't matter. Then we had a disagreement because he wanted me to leave Les Pavots to live with him in his villa."

"Ha! You see! I was right!"

"No! It isn't what you think!"

"How naive you are, you poor thing!"

Anna seemed desperate to be understood. Everyone was accusing her, but she simply wasn't able to defend herself. "To think I left him alone in his office! He was so moved, so upset by our conversation. And I just ran away without giving him a second thought."

"You do realize you're facing the death penalty, don't you? Or at best, deportation to some island?"

She nodded and sat down on the bench with her head in her hands.

"If you don't tell us everything, we can't help you," Lola continued.

Anna had withdrawn, but then something appeared to change within her. She looked up and sputtered nastily, "This is all your fault."

Lola was bewildered by this. She looked at Maupassant helplessly. The writer was outraged by the girl's words and demanded she show her elders some respect.

Anna laughed. "Ha! You're defending her?"

"Where have you been hiding since you disappeared?" he demanded.

"You don't have to pretend to care about me. I'm on my own now. I'll face this alone. I lost the only person who could have protected me."

"Guy," said Lola, deeply wounded. "Stay out of this."

She then addressed Anna gently. "Do you need anything? Have you eaten? I'll make sure you are treated properly, and I'll have your meals delivered to you. Please watch out for Rodot and make sure you're never in a room alone with him. Understand? There always has to be someone else with you—even if it means causing a scene. Miss Fletcher or Rosalie will bring you a change of clothes. You're filthy. I won't come see you again until you say so. I don't wish to upset you. But know that I'm not abandoning you. I will do everything in my power to prove your innocence."

"Did I say I was innocent?" Anna whispered.

Swallowing a sob, Lola left the room, followed by the two men, as the guard locked the door behind them.

21

IN SEARCH OF LECERF

After receiving Lola's note from Basile, I rushed out to the Faisan Doré. My thoughts had turned to Mario and how desperate he must be feeling. He could do nothing to help Anna. His boss had seen to that.

The delicatessen's shutters were closed, and a sign on the door said, "Temporarily Shut due to Municipal Event."

What a strange way to put it. It was hardly an "event." I couldn't help but smile, despite my concerns. Only in Cannes would you see such a thing—a shop closed so the staff could join in the fun of a memorial to the dead.

I heard some noises coming from within the store and went around back to see where the service entrance was located.

As I neared the door at the rear of the building, I noticed two carts. One was laden and ready to depart, while the second waited to be loaded. Both were decorated with the "Faisan Doré" sign on the side of their tarpaulins.

"Can anybody assist me, please?" I asked several nearby workers.

I watched as one of the storekeepers, who was paying no attention to me, entered the storage area behind the shop. I followed him. The place was full of perishable and canned foods. At the back of the space, there was a huge kitchen with dozens of people rushing to and fro. I hadn't expected this.

A man wearing a strange white hat hollered at me.

"Madame, you can't stay there. You're in the way. If you wish to enter any farther, you will need to put on one of those white aprons on the wall there."

"I'm looking for a fellow named Étienne Lecerf. He's one of your runners here, I think. Or perhaps he works the books? I don't know."

The man altered his tone when he heard my English accent. I often cause this change in attitude whenever I speak. My eccentric dress is more than a little odd in the eyes of the people of Cannes, but being English is, in their view, a mark of superiority. Tradesmen, in particular, are sensitive to this fact.

With deference, he answered me. "He did, madame. However, he is no longer at our service."

"Has he taken ill?"

"No, madame. He lost his job because of a misunderstanding."

"How so?"

He looked offended by my questions. "Madame, I can't tell you more without violating my employer's rules. I must maintain loyalty and discretion at all times, you understand. Please excuse me, I have a crayfish soufflé in the oven."

He turned and went back to the kitchen. I walked slowly toward the exit, looking at the shelves filled with jars of fresh tomatoes decorated with Auguste Escoffier labels.

A young boy of no more than twelve, I imagine, was filling a crate with foodstuffs from the shelves. He put in jars of asparagus, lobster soup, foie gras, as well as several bottles of champagne. On the delivery note, I read, "Caserta, Marie-Thérèse."

I approached him. "Do you know Étienne Lecerf?"

"That drunkard!" he said with contempt. "Of course I know him. He's a wrong'un. He got fired, the dunce. They found him fast asleep here in the middle of all the boxes. He'd been at the wine, no doubt."

I smiled at the cheeky way he spoke of this Lecerf. "Do you know where he lives?"

The address given to me reminded me of my own past misfortune. Lecerf lived not far from the goods station, near Place de Châteaudun, the same neighborhood I'd ended up in when I sank to an all-time low before meeting Lola Deslys.

I was afraid to go there, but since it was only a few streets away, I had to get over my cowardice.

I took some deep breaths. With any luck, I might be able to get him to talk, and we could then demand our Anna be freed.

Anna had already gone through more than enough difficulties in her life. The fire on the farm where she'd lived as a child had robbed her of her parents. She'd then faced years of hardship and hunger at the Sacré-Cœur orphanage. The most distressing part in that dreadful place was certainly the death of her best friend. It was after these shocking events that she had taken refuge with us.

I could not bear the thought that rotten luck had caught up with her again and that she was now being accused of murder. It was up to Lola and me to get to the bottom of this, and if I had to go back to the hell from which I'd come to achieve it, then I'd do just that.

I passed my former boarding house to reach the one where Lecerf lived. The entrance led to a decrepit courtyard and a sign indicating that the concierge wasn't there. I slowly climbed the filthy steps toward the backyard and met with an extraordinarily thin woman coming down with full, stinking chamber pots at the end of each arm. She must have been going to empty them somewhere outside. I didn't want to know where.

She was bending under their weight, and I feared she would collapse.

She failed to greet me, so I stopped her. She balanced the pots precariously on the edge of a step, and I moved for fear they might spill. The smell was pestilential, and I now regretted having bothered the poor soul.

"Hello, excuse me, but I'm looking for Monsieur Lecerf's apartment? Does he live here?"

"That man who's always drunk?"

So everyone was unanimous in calling him an alcoholic, it seemed.

"Lives up there, second floor, on the left. He told me he was going on the run, but he hasn't run yet. He's good at running to the inn, though! He went out not so long ago."

She laughed at her own joke and picked up her stinking pots again. I moved to one side to let her pass, cross that I'd missed him.

"I'll wait, in that case," I said.

She didn't even turn around but mumbled under her breath, "Well, fancy that . . . Never mind . . . No harm done if that's the type he goes for."

I went up to his room and turned the handle. The door was unlocked. Inside, the place was a mess. There wasn't a stick of furniture, just a huge trunk in the middle of the floor, full of miscellaneous, seemingly random objects. Nothing of note. They looked like objects he might have liked rather than needed. Was his departure imminent?

Although I was afraid of catching fleas or being bitten by vermin, I searched everywhere in hopes of finding a clue. But apart from empty bottles lying in corners, there was nothing of much interest. I was just about to give up when I decided to take a closer look in the trunk. I rifled through what was in there and spotted a framed photograph of a family.

A woman sat with a baby on her lap, and a man stood behind her. If the man was Lecerf, the photograph must have been more than twenty years old. He would have changed since then. Nevertheless, it was all I could find, so I took the image out from behind the glass and slipped out the door.

He had probably gone, as his neighbor had suggested, to a nearby drinking den. My mission was to get this man to talk, which meant I had to find him. There was a café directly across the street, so I headed there.

As I entered, all eyes turned to me, and I heard more than one inappropriate remark from the numerous males present. I could see four men playing cards, watched by a bright-eyed boy; three others at the bar, chatting with the proprietor; and a sad and lonely looking woman at a table in the back with a glass of absinthe in front of her.

I must have seemed uncomfortable, which the men found amusing. It was fair enough, I suppose. I didn't exactly appear like I belonged.

"I'm looking for someone called Étienne Lecerf?" I said.

The laughter stopped. The boss shouted, "Don't know him!"

I realized I would likely get no more from them, but I walked around the room, showing them the picture. They had to have at least seen him, I thought. He lived just across the street. Their faces, however, remained closed.

I didn't feel discouraged. But the scene was repeated in an almost identical fashion in the other cafés and cabaret bars throughout the neighborhood. The types of folks I encountered changed somewhat as I moved away from the Châteaudun area, but their reactions remained the same. I knew that to find him, I wouldn't be able to count on help from anyone. Only fate would bring me to him—that, and the fact that I would need to rely on a twenty-year-old photograph as a guide, for my brief glimpse of him at the station was too blurry in my memory for me to identify him with any confidence.

While following this seemingly never-ending trail, my mind was occupied by Lady Sarah. What had really happened to her? What exactly was that scene I'd witnessed at the port?

As I continued the search, Lola was still at the town hall, trying to compose herself after having left Anna.

She asked Maupassant and Murier to wait for her in front of the building while she made her way back toward Rodot's office.

22

A Dangerous Tea

Lola opened Rodot's door without knocking.

"Goodness! A visitor!" he exclaimed. "What do you want? You want me to look kindly on that little killer of yours, I imagine? Don't worry. I have something for her, all right."

While speaking, he licked his lips.

Lola's heart began to beat furiously. She was consumed by both fear and rage.

"I must warn you, you worm," she said, closing her eyes so she would no longer see his repulsive face. "Don't you dare go near her if you want to keep your equipment intact."

She knew he would laugh at her, but as she opened her eyes again, she saw he wasn't even smiling. His expression was furious. He had always despised her, but he usually enjoyed belittling her—it was his way of exercising his dominance. But this time, he was clearly about to unleash a torrent of hatred upon her. It was the hatred of a man who wishes to be all-powerful when a woman dares to defy him.

"Did I hear that right? Are you threatening me?"

Lola felt it was necessary to hit harder, to go further. She had opened a door she knew would never be closed again. Had she made the right decision?

She remained calm as she responded. "I know all about you, and I have a journalist friend. Touch one hair on Anna's head, and all your infamies will be made public, including your little visits to the Rat Noir and your . . . special relationships. Do I make myself clear?"

Maupassant called out, "Are you coming, Lola? I have other things to do with my time, you know?"

Without awaiting Rodot's answer, Lola turned, marched out of the office, and slammed the door.

She passed in front of Hippolyte, whom she had met during Rodot's search of Les Pavots. He was sitting behind a counter. He looked at her with understanding, as if he knew everything about Rodot's behavior and disapproved of it.

As she stepped outside, Maupassant took her by the arm with a smile, but his expression quickly changed when he noticed she was shaking.

"What's the matter? Whom were you talking to? Was it that Rodot fellow you warned Anna of? Who is he? Why does he scare you so?"

"Come now, Guy! You know I'm not afraid of anything!" But her voice quivered, and the trembling only stopped when they found themselves far from the town hall.

Murier had already left Maupassant in order to return to his newspaper to write his article.

"I can't leave you in this state," said Maupassant. "Miss Fletcher would never forgive me. Come with me to the *Bel-Ami*. It's where I go when the vicissitudes of life become too unbearable. That boat heals me, you know. She washes away my woes and galvanizes me so I am ready to face the world. Come! You can tell me what's going on with this brigadier fellow."

Lola allowed herself to be guided by her friend.

They arrived at the dock in front of the yacht, and in the absence of his crew, Maupassant pulled on the mooring line to bring the boat in closer. Lola, who usually made a big song and dance when getting on board in order to be assisted by passing gentlemen, hopped on without any trouble.

They went below deck and settled beside each other on one of the comfortable benches. Maupassant offered her tea. He found the ingredients by snooping around in the cupboards. This was usually François's domain, and it was rare for Maupassant to have access to such things. He managed to light a small stove on which he placed a kettle full of water. He felt rather proud.

As soon as he started questioning her gently, she felt herself melt. Touched by her distress, he approached her to take her tenderly in his arms, just as one might comfort a small child.

But Lola's feelings for Maupassant were on a different level than this. It was precisely the comforting, fatherly side of him that attracted her, and she felt in great danger as soon as he showed her these little attentions.

She wanted nothing more than to lower her guard, to rely on a man who would understand her and protect her from the turpitudes of life. It would take so little for her to open up and let her love for him speak for itself. But this was precisely what a girl like Lola could not afford to do, especially since she knew that underneath his solid appearance, Maupassant was hiding another side of himself. That of a seducer, a consumer of women, a bon vivant. She knew he made fun of the idea of attachment. He often stated that there was no such feeling as love.

She leaned her head against his chest, and he stroked her hair gently. Lola felt a sensual warmth invade her, and shuddered. Her friend's breath became more shallow. She began feeling dizzy. Was this really about to happen? She sought out his lips passionately. Maupassant took her mouth with fervor as his hands stroked her bodice, seeking out her skin, her generous cleavage, then farther down . . . her silk-sheathed legs.

Lola, in the grip of blind desire, did not recognize herself. Her sudden abandonment terrified her while at the same time filled her with utter delight. She had to resist. She couldn't just give herself to this man. The image of a woman in gray with a baby in her arms passed before Lola's eyes. She remembered seeing him with her at the station years ago.

Knowing that this revelation would irreparably break the spell that bound them to this moment, she ventured, "That woman, Guy . . . The woman in gray at the station. Who is she?"

He stopped abruptly and laughed but avoided answering the question.

He pulled back so he could look her in the eye. He must have been wondering not whom she was talking about—for he would have immediately understood that—but rather how she had learned of her.

"What woman?"

"You know who, Guy. The mysterious woman in gray. She had a baby."

The struggle he appeared to be having with himself suddenly subsided, and he motioned for her to put her cheek against him again as he placed his powerful arms around her. All traces of desire had now vanished.

He whispered, "I know that nothing escapes you, my *Belle Amie*. Yes, there is a woman who holds a special place in my life. And we have children. But how can I, with the name of Maupassant, marry my Joséphine? Her name is Litzelmann, for the love of God! I have told not a soul, of course."

"When do you see her? You have such a busy schedule."

"She lives near my house in Paris, and sometimes she follows me on my trips. Not even François knows of this."

Lola couldn't believe what he was saying. She envied this Joséphine. And she knew now she could never give herself to him. There was a moment of silence as they tried to regain their composure. Maupassant gave a slight cough before venturing further into the conversation.

"Now," Maupassant said, clearing his throat and pulling Lola from her thoughts, "I want to talk of that brigadier fellow."

She did not answer his questions about Rodot with the truth, fearing she would reveal too much of herself if she told him how the brigadier had abused his power. She felt ashamed.

When she felt able, she stated, "Rodot is a despicable man. I know him well, as does everyone in Cannes. I fear for Anna, that he will force her to . . ." She lowered her head.

Maupassant couldn't fathom this. He had known Anna since she was twelve years old, and although at fifteen she was fast becoming a woman, he still saw the child in her.

"I'll have a word with Valantin. He'll make sure that nothing happens."

"Because you think Valantin doesn't know about Rodot's character?" she scoffed. "Don't worry, I'll handle it my own way. I feel so awful about this. Anna thinks I'm her enemy, but it is Rodot who is supposed to represent the law, who is in fact a danger to her. But none of this compares with the real threat here."

"What do you mean?"

"The guillotine, Guy. A young orphan with no protection other than that of a courtesan and a woman who has been rejected by all good society stands accused of murdering a banker? You know as well as I that they won't even consider prison. It will be the death penalty with no plea."

Maupassant felt powerless to save Anna. Just as he felt when it came to saving Lola and his brother, Hervé. As for Joséphine, although she never asked anything of him, he knew she wanted her children to be secure, and just perhaps, she dreamed of marriage at some point. Some friends who were working to become successful writers and poets relied on his regular payments to survive, as did his whole family, who led a decent life thanks to the income he provided.

All these charges seemed too much for one man. Too much for him, in any case. What would happen to them all if he, too, became sick? For he had realized some time ago that his body was starting to betray him.

He stood and put their used cups and saucers into a ceramic basin. His crew would take care of them when they came aboard later.

He suddenly wanted to get home and reflect on his woes. How would he ensure everyone who depended on him was financially stable, including Joséphine? He felt selfish for having to leave Lola and thinking of his own sorry state of affairs.

Lola stumbled to her feet, blowing her nose into her handkerchief noisily. She wiped away her tears and thanked him for the tea.

"Come," said Maupassant gently. "Let me put you in a cab, and you can go home. I have matters I must attend to. My apologies, Lola."

"Thank you," she replied, avoiding his gaze.

23

A Thoughtful Gentleman

Lola stepped down from the cab and rushed into Les Pavots, heading straight for the kitchen.

Some rockfish stew was simmering on the stove under Sherry's watchful eye, filling the room with a comforting smell. On the sideboard, an unbleached linen cloth covered the homemade cake that had been made for dessert, protecting it from insects and dust.

She was greeted by Rosalie, who took her into her arms when she saw the defeated look on Lola's face.

"Why the sorrowful look, my lovely girl?"

Lola was finally able to release her pain. "They're keeping Anna locked up. Can you believe it? Our little one?"

"There, there . . . ," said Rosalie, stroking her hair.

"I'm going to bed. Would you come and undo my corset? I just don't have the strength."

She removed herself from Rosalie's arms and began to search through the cupboards and along the shelves for something with which to drown her sorrows. She found a bottle of cognac and some port wine. She mixed them together in a chipped bowl and took it up to her bedchamber.

She unpinned her hair as Rosalie untied the strings of her underwear, before slipping on a nightdress and climbing into bed.

"Miss Fletcher isn't home yet, I understand?"

"No, not yet. She left right after she received your message to see that Lecerf fellow, just as you asked her to."

"I hope he doesn't kill Miss Fletcher," said Lola with a certain finality.

"What?" cried Rosalie. "What nonsense is this?"

"Well, he's the killer, isn't he?"

"Now, that's enough. You are being quite self-indulgent dwelling on misfortune. You're stronger than that. It will take more than this ridiculous business to bring you down. You always have the last word, don't you?"

Lola felt moved by these kind words and wiped the tears from her cheeks with the corner of the sheet.

"If you only knew, my beloved Rosalie! This time it's going to be hard. Cousin wasn't after Anna for . . . you know . . . There was something else going on. A secret. Anna knows it, but she won't tell me. If only she kept a journal. Can we look through her affairs?"

"I'll check. If she has one, I'll find it," said Rosalie.

"And please wake me when Fletcher returns home. She'll be able to tell me what to do. The English are so pragmatic. They never get burdened by emotions. They have such gumption."

"I promise I'll bring her to you as soon as I see her."

"And with Anna . . . we have a real war on our hands, Rosalie. I shouldn't have lied to her."

"You have nothing to be ashamed of. You've always done the best you could."

Gradually, the mélange that Lola had just ingested started having an effect. She felt more and more relaxed and began to talk about Maupassant and his secret love.

Surprised, Rosalie questioned her, but Lola's answers were becoming increasingly disjointed. Half-asleep now, Lola started on the subject of Rodot instead.

"And the one who's guarding her . . . It's . . . He's the one who . . ." She had become impossible to understand.

Rosalie was crying now. "I wonder where she was all night long, our poor little love. *For heaven's sake!* All this is just so upsetting. I'll search the house. I'll search all of Cannes. I'll search the whole world. I'll start right away!"

"What for?" asked Lola, numb.

"Her journal! All young girls keep a journal in this day and age."

"Go to bed. Remember the soaps," Lola muttered. "Embroidering . . . the lace bags."

"I'll do it tomorrow with Miss Fletcher," said Rosalie, leaving her mistress in peace.

Shortly after, Lola was on the brink of falling into unconsciousness when there was a knock on her door. She stirred at the sound.

The handle turned slowly. It was Ferdinand, the handsome baron.

Rosalie had let him in. Lola opened her eyes and noted that Ferdinand's own appeared filled with a burning light. He kneeled before the bed.

"My dear, are you unwell? I waited for you. I looked everywhere. Can't you see how enamored I am of you?" He took her hand, lifted it to his mouth, and kissed it. "What's the matter with you? Are you ill?" he continued.

Lola managed to answer him laboriously, "You can't stay here. I'm in no condition for that. I need to be alone."

"But I fought for you this morning! You know that, don't you? The duel versus Philémon Carré-Lamadon? Paul Antoine told you, didn't he?"

She felt a little more sober by this point and able to speak, albeit wearily. "Did you kill him?"

"I didn't kill him," he said, smiling.

"So, don't come here to talk nonsense to me in that case. Such childish matters are quite grotesque."

"But it was not through want of trying. He collapsed in fear before we'd even started. The shame is so very great that I doubt he will ever show his face here in Cannes again!"

"That's fabulous. You're an angel. But he was at the ceremony earlier. He looked as dashing as ever. And more arrogant than ever. He kept me from entering the gathering in the town hall. Leave now, please. I must sleep."

"You can't push me away, you know. I love you too much. Tell me what's bothering you."

"Don't worry, I'm just tired. It has been a difficult day for me. I think I've had too much cognac."

He must have smelled it on her breath and known her to be telling the truth. "I understand the need to have the odd tipple, but you mustn't overdo it with liquors. They take away your will!"

He rushed out in much the same way as he had come in. She couldn't hear him as he walked down the hallway and stairs, for when Anna had come to live with her, she had placed a thick velvet curtain in front of her door so that the rest of the household would never hear what was happening when gentlemen came to visit.

But this meant she did not hear him on his way back. He waltzed into her room several minutes later with three huge bouquets of flowers, which he threw onto the bed. He had left them downstairs until he was sure he could see her.

"These are for you. Nothing will ever be too good for you, my Lola."

"I already told you . . . It's nice of you, the flowers and all that . . . but . . . come back tomorrow. Be a sport. I must sleep now."

"Allow me to remain near you tonight. I can stroke your head or hold your hand. Or I could lay myself down by your feet . . ."

The tone was so exaggerated that Lola could not help but smile.
He was so kind and sweet. She couldn't resist him. He lay down
beside her, fully clothed, only removing his shoes.

He caressed her shoulder as he whispered, "We'll go to Paris. You
will be my queen. I will have a private mansion built for you on the
Champs-Elysées. All of Paris will be desperate to meet you."

Lola repeated a few of his words dreamily. "Paris . . . All of Paris . . ."
She fell into a deep sleep with Ferdinand at her side.

24

SALVATION

It was already the middle of the night by the time I entered the Poussiat district. The alleyways were dark and dirty, and no matter how careful I was, it was difficult to avoid the muddy puddles. My short outfit really served me well and kept me from getting too much of the fetid filth on the bottom of my skirts. The lighting was poor. Indeed in contrast with the gaslight down on the Croisette and the electricity along Boulevard de la Foncière, it was all but nonexistent. Fortunately, I always have my matches with me.

I lit one whenever I heard a suspicious noise. I expected to be attacked by scoundrels at any moment, but in all likelihood, the noises were being made by rats. I now understood why the cabaret bar that I was making my way toward was called the Rat Noir!

I decided it would be the last place I'd check before going home, because I simply couldn't take it anymore.

Maybe this whole frantic race of my own making would be in vain? Maybe Lecerf had already gone home? Perhaps he'd even left Cannes for good?

But the laws of searching for something lost dictate that it's always found in the very last drawer in which one looks. And thus, I hoped to find Lecerf at the Rat Noir. The establishment was run by a lout named Roussel, whom Lola knew well.

Raids were frequent there, and I hoped none would take place while I was on the premises. After being received wherever I had gone with indifference at best, and outright nastiness at worst, I had gotten used to the general tone of the local bars and cafés, and I knew that my best defense was to speak as loudly as possible so that everyone could hear my English accent. It was like a magic formula. Everyone would turn away, believing I shared the same eccentricities that they acknowledged in my compatriots.

As soon as I opened the door, I was met with silence. I quickly looked around and pulled out the photograph. The law of the last drawer, once again, had panned out. Lecerf, drunk out of his mind, seemed to be waiting for me. He had, in fact, changed little since his portrait had been taken. The only notable difference was that he'd put on some weight. Roussel looked me up and down. When I opened my mouth to speak, he turned his head away.

I stood next to Lecerf and asked for a sherry. Lecerf didn't seem concerned by my presence. On the contrary, he seemed to be pleased that I might make the ideal drinking partner. His intoxication was advanced enough that I hoped my questions would not bother him. He was in a rather talkative mood. I asked why he had been fired from the Faisan Doré, and he did not seem at all surprised by my question. It was Roussel who interrupted our conversation.

"But how do you know about that?" he asked suspiciously.

I imagined he was thinking that if the police were now employing women, his life was about to get complicated. In fact, I realized that it might help my cause if doubts arose as to my possible membership in the forces.

"I was told . . . by a friend."

But the more I talked, the more he seemed convinced that I had received my information from an official source and that I had been assigned to investigate Lecerf.

He looked worriedly around room, at the gambling tables and the men who were disappearing behind a filthy old curtain at the back.

He nodded to two of his employees, hefty men with unattractive faces, and then came out from behind his counter, crying loudly, "We're closing! Everybody out!"

Within a few minutes, he'd managed to drive out every customer, including Lecerf and myself. I quickly realized that my new companion wouldn't get far on foot as he stumbled into the gutter, clearly intent on sleeping it off quietly.

I stood in front of him, urging him to get up.

Roussel was outside now, closing the shutters on his windows while throwing the occasional dark look in my direction. He stomped back into his bar through a small door at the side of the building, and I heard him climbing the stairs inside with a heavy step. I didn't understand. This cabaret was not known as a brothel, but I could hear voices coming from upstairs. I recognized Roussel's. He was yelling at a man in one of the rooms at the front of the building.

I could only capture a few words. Mere fragments. "Double game . . . Finished . . . Refund . . . Dangerous . . ."

While Roussel's tone was very aggressive, the man responded calmly, "Are you threatening me? Whom do you think you are to . . . ?"

I recognized that voice.

Lecerf laughed. "That Rodot won't be shifted. He's a pig."

"Brigadier Émile Rodot?"

"That's right. He comes for the girls. And that scoundrel Roussel gets protection."

"That's extortion!"

"You're not wrong there. But the boss thinks you're one of them. So he's having a go at Rodot about it."

I pretended I didn't understand. "One of whom, exactly?"

"You nick people. You're a flatfoot. But a girl all the same."

Since knowing Lola, I had become familiar enough with some of the popular terms to understand local parlance. Despite the drink he must have consumed, Lecerf was rather clear in his reasoning.

As he ranted, I got to thinking. I didn't want to witness a fight between Rodot and Roussel. I didn't want to run into Rodot at all, in fact. So I grabbed my new friend's elbow, hoisted him to his feet, and started to push him forward.

Although I made it look like I was clinging to his arm, I was actually holding all his weight as I guided him through the alleys to his quarters on the other side of town.

The fresh air did him some good, and as I began once again to question him, he started giving me more coherent responses.

"Where was I? Oh yes, my former master at the Faisan Doré. When I think of all the advantageous contracts I set up for him, back when I was the one selling him bottles! I know a lot about him. I could tell you some things, but I'm an honest man. Just because I lost everything doesn't mean I wish the same on others. He fired me. What a short memory he must have, eh?"

"But why were you asked to leave?"

"What do I know of it? I had to load crates and take them to the customers. That's it. Then I mislaid one of the addresses, so I went back to the warehouse. And I opened a bottle to give myself a little snifter. And then the mangy dog screamed at me! If I'd known he treated his employees like that, I'd have never helped him as much as I did back in my day!"

"But he wouldn't have fired you over a simple lost address, would he?"

"No, but you know how it is. One bottle precedes another. I ended up trying a few, and then I fell asleep on the job. But it's not exactly the worst thing a man can do, is it? But there you go. He's a cold one. A bastard. Excuse my language, mademoiselle. But there are no other words. To think that . . . Back when I was someone . . ."

"When did this happen? And at what time?"

"It was in the afternoon, two days ago."

It was then that I realized he couldn't have been the one who attacked Anna. When it came to the murder, though, there was still a chance he could have committed it.

"And what did you do then?" I asked.

"Well, he caught me in the warehouse, and he woke me! And he forced me to catch up on what I should have done in the afternoon. Even though I was in no condition."

"Maybe the customers were waiting for an order?"

"Some food was perishable and had to be delivered by the next morning at the latest."

"So that's what you did, is it? You worked alone?" I was hoping to get an affirmative response, for it would mean he had no alibi.

"No," he replied shamefacedly. "He made the head storekeeper, another mean piece of work, stay with me in the end. He just stood there watching me. He didn't lift a finger to help. He was furious that he'd had to work the night shift. But was it really my fault that the boss was so angry? When we got back from our deliveries, the boss was waiting for us, and he let me go there and then. When I think about what I'm now reduced to! All because of that Cousin. What a con man. Have you ever known the like?"

"That's the reason I'm asking you all these questions."

"I guessed as much. They're the same questions the police asked me. But they let me go, you know. Are you part of a private agency or something? I hear it's common practice to employ women at those places."

"No, I'm looking for people who were financially ruined following Cousin's operations. You're one of them, which is why I will check everything you have just told me. You might well have wanted to take revenge on the banker."

"Oh yes, I wanted revenge. More than wanted it, I needed it. If I could only have seen him die. It's not like I had a whole heap of other savings and properties to fall back on. Like that Vidal . . ."

"Vidal?"

"The fellow who has that asylum out on the islands. It's all fine for him. He was able to get back in the saddle pretty quickly."

"I understand your son is suing you?"

"You know everything, don't you? Bad news travels fast."

"Trials are public affairs. There are no secrets in court."

"Yes, and now I'll have to go on the run because of that cur. The shame of it, going after his very own father! It's his wife. She's a bad influence on him. She was hoping to get her share of the pie, and now that I'm a broken man, she's enjoying her revenge. I have no salvation other than escape. I have no money, so they must want to see me in debtor's prison."

"Where will you go?"

"Algeria. I can rebuild my life over there."

He remained quiet for a moment, appearing lost in thought. We were approaching Place de Châteaudun. As we stood in front of his building, he said, "At the end of the day, I'd rather be in my position than in Vidal's. I still have a wife who loves me. She says she'll come with me. God knows I don't deserve her." He was tearing up, sniffing loudly, in the grip of one of those embarrassingly sensitive performances drunks often give. "Do you realize that she supports me and everything I do? When our son has turned against us? But that Vidal, the poor bastard . . . He lost a whole lot more than I did."

"You said he'd landed on his feet."

"All right, all right! He has recovered enough to create that lunatic place, but . . . It is his wife's inheritance, you understand . . . He lost a lot. So much more than I did."

"How so?"

"Well . . . his wife and daughter. They died because of the dishonor of it all. When I say died . . . you understand . . . they invited death to come for them . . . if you get my meaning."

I shivered. Images of my father's end flooded my mind. This story had now gone too far for me. Anxiety rose inside my throat, about to destroy the progress I thought I'd made. Was this my own destiny catching up with me?

I left him without saying goodbye, absorbed by my intense pain. I didn't even have the strength to seek out a cab. I hobbled home like a woman three times my age.

25

THE SHATTERED PORTRAIT

When I entered the kitchen the next morning, with my ash bucket in hand, I found Rosalie crying in front of the stove. It looked as though she'd been finishing embroidering the small pouches for the orange-blossom soaps. We were supposed to deliver them to Paul Antoine's store on Rue d'Antibes in the afternoon. Even though we hadn't had the opportunity to work much on the soaps of late, we still wanted to fulfill our orders as best we could.

"It's so hot in here! I was half-frozen to death up in my room," I said by way of greeting, acting as if I hadn't seen her in her sorry state so as not to cause her any embarrassment.

She looked at me, her eyes drowning in tears, and responded mechanically, "It's always colder under the eaves."

"That hot chocolate smells so good I can't resist it. No coffee for me today. I'll have the same as our mistress."

My request brought a smile to her face. "I'm sorry you've caught me off guard here. It's just that nothing's going well anymore, Miss Fletcher. Already, there was much left to be desired with this place and how we all live, but it seems that everything has gone wrong. All the fighting and bad tempers. And now I'm so afraid for the little one."

"I know, Rosalie, but you have to believe that there's a way out. You know Lola as well as anyone. She's going to get Anna out of this predicament."

"Oh, but she already has. It's this Lecerf fellow, according to her."

As she watched me lower my head, she anticipated my answer. "No? It isn't him, then? So how are we going to do it? Yesterday, I searched the entire house, looking for a trace that Anna might have left without knowing it. Her journal, for example. At first, Mademoiselle Lola thought the old man just wanted to have Anna in his bed, but now . . . she doesn't think that."

"Why not?"

"Anna told her there was something else, but she doesn't want to say what it is. So Lola doesn't think it was anything to do with seduction. She thinks there's a real secret and that we have to uncover it. She's sure we can find clues in the house if we look hard enough. Yesterday, I searched Anna's room in the wardrobe, her cupboards, under the benches, the pillows, everywhere. Nothing. The living room, the library, everywhere. I opened every single book. I turned every page. Nothing! I wanted to look in the mistress's bedchamber, too, but she had company, so I couldn't take the risk. I looked in, and they were sleeping like little dormice."

"Who? Mario?"

"Oh no! Mario came by early this morning before work, but it was to find out what he could do to help. He won't rest until he finds her attacker and kills him. He went back to the Pantiero, though. He had little choice."

"Then who?"

"That young pup. The one who's head over heels for her. That Ferdinand. He slept with his clothes on, over the sheets next to her. He was holding her hand. She had a lot to drink, you know."

To hide my annoyance, I ventured into the laundry room, which also served as a small workshop for our soap making. I picked up my basket of lace fabrics, my scissors, and my thread and took a few deep breaths. I came back to assist her with what was left of the embroidery work. The simple, serene gestures required a concentration that emptied my mind, calmed me down, and helped me to find a semblance of peace.

Rosalie's sniffles and the ticking of the kitchen clock punctuated our actions. The pile of finished pouches grew steadily.

We didn't exchange a great many words, each of us lost in our own worlds. From time to time, we heard noises above our heads, and Rosalie would say, "Oh, is that her? Do you think she's awake?"

I, too, would look up at the ceiling, but silence ensued, and so we would start up our task again, both of us feeling disappointed.

Sherry suddenly entered the kitchen with his tail in the air, meowing imperatively. Rosalie got up to serve him a small bowl of milk, which she put near a cushion on the floor next to the stove. After a few laps, he left the saucer alone and continued to meow with impatience.

"What's the matter, boy?" Rosalie asked. "Isn't the milk fresh?"

He looked at her and jumped up first onto her knees and then to the table. He purred, knowing it would soften her mood and he would be allowed to stay put. In general, he was not permitted to sit on the table, but he seemed to know that these were exceptional circumstances, and neither she nor I prevented him from doing so.

He waltzed between the cups, the bread, and our baskets of thread and fabric. Twice he kicked the pile of pretty finished pouches to the floor, which made Rosalie exclaim loudly.

He approached my basket and sniffed it curiously.

"There's nothing to eat in there," said Rosalie. "What's the matter with you?"

After examining its contents, he tested it with a paw, as if he were going to sit there to take a nap.

"Ha! Not a chance, you little so-and-so," said Rosalie. "That's not your basket. Look, your cushion's by the stove! Don't let him settle in there, Miss Fletcher. He'll leave fur and fleas everywhere."

I tried to shoo him away, but he refused to budge. He jumped into the basket, but he was too heavy for such a maneuver, and it slipped off the table and fell to the ground, its contents spilling all over the tiled floor. Strangely enough, the sound of broken glass accompanied this fall.

At the bottom of my basket, under the lace fabrics, were various sheets of paper with embroidery designs that came to me from my mother and two notebooks with illustrations and instructions that had also belonged to her. Nothing that could have caused such a noise. Yet glass shards littered the kitchen floor among the thread, needles, and other bits and pieces.

Sherry had run away as fast as he could to avoid being reprimanded. I crouched down to put everything back in order, surprised to find a portrait in the middle of the mess. It was in a wooden frame, but the glass had shattered into hundreds of pieces.

"Well, look at that. I've never seen this before. It's Anna!" said Rosalie, taking the paper from the frame and holding it out to me. There she was, our little Anna in a Second Empire–style headband and crinoline dress with a photographer's decorative canvas behind her. "When did she dress up like that? I don't remember her ever going to a ball."

I grabbed the photograph in surprise. "She's never been to anything like that, Rosalie. You know she's not yet out." I looked more closely at Anna's features, detecting several small details that were not exactly like her. "It's strange. It's almost as if she is trying to look older, isn't it? Her eyes are more . . . mature. Don't you think so?"

Rosalie grabbed it for closer inspection. It was then that I saw the back of the portrait. There was a photographer's stamp and an address with words underneath written in a light, elegant style, followed by a signature.

The stamp read, "Karekine Noubarian, photographer, Rue Franque, Smyrna."

And the words delivered a promise: *Forever yours, Emina Aba-Melech de Caravel.*

I turned it over in Rosalie's hands to show her. We exchanged a disconcerted look.

"She's never been to Smyrna, has she? Or maybe I missed something," said Rosalie. "Where is it, anyway?"

"It's in Turkey," I said. "She couldn't have falsified a photographer's stamp, could she? This can't be her. The lady's name is Emina. Have you ever heard of a name like that?"

"We must show this photograph to Mademoiselle Lola right away," said Rosalie, rushing up the stairs.

Before leaving the kitchen, I noticed Sherry skulking in the pantry. "Thank you, Sherry," I whispered to him.

He gave me an eyes-half-closed look, as if to say, *You're quite welcome, my dear! Think nothing of it.*

"Don't walk around here, for you may hurt your paws," I told him.

I grabbed a small, dented metal shovel and a brush and began to sweep up the pieces of glass.

As she walked up the stairs, Rosalie shouted, "Mademoiselle, mademoiselle, wake up! Come and see this!"

I went up to join them after verifying that the floor was clear. We didn't have to wait long in the living room before Lola appeared in her nightdress, hastily putting on her red silk Chinese bathrobe. A man followed behind her—glued to her, one might say. Ferdinand! How had I already forgotten him? He rushed around like the last time he was here, not having the first clue how to please her.

"Gracious, Ferdinand, please stop! I don't need to sit down! I just got up! Let me be! Take this chair! Sit! Leave me to concentrate on my business, will you?"

He blushed violently and sat in the chair she pushed toward him. He made no reply, but his face expressed annoyance.

"And don't sulk," she added. "It doesn't suit you at all." She grabbed the portrait and examined it carefully.

"At first we thought it was Anna," I explained.

"She looks a lot like her, doesn't she?" said Rosalie.

"Yes! Oh my gosh! But where did it come from?"

"It was Sherry. He knocked over Miss Fletcher's basket."

"This was in your embroidery basket?"

"Yes. Under my patterns and threads and the like. But it can't have been there long, because I use my basket a fair amount. I would have noticed it."

She turned the portrait over, just as I had done. "He's not a local photographer," she noted.

"Indeed. He's from Smyrna. It is a Turkish city."

"But where could it have come from? Emina Aba-Melech de Caravel," she whispered pensively.

Ferdinand raised his head. "I know that name," he said. "The de Caravels. They're Italians. My uncle knows them well."

"Ferdinand, please. I know you want to make yourself useful, and I appreciate it. You are very charming, but even so, you mustn't interfere."

"It's true, my sweet! I even remember—"

But Lola was no longer listening. "What strange fashion," she said, further inspecting the photograph. "She doesn't look French, does she? Nor Italian like many of us from these parts. She looks like a Gypsy."

"Just like Anna," I replied.

She fetched her purse where she'd placed Lady Sarah's contract and slipped the photograph in beside it. She put it on the dresser next to Ferdinand and walked back to us.

"I'll go see Murier later. That man is an encyclopedia. He knows everything about everyone. Rosalie, could you bring us up some food, please? Are you hungry, my sweet?" she asked the young man.

He looked agitated. "Why not? Yes, that's a good idea."

"But whatever is the matter? Is it because of what I just said? About interfering? Or because I didn't listen to you? What did you want to tell me? I'm listening now."

She leaned forward to embrace him. In a clipped voice, he explained, "I just wanted to say that I remember going to his funeral at the Grand Jas cemetery a few years ago. I was a teenager, but my uncle wanted to attend, and as I'm his only family, he forced me to accompany him. He cried a lot at the graveside. The man must have been a close friend."

"Do you really not follow? What man? We're talking about a young woman named Emina."

She had moved away from him, possibly to think more clearly. He looked so saddened to have been rebuked by Lola. With his lips pinched, he reached out his hand to her, but she lightly pushed it aside and made her way toward me.

Rosalie's footsteps were getting louder. Lola went to open the door for her. The smell of freshly ground coffee tickled our nostrils. Lola held my hands and looked at me intensely. I understood exactly how she felt.

"If it's not her, it has to be her sister," I said.

Lola whispered, "Anahita . . ."

"Or even her . . ."

Just as I was about to say the word *mother*, Ferdinand stood suddenly and, in three strides, crossed the space separating him and the door.

"But," said Lola, amazed, "where are you going? Are you really so cross with me?"

Without responding, he rushed down the stairs, pushing Rosalie out of the way, and she almost dropped her tray.

"For goodness' sake! What has gotten into that one? Will he not breakfast with us?" cried Rosalie.

Lola hurried to the window and called out to him as soon as he appeared on the pathway. "Ferdinand? Ferdinand? Where are you going?"

After a few seconds of silence, she returned to us. "Oh, let him sulk if that's what he wants. He's just a little boy, don't you think? I have far greater concerns. And as my grandmother used to say: *Passeràsene prima che mi riprende.* He'll be long gone before I start caring."

26

AT THE GRAND JAS CEMETERY

Lola drank a large cup of coffee as quickly as she could, and I, too, took a second cup as I lit one of my cigarillos.

She then rushed into her bedchamber to get dressed, calling out to me for help with her corset. She dressed soberly in a dark-blue dress that nevertheless boasted a décolletage more suitable for the evening.

"What are your plans for today?" I asked. "And what can I do to help? Although, I must say, I don't know what can be done at this point. The Lecerf theory seems to have come to a dead end."

Lola wasn't listening to me. I had such a great deal to tell her, but I knew I would have to choose my moment.

"As I said, I'm going to go ask Murier some questions about those people," she muttered.

"Would you like me to come with you?"

"I'd rather you went to visit Anna," she said. "I'm so worried."

"Of course. It would please me very much to be able to console her. We don't want her to feel abandoned. She may even tell me her secret."

"I won't go if she doesn't ask for me, but I still need to know how she is and that all is well," continued Lola. "Take her some food and clothing, and keep your eye on Rodot, please."

"I will. It will be good for him to understand that our girl is not without her protectors."

"Yes, but I'm rather concerned that our protection may appear weak. They may not let you see her if you go alone. Could you ask Maupassant to go with you?"

I agreed to her suggestions and was looking forward to getting started.

"They may keep you waiting a long time, so take some reading materials, and eat before you leave. You don't know what time you'll be back."

She covered herself with a hooded shawl and hollered out to Rosalie as she left the house, "Miss Fletcher will see Anna. Make up a basket for the little one. She must be half-starved in that place. Why don't you make her a pissaladière? She adores that! And fruit. And chicken. And a little wine."

I went upstairs to get ready, and from my little window under the roof, I watched her energetic figure heading toward the newspaper archives just across the road and up the hill.

As Lola later told me, she didn't use the main door but sneaked in behind the building and entered the basement. The concierge recognized her and let her pass without so much as a blink. She walked farther into the offices and asked the clerk for Murier.

"I haven't seen him yet. It's still a little early for that one. Can I help you with anything?"

She knew she couldn't wait indefinitely for Murier, and she had no intention of chasing after him from café to café all over the city. She didn't know where he lived either. Should she go to Maupassant and ask him for Murier's address? No. She would lose at least an hour, and she wasn't even sure he would know.

Lola thought that perhaps she should take advantage of the information at her fingertips and act as a journalist would.

"Yes, if you would be so kind," replied Lola, undoing her little cape. "I'm looking for something that would have perhaps been printed the 1870s. Could you help me look through some of the main publications?"

"It would be my pleasure," he said with a smile.

That was easy! she gloated inwardly.

The employee escorted her to the back room and sat her down at a huge central table. He brought her several boxes and left her in peace.

She decided to look through the newspapers in order. She was mainly looking for the arrivals of personalities in Cannes. Might the lady in the portrait have come here as a visitor? Had she been someone of renown? Lola scanned the papers one by one.

After some time, she went into her purse to pull out the image, but simply couldn't find it. *I know I put it in here,* she thought, perplexed, rifling. Where could it have gone? *Oh, it doesn't matter!* she finally decided. *I know her first name was Emina and her surname was something like caravan.* That was it! She'd seen it somewhere. The name *de Caravel* appeared in several articles. She'd seen the name Ernesto de Caravel. He had to be a relation. He had a villa on the hill above the La Ferrage grounds.

And then she found what she was looking for: the announcement of his engagement to a certain Emina, which had given rise to a beautiful celebration at the Caserta family home. It was specified that Emina was a young lady of Armenian nobility. Birth name: Aba-Melech. Ernesto was a widower when he married her and already a father of married children. He had started out as a wealthy landowner with property in both Italy and Turkey and then gone on to become a silk trader. He controlled the entire process from his silkworm farmlands in Turkey to his spinning mills in Italy.

Lola made a face when she thought of silkworms. But perhaps it was the idea of young Emina's engagement to a man old enough to be her grandfather that brought about the feeling of disgust.

In 1871 and 1872, the de Caravel family came to spend their winters in Cannes. There were a great many celebrations, and it seemed they were invited everywhere. In 1873, their name was only mentioned on the day of their arrival. Throughout the season, traces of them became very scant in the society pages. It was as if they had remained shut in their villa, no longer invited to dine with other families, nor receiving guests in their home. Lola was aware of this phenomenon. It likely had something to do with an illness in a family.

Anna was born in 1873, she thought, recalling what they knew of Anna's past from the orphanage documents. *Where was this Emina while Anna's mother, Madame Jeanne Martin, was supposedly giving birth to the little girl on her farm at Camplong?* As she continued to look through articles from that year, she learned that Emina Aba-Melech de Caravel had spent the winter in Cannes without her husband, who had been held back by his business. *Goodness! Perhaps Ferdinand had been speaking the truth. Could this de Caravel really be buried in the Grand Jas cemetery?*

It seemed that Emina began living as a recluse in Cannes. Her arrivals and departures from the city were noted in the papers, along with those of all the other *winterers* of good breeding, but then that was all. Her husband no longer accompanied her.

There were no more parties and no more public outings. The Italian trader and his wife had no children at the time these newspapers were published. From 1877, Emina was no longer mentioned even as a winterer. Lola got tired of soiling her gloves with dust.

"Could you tell me the time, monsieur?" she shouted through the door.

The clerk appeared in an instant and put his hand in his pocket to consult his watch. "Almost three o'clock, madame."

She noticed a writing desk in a corner of the room. "May I?"

"Please."

She took a sheet of paper from atop the bureau and dipped a pen in the inkwell to write a short note for Murier. She regretted missing him and hoped they would meet again soon.

She wanted to maintain good relations with him because a well-timed article on a young lady such as herself, with all the innuendo in the right places and without any breach of decorum, could do her an immense service. She was delighted to have found a new journalist friend.

She finally got up and, with her most dazzling smile, said goodbye to the archives clerk.

She walked down to the Boulevard de la Foncière and hailed a cab, asking the driver to take her to the Grand Jas cemetery. Perhaps Ferdinand had been right. She wanted to see de Caravel's grave for herself. Was it really the same man she had found in the newspapers? She needed as much information as she could find about this couple.

The cab turned around on the boulevard, then took a right onto the Route de Grasse.

The ten-hectare park that housed the Grand Jas cemetery was located far from the city center. It had been granted to the city in 1866, and parts of it still looked like abandoned fields. They had planned for it to be very big, indeed. It must be said that a great number of visitors who came to Cannes for respite never left.

It was as if the sky were sharing Lola's thoughts, as it began to rain large, slow, heavy drops.

She asked the coachman to wait for her, bought a bouquet of violets from the lady standing at the entrance, and entered the gloomy park. She meandered between the graves for what seemed like ages. She should have asked the guard who lived in a small lodge near the entrance for the exact location of the grave, but she hadn't thought of it, and she didn't want to retrace her steps. She was convinced she would stumble upon the tomb of the de Caravel family by chance. She just hadn't envisioned it would take this long.

She tried her utmost to shelter herself from the heavy rain with her lace umbrella, but it was really not up to the task. She finally found what she was looking for after more than an hour of wandering.

The tomb was superb and stood proudly among those of other Italian nobles. It was capped by a tall turret and magnificent bust. There was a gate leading to a crypt under the stunning edifice.

As she approached, Lola noted another name at the bottom of the stone, under the sculpture—Emina Aba-Melech de Caravel, Ernesto's wife. Emina had died in 1877, at the age of twenty-seven. Her husband had followed her into death two years later. But he had been seventy-three years old.

How had the photograph of this lady ended up in Miss Fletcher's sewing basket? To whom had the lady written those sweet words: *Forever yours* . . . But above all, why was the resemblance between Emina and Anna so striking?

Before leaving, although soaked through to the bone, Lola made a detour to the corner where the paupers were buried. There was no trace of her friend Clara Campo here, for she had been buried in an unmarked grave.

Lola placed the bouquet of violets at her feet and left the cemetery to join the carriage that was still waiting for her.

I was already home when she arrived back at Les Pavots. My visit with Anna had broken my heart. I had had to deliver the soaps to the perfumer after my return from seeing the girl despite being in no mood for such an errand, but we now had a pretty sum of cash saved away.

Sherry was washing himself quietly on the rug in my bedchamber. From time to time, he would look at me with insistence and blink to let me know that he shared what I was feeling. He must have been worried by Anna's absence too.

When I'd arrived home, I'd been overcome by the desire to put pen to paper and write of the ordeal we were going through. I tried to put in order the sequence of events as we'd perceived them, starting with the nightmare I'd had, which forced me to see the murder as if I'd in fact been there.

So I noted all the events that had taken place since Anna had been attacked. It seemed to me that it had all started at that precise moment.

But as the words started to flow, I was struck with different ideas. I believed that it had really all started the day we visited Cousin, taking Anna as bait.

But if I really wanted to be logical about matters, it had all started the day Lady Sarah asked Lola to steal that file.

Did this mean Lola was right? Was Lady Sarah at the heart of this case?

Or maybe it all started when we saw the altercation at the train station?

The real reason behind this copious note taking was my inability to save Anna. It kept me from dwelling on her situation, for the very thought of it haunted me.

I had to try to remain optimistic and believe that Anna would soon be out of police hands and that I would be using my writing to entertain friends and even make a second novel out of it.

I heard a cab stop in front of the house. I peeked out of my window and saw Lola running to the front door. The rain was falling harder by the second. She would be drenched through.

She must have asked Rosalie for some hot water, for there was a great deal of to-ing and fro-ing between her bedchamber and the living room.

At around seven o'clock, I heard Lola shouting down to Rosalie, "No need to set the table up here! I'll eat in the kitchen with you."

With Sherry in my arms, I went downstairs to see what was going on. A smell of court bouillon filled the house.

Dinner in the kitchen was upsetting, to say the least. Rosalie wept as she served us. Lola did so, too, from time to time. Sherry was the only one enjoying himself as he snaffled up some pieces of fish that had been placed on the floor for him in a saucer. I conducted the conversation as best I could. I told them of my meeting with Anna. She had hardly spoken but had eaten every morsel of the pissaladière. She had, however, remembered to tell me to thank Rosalie. As I mentioned this to Rosalie, more tears came. I also told them about the money we'd made with the soaps, but it brought them little relief.

I couldn't think of what else to say. I ventured a few words on Vidal, for I remembered I hadn't discussed this subject with Lola the day before. I recounted what Lecerf had told me.

Lola suddenly became engaged in the conversation. She seemed very interested in Lecerf's version of the events.

"Maybe Lecerf is right. Vidal has more reason to seek revenge on the banker than he does, after all. Yet they were good chums, were they not? Didn't Cousin put up the money for that home of his? I haven't done enough digging. I should have gone to the commercial court to find out exactly how that place was built and who paid for it."

Rosalie, who was not listening to us, diverted the subject as she put forward her own thoughts. "I cannot help thinking that the lady in that picture is our Anna's sister or mother," she said.

"It can't be her mother," I replied. "Jeanne Martin was the name of her mother. It's on her papers from the orphanage. Jeanne died in a fire at Camplong."

"I found out a little more about our portrait lady," explained Lola. "She's dead. The resemblance is disturbing, I'll grant you, but we'll never be able to ask her. Nor her husband." She went on to tell us everything she had discovered about the de Caravel family.

"Above all," I said, "how on earth did the portrait end up in my embroidery basket?"

"We need to rest," said Lola. "A good night's sleep will help us think. Tomorrow will be the day we prove Anna's innocence. I maintain this is the revenge of a ruined man. We'll go to the island and corner Vidal. If we can't get anywhere with him, I'll go see Lady Sarah."

"You still suspect her?" I asked.

"I suspect everyone but Anna," said Lola.

"Perhaps Maupassant will agree to take you to the island tomorrow on the *Bel-Ami*?" suggested Rosalie.

"Good idea. I'll send a message to him first thing in the morning."

27

At Sea

As Lola later recounted, when she awoke at three in the morning, the rain had stopped. She couldn't get back to sleep. Something was pushing her, motivating her, to rise and ready herself for action. She knew that waiting for dawn to come would be too much for her.

She got up discreetly, put on her plain brown dress she wore when she traveled to the old town, and forwent her corset so she would feel more free in her movements. She put an old navy-blue woolen coat over her dress and gently descended the stairs so as not to be heard.

I was still sound asleep and so was Rosalie. Sherry would have been the only one to see her leave. She walked in a hurry, meeting with the odd cart loaded with wares heading to the market as well as a few half-asleep fishermen making for the docks.

There were also several revelers, some wobbling, who were on their way home after a night of heavy drinking. It was that time of day when people who wake up too early meet those who stay up too late.

The cafés and cabaret bars kept their lights on low, indicating they were still open for business. She saw some men she knew coming out of a bar near the docks, opposite the Grand Café on the Allées. They waved at her enthusiastically.

On Rue de la Vapeur, three working girls out on the sidewalk nodded hello lazily. She smiled with indifference.

But overall the city was calm. The nighttime patrol officer who was driving around the streets on a loop looked at her suspiciously and stopped his vehicle. She made an effort to look like she was on her best behavior. This was no time to get rounded up for working.

She had made the right decision to slip on her trusty brown dress with its old maid's décolletage. She knew she looked like an honest woman, but the question would be, What was she doing out at that time? She prepared a lie so that there would be no hesitating should she be interrogated by the policeman. But he let her pass with a kind smile. He hadn't recognized Lola Deslys.

She went straight to the Pantiero, where Mario and his boss, Pierre Gaglio, were about to head out trawling. She explained to them that she wanted to go see Dr. Vidal at his Grand Jardin sanatorium. She asked if they might drop her off on Île Sainte-Marguerite. Gaglio had known Lola for a long time. He agreed without asking further questions. She explained, however, that it had something to do with Anna. He knew the situation and pitied the girl. For him, either she was innocent or, if she had killed the banker, she'd had her reasons and done what needed to be done. He wasn't one for nuances.

Fishermen often ferried visitors over to the islands but would ask for a fare. They weren't usually in the habit of taking people on board this early, however. Gaglio refused to accept any payment from Lola. Mario was frightfully agitated. He would have liked to go with her, but he couldn't leave his work.

She waited until they were ready, climbed into the big boat, and found a makeshift seat for herself near the front. She settled between the traps and nets, trying to not bother them.

After untying the mooring line, they unblocked the oars and slid the boat out to the end of the pier. Gaglio positioned himself in the skipper's place at the helm, and Mario stood by his side, making sure he was facing the wind as he hoisted the sail.

They felt the difference in temperature as soon as they passed the small lighthouse. The tide was coming in, and the sea felt rough. An unexpected wind was starting to blow rather strongly, coming in from the east.

Vidal's sanatorium was located on the far side of the island, due south. It stood facing its sister island, dominating the natural passage between the two. Lola knew there was a private jetty attached to the home, but Gaglio refused to take her there because he said he had to head for the Gulf of Juan.

"I don't want to be too long!" cried Gaglio. He kept scanning the sky and the surface of the water. He seemed worried. "Are we coming back for you?" he asked.

"No. I don't know how long I'm going to stay. I'll go home on the steamer."

"Good idea. Can you see that squall? We're not going to hang around here for long. I don't even know if we can fish in this."

As they neared one of the mooring ramps on the west shore of the island, Lola jumped down without making a fuss, while her brother held the boat steady for her. It was good fortune that she hadn't gotten terribly wet during the crossing. The waves hadn't been very high, though the foam had still sprayed her.

She watched them sail away, focused on their task. Mario turned to wave at her. She saw the concern and frustration in his eyes.

28

An Old Acquaintance

Lola walked inland. To her left, she spied a few boats in front of a fort. She hadn't known there was a military presence on Île Sainte-Marguerite. She left the coastal path bordered by a few fishermen's cottages and went down the recently traced track that crossed the island. It had been planted with eucalyptus trees imported from Australia, but they were still young.

It was as if every living thing were asleep—every plant, every bird, every insect. Only the umbrella pines were watching her, leaning in, their leaves hissing at her in the bare light. She hadn't thought of taking a lantern, but fortunately, dawn was now beginning to break. There was nothing welcoming about this place. She shivered, still damp, and realized just then that the wind was strengthening by the minute.

She walked a little farther, and the southern coastline came into view.

The sight of the gray water surprised her. During the twenty minutes she had been walking, the surface had changed dramatically. The sound of waves crashing on the rocks was stupendous.

On her left, the first glimmers of sunrise became apparent. She didn't know the exact location of the Grand Jardin asylum but sensed it couldn't be far. Closing her coat more tightly around her and struggling against the gusts, she had to change directions and turn back several times through the trees before finally happening upon the high walls surrounding the property.

She hesitated. Should she ring the big bell, waking those inside, and ask to be received right away? Or was it better for her to wait for a more decent hour? If she chose the second option, she would have to find a hollow in a tree or in the wall to protect herself from the increasingly strong winds.

She was getting colder and colder, and the sun would be up soon enough, wouldn't it? Finally, no longer able to stop herself, she grabbed the rope on the big bell and pulled it with force.

She could hear heavy footsteps arriving. The solid wooden gates shook, and a man's voice grumbled, "Very well! Very well! There's no rush!"

A key turned in the lock, and a watchman appeared from the other side. He looked at her with suspicion. He was an old fellow with his nightcap still on and a dirty shirt sticking out of his trousers. He held an oil lamp, whose flame was protected by glass.

"What do you want?" he bellowed.

"What do I want? I have to see the doctor! Hurry! This is urgent. And it's a private matter. What's your name, by the way?"

"Aristide."

"Good. I'm Lola. The introductions have been made. Let's go!"

Her accent must have reassured him, although he looked right and then left before letting her in.

There was a small building on the side that served as his lodge. Then, to the right of a large, partly paved courtyard with grass and various plants, a superb Gothic structure loomed over them like a huge keep framed by four fine square towers. There was something mysterious but almost malevolent about the place.

Adjacent to it, at the end of the courtyard, was a large bastide with a sober facade, pierced by a few windows. It made the place look less oppressive. A vast cultivated area extended around the buildings, justifying the name of the property, Grand Jardin.

Aristide closed the huge gates behind them. The sound of the heavy lock being secured echoed in Lola's head. It felt as though she'd never see freedom again.

Aristide led her to the main building and opened the front door. As soon as they entered, the smell of coffee and something more caustic that Lola couldn't quite put her finger on struck her nostrils.

A vast corridor opened out onto a number of doors. At the end of the hall, a huge wooden crucifix was fixed to the wall between two large windows. The rising sunlight from outside illuminated the crucifix and reflected on the floor of waxed terracotta tiles.

He took her to an expansive living room, where several sofas were arranged. They hadn't seen anyone in the hallway, but she'd heard the clattering of dishes, as if there was a kitchen nearby. Or a dining room where residents ate breakfast?

As he invited her to take a seat, his previously rather mournful features seemed to come to life.

"Are the staff already at work?" asked Lola, smiling. "Or did they fall out of bed?"

"It's the staff's morning meal," said the man. "They get up early to put the bread in the oven, empty the chamber pots, and light the fires. They eat before they start their day."

He hesitated, scratching his badly shaved cheek before turning away.

"Well, I'll leave you to it. The doctor will be with you in time." Before exiting, he asked, "You'll want coffee?"

Lola was touched by the attention. "How very kind. Thank you. I'd enjoy that."

As he walked down the hallway, she heard him talking to some servants. He returned holding a tray on which there was a bowl of coffee with milk and a buttered slice of bread.

"You are very welcoming," said Lola.

She was amazed to see him blush. He looked down like a shy young boy as he said, "Well, I know you, that's why. Of course, you wouldn't remember it, but I first met you when I worked at the perfumery. You were knee high to a grasshopper. You've certainly prospered since then. I'm happy for you, Lola. That's your name now, isn't it? It used to be Filomena! When I go to the mainland, I sometimes watch you on the Croisette."

Lola put her finger to her lips and winked at him. "Hush now! Don't go telling the doctor. He doesn't know who I am." She was flattered to have been recognized. Then she remembered. "Why, yes, Aristide! Of course! You didn't stay long at the perfumery."

"When the boss wanted to get rid of me, you were the only one who defended me. My wife was sick, so I had to stay home with her. And I was fired for it!"

"Those people have no heart, have they?"

"And you, even as a child, you weren't afraid of much. You talked to the boss about taking me back on."

"It didn't do much good, though."

"Maybe not, but it's the gesture that counts. I've always hoped life turned out well for you. If you need me, you come and ask for Aristide. I'll always be here for you."

Lola was touched and whispered in a weak voice, "Thank you, Aristide."

"I don't know when the doctor will come, but you can wait for him here. Someone will be in to light the fire. Adieu, Mademoiselle Lola."

"Adieu, Aristide!"

He walked away slowly, looking back at her one last time and putting his finger up to his lips just as she had. He wouldn't say a word.

The door slammed shut.

Although Lola was still shivering in the cold room, she removed her damp coat. And thanks to the hot coffee and Aristide's kindness, she felt slightly warmer than when she'd entered.

For now, apart from her intuition giving off warning signals about the place, everything was going well. She smiled to give herself courage.

She felt as though she were about to fall asleep in front of her empty bowl of coffee when Dr. Vidal arrived. He stormed in moodily, startling Lola. He was already dressed as though he had pulled out all the stops, which, for this hour, impressed Lola. She could see he was the type of fellow who was probably always well attired and that such apparel was not reserved only for outings to the city.

His voice was tense, yet his words were kind. "Madame! To what do I owe the honor of this morning's visit? Has your friend Monsieur de Maupassant made his decision regarding his brother? Is he with you?"

Believing he must have mistaken the reason for her visit—as Lola made no answer—he simply smiled at her politely. The concern she detected in his voice came from worries other than her presence. She was sure of it. *I'm not surprised by his torment,* she thought. *When you've killed someone, you must feel something. It's called guilt.*

He bowed down and kissed her hand delicately before walking her to his private office.

29

LOST SOULS

They walked through the dining room, and she observed the servants setting several long, waxed tables for breakfast.

Once seated in the doctor's office, Lola explained that Maupassant hadn't been able to come, as he'd urgently needed to correct a manuscript, but that he had sent her in his stead. She was trying to establish a less distant relationship with Vidal, and he certainly appeared more at ease now that she had spoken. Her aim was to lull him into a false sense of security and have him talk about Cousin.

"I must give him as accurate a report as possible," she declared. "Fortunately, I have a good memory. But I'll need to see everything."

He tittered nervously, and she wasn't convinced he had fully warmed to her. His mind, she believed, was elsewhere. His answers were almost automatic. *This man is as dull as dishwater!* she thought.

She looked around the room. On the wall, she noticed an oil painting of a family. It was Vidal with his wife and child. The doctor was standing in front of a mansion surrounded by cypress trees. Next to him, a lady in crinoline was sitting in a large wicker chair, her wide skirt spread out around her. On the grass in front of them, a little girl smiled. She had a hoop in one hand and a luxurious doll in the other. Everything in the painting spoke of the joy of life. Even the little dog, resting on his mistress's lap, looked delighted, with his periwinkle-blue bow around his little neck. It was complete harmony and domestic happiness. This was in stark contrast to the office itself, which was dark, confined, and sad. In fact, it was as gloomy and tired as the rest of the property.

"I'll start by giving you the rules and explaining what my method is," Vidal stated.

"I understand you don't practice isolation and that you don't use straitjackets or restraints?"

"We do, but only on very rare occasions, indeed. My electromagnetic invention helps much more. It is an essential step in the treatment of any person entrusted to me, if he or she wishes to recover, of course."

"And how many of your patients make a full recovery?"

He stared at her without answering. She shook herself in the hope that it might free her from his hypnotic gaze.

"What is your method . . . uh . . . the electric thing you mentioned? I must admit I have difficulty imagining how electricity can have any sort of positive effect on human beings, but then, I don't have your scientific knowledge."

"I apologize for my use of jargon, but my work with Duchêne has allowed me to determine that hysterical conversion, among other things—"

"Sorry? Hysterical conversion . . . I'm not familiar with that term."

Irritated, Vidal explained, "When a patient is afflicted with contradictory feelings that are too powerful to cope with, it's like a circuit gone wrong, you see? What I do is use an electrical process to achieve the opposite, to correct the electrical short circuit. It's a very cathartic method. We send an electromagnetic pulse into the body to restore a good mental state. It fires things up again, so to speak."

"That's fabulous! What a visionary invention. Your work here must have received a great many awards."

He flashed her a bitter smile. "I'm afraid I might be too ahead of my time for that. Or perhaps it's the fact that I reside in France. No one is a prophet in his own country."

"I am sure that Hervé could be cured through this ingenious method. But do you think that if the problems were brought about by a sunstroke that this type of treatment is recommended?"

"I have had good results with cases of mania, melancholy, hysteria, feelings of persecution, dementia, and even progressive general paralysis, which is usually considered irreversibly progressive. Do you want to know the rules of our establishment?"

"No," replied Lola, as all this was beginning to bore her deeply. "I'm sure it's all in order."

"We currently have nine ladies and seven gentlemen who reside here long term and many others for more temporary periods."

"Do you have a specific room where you perform these electrical experiments?"

"Yes, I have a laboratory where I've installed my machines. It's near the hydrotherapy rooms, sulfur baths, and so on, in what we call *the tower*."

"How successful are your treatments?"

"The surest way to a cure is still the human touch, madame. Nothing beats attention and kindness to these poor, temporarily lost souls."

A forced smile appeared on his drawn features. It was clearly taking a lot of effort to have a polite, normal conversation. The man was truly exhausted.

"You are a pioneer, Dr. Vidal. Your approach is admirable."

"There's little merit in it," he said wearily. "I went to a good school with Dr. Blanche and . . ."

He seemed to give up explaining, no doubt realizing Lola would not understand what he had to say.

"Uh . . . if you agree, I could give you the tour?" he said gently.

He stood, strode to the door, and waited for her to join him. She followed him down the hallways, wondering when she would be able to change the conversation to Cousin.

From the large windows along the gallery, she looked out at the trees and noticed that the wind had further strengthened.

"I think a violent storm is on its way," said the doctor with the same voice he might use had he said, *The soup is a little cold today.*

This can't be good, thought Lola. *How will I get back if the steamer can't dock?*

All the rooms she was shown were clean and airy. She watched as efficient staff, although slow in their actions, busied themselves in silence. It did feel odd. Not a word was spoken between them. Nowhere did she see groups of nurses discussing their family concerns or young servants in huddles, gossiping of an upcoming ball or their secret lovers. They were model employees.

"I see that you can count on your staff. They seem so very hardworking. It's just perfect."

"Yes, I'm quite proud of them. This is due to the way they are selected. I don't settle for mere references, for they can be easily falsified."

What an odd thing to say, thought Lola.

"I ask them about their family history, and I insist they comply with my methods. I only keep those who answer my questions coherently and who are prepared to accept my demands."

"What are your demands, if I may be so bold?"

A sudden gust of wind broke into the room, causing the curtains to float up in the air. Lola jumped. A window had blown open. As a servant rushed to close it, a piece of paper from who knows where flew across the floor.

As if he hadn't noticed a thing, Vidal continued. "Here, madame, we believe in my methods to such an extent that we all undergo electrical treatment once a week. I see it as a kind of cleaning up of the pollution within our cervical cells."

"Ah! Now I better understand why your employees are so very well behaved," said Lola.

The truth was, of course, that she better understood why they all looked like specters.

"In fact, everyone here seems very contented," she continued.

"Don't they just?"

Vidal suddenly looked very contented too. He regarded her with a kind of tenderness and appeared grateful for her words.

But they were quite the opposite of what Lola was thinking. She had never seen a place that radiated more sadness. The silence was unnerving and the gestures of everyone too precise. However, there was a certain despair behind every movement, behind every glance exchanged. It was as if the very souls of those present had died.

As they left the women's ward, where he had taken her to visit a patient who was painting with watercolors in front of a bare wall, they passed a heavy tapestry curtain. Lola wondered what it might be hiding. Her question was answered as she heard a rustle and turned around. A nurse was coming from behind the hung fabric with several wet bath towels on her arm. Lola glimpsed a padded door behind the curtain. The nurse tried to shut it quickly.

"Is there a door there?" she asked. "What is it? Have we already visited that room?"

For the few seconds the door was ajar, she had heard some unusual noises. Muffled moans.

But Vidal didn't answer. When she realized they were on their way back to his office, she insisted. "We didn't visit your machine room. I must say again that if Hervé de Maupassant comes to you, it is important that I see exactly what the treatment consists of."

Vidal suddenly seemed to emerge from his state of apathy.

"Your visit was quite unexpected," he said curtly. "The room is not presentable at the moment. Come back with Monsieur de Maupassant, and we will visit it together. But let me know first."

"On the contrary! The whole point of a visit such as this is that it be impromptu, don't you think?"

The first drops of heavy and violent rain hit the windows.

"I accept your reasoning, but you, too, must accept that I have to respect my patients. They are not spectacles, and all treatments are received in private. This isn't the Salpêtrière, you know."

Desperate to transition into the conversation she had come here to have, Lola threw herself in headlong. "A question comes to mind, if I may? I met the late Henri Cousin some time ago . . ." Despite the doctor's suddenly sullen face, she continued. "May his soul rest in peace. What a terrible business . . . What was I saying? Oh yes! I met him shortly before his death, and we talked of you and your work, of course. He told me he had never witnessed any of your experiments. Is that true?"

The doctor paled. Lola seemed to have touched a raw nerve.

"What are you implying? That my invention might be pure fiction? Madame, please believe that I would not have such incredible results, far beyond the average of other establishments of this kind, without this invention. And Henri came here often. He knew my facilities very well, indeed. He knew his money had not been invested at a loss. I told him about the imminent release of . . . of . . . But why am I telling you all this?"

They were now back in his office, and Vidal appeared more composed.

"When was the last time you saw Henri Cousin?" asked Lola.

The doctor appeared close to losing his temper. His gaze wandered around the office as if looking for an exit. *He's panicking,* Lola thought with satisfaction. *That's one point for me. Why was he so surprised by my question?*

Vidal stammered, "Uh . . . let me think . . . I don't remember . . . That's the day he came here to visit . . ."

"What was he doing here so often, anyway? Whom was he coming to visit? What is this release you mentioned? Do you keep a register?"

"I'm astounded by your questions. I don't see the connection between your visit and your . . . requests."

A lightning bolt illuminated the sky, and a few seconds later, thunder broke out so loudly that the windows trembled.

"And I'm astounded that I can't get any answers from you," Lola continued.

He had regained his stiffness and his indignant tone. "In our business of dealing with family secrets, one of our most reliable guarantees is the confidentiality we grant each of our patients. Not only are we deeply concerned about the sensitivities of the human brain, but we know how to keep silent on certain matters. Even our registers don't show every detail of the conditions of certain patients, for some are considered too sensitive to be displayed in a logbook intended for public use."

"But you need clarity when it comes to keeping records—inputs, outputs, diagnoses, and the like. Surely, it's the law!" said Lola.

"Of course, but when we want to be discreet, there are a thousand ways of going about it." He sat behind his Empire desk and pointed to an armchair for Lola.

"I see," she said as she sat down.

"You don't see anything at all. I am telling you this so you know that your friend's brother will be treated in the strictest confidence and that journalists will not be able to sniff anything out."

Was that a threat?

Suddenly, in the hushed world of Vidal's sanatorium, a violent crash rang out, without the storm as the cause. Lola heard screaming.

The doctor stood and ran to the door. "Albert!" he shouted. "What's going on?"

Lola heard rushed footsteps, furtive exchanges, and a struggle of some kind. The doctor had disappeared into the hallway, rushing to help his nurses. Lola didn't waste any time. She stood and peeked out to witness what was going on. For an asylum, she'd imagined there'd be a certain amount of screaming and fighting. The calm of earlier had worried her much more than this turn of events.

She left them to it and rushed behind the doctor's desk. This might be her chance. She began to feverishly search the documents on his desk, opening the notebooks and journals, turning over every piece of paper. She didn't know exactly what she was looking for. Perhaps something with the name of Henri Cousin on it . . . or recent patient admissions? She then opened the drawers, rummaging to no use, for she found nothing of interest. She had little time, and the sound of the storm prevented her from listening for the doctor's return.

Finally, she came across an annual accounting book. She didn't understand anything of the rows and columns of numbers, but a pinned note caught her attention. It had been signed by Henri Cousin, and it summarized the banker's contributions over the previous year. He specified his commitment, that for a quarter of the income raised from patients, he himself would finance the remaining three quarters.

He was surprised that the funds had not yet been reimbursed and that the patients were not meeting financial expectations.

This man was holding the house to ransom, Lola thought. *There aren't enough patients, perhaps, but we're not exactly in a capital city here! We have nowhere near the numbers that similar homes in Paris might attract, despite the winter season and its share of wealthy migrants.*

Although not particularly gifted with numbers, she nevertheless noticed that the money coming in from Cousin was divided into three parts: donations, investments, and bills paid for a resident. He was paying for the treatment of a permanent patient. That must have been what the doctor almost let slip. Cousin had placed a family member here. The patient's name appeared only as initials: FdB.

Now that Cousin was dead, who would finance this place?

30

Chloroform

Lola could hear the doctor's voice out in the corridor, and with her heart pounding, she barely had time to move from behind the desk. Instead of sitting down, knowing it would be too difficult to compose herself, she rushed out of the room and looked around worriedly, twisting her hands together.

Just in time! The doctor was there.

"Do you need some help?" she asked. "What's going on? I have nursing experience. I used to help Dr. Buttura."

Vidal was in an even darker mood than before. He guided Lola back into the office. "Madame, I think I'll have Albert take you to the pier. The steamer should be here soon, if it can dock. The sea is rough out there. If the crossing to Cannes isn't running, you will find some fishermen who live at the foot of the fort. They will be happy to take you in. Or someone in the fort itself may assist you. You'll excuse me, but I think you have all the information you need to report back to your friend. Unfortunately, duty calls me. My apologies."

"Of course. I don't want to waste your time. May I ask you one last question?"

"Please," said Vidal, a pinch of annoyance showing on his mouth.

"Do you have patients enough to get by without Cousin's contribution?"

"What exactly is your meaning?"

"Well, now that the man funding you is no longer with us, how will you do it? I'm sure this place is flourishing, but Cannes isn't Paris, is it? Did Cousin mention you in his will? Has he made a donation to your establishment to assist with its sustainability?"

The doctor sat down heavily in his chair. "No, but . . . uh . . . his heir . . . I'm in touch with him. He will continue the work of his uncle."

But he was hesitant. He didn't seem sure.

"Do you have a signed contract? You understand we cannot place Hervé in a home that may well close in the coming weeks. What exactly was your arrangement with Cousin? Why did he finance you, by the way?"

Vidal put his head in his hands. "Madame, I say I've come a long way. The truth is, I've not come far at all. I didn't come back. I'm still there, in that faraway place, that limbo. I stayed there with them."

"Whom are you talking about?"

"Do you think I wear this mourning outfit for show? Your questions are forcing me to return to that deep sorrow. I lost everything, madame. When I say everything, I'm not just talking about my fortune or my position. Those are trivial. I lost my beloved wife and daughter."

Lola emanated compassion, but in fact, she was thinking, *Maybe this turned you into a killer. I don't care, maybe you did the right thing. But Anna won't pay for your crime!*

"How did this tragedy happen?"

"If you are from Cannes, you must have heard about all the so-called real estate possibilities in and around Boulevard de la Foncière?"

"Of course."

"Well, I was involved in that. I can't complain, for I was largely responsible. But on the advice of a friend . . ."

"Cousin?"

"Yes, Cousin. My wife, Constance, was a childhood friend of his family. When we came to Cannes, she would visit Cousin, and they reminisced about their childhood. He advised me to invest everything in Boulevard de la Foncière. I even had some houses built. This swallowed up a good part of Constance's dowry. After my ruin, Constance couldn't tolerate our downfall. She experienced a profound melancholy. It was at that time that Cousin, knowing my background with Dr. Blanche, suggested I open this asylum."

"And treat your wife here?"

"Yes. It would mean I could experiment with my inventions too."

"Did you manage to cure your wife?"

"Alas, no. She died on a day very much like this one. It was quite stormy, but she insisted on going out. She was accompanied by two nurses, but they were unable to do anything. She fell off the top of the cliff on the north side of the island." His voice broke. "My daughter, my Clotilde, was with her. They both slipped and fell."

"How terrible!" said Lola.

But she knew the rumor was that they'd committed suicide together. So it seemed that the doctor's invention was not so effective, after all.

"Cousin must have been very disappointed that his investment hadn't been able to save your wife. It must have been bad publicity for the place. I imagine he expected a substantial financial return. A banker doesn't assist a person without expecting something back, does he?"

"The truth is his nephew needed my professional help. His sister's son—" He stopped abruptly, as if he'd said too much.

"Cousin's nephew was ill? So he's the heir you spoke of," whispered Lola. "And is he here? Are you keeping him locked up? Is that what you mean?"

"Whatever would give you such an idea?"

"Is he or isn't he here, monsieur?"

"Yes, he is. But as we speak, he is preparing his effects. He is to leave immediately. He's cured, you see."

"Since when? Did Cousin know this?"

"Of course! That's why he came to the island the other day. He wanted to see for himself."

"But why was his nephew's health compromised to such an extent as to need to stay here?"

"The poor boy had a difficult childhood. His mother died in childbirth. His father, the baron, died in a duel in the Bois de Boulogne. Cousin raised the child alone. As he himself had no family, he gave it his all. An English nanny, the best boarding schools, a prestigious military academy. As an adult, the young man inherited from his father. But what with the risky businesses, the women, and then the casinos—his income just wasn't enough. He started selling property. His farms, in the main. He used the money for racehorses, expensive trips, courtesans. He sold everything, building after building."

"And how were you able to help this young man?"

"After lending his nephew large sums of money, which were never paid back, Cousin decided to impose restrictions on him in exchange for a regular income. He made him train as a banker. He provided employment and a mansion in the countryside. The nephew refused to accept the arrangement. I'd told Cousin about my invention when we'd dined together. To my detriment, he asked me to examine the young man. I diagnosed both melancholia and monomania. We had to isolate him as soon as possible. That's the real reason Cousin financed this institution."

"I understand. He wanted his nephew incarcerated here so that he could reshape him. It was to suit his own needs, really."

"That's not the way I see it," the doctor snapped.

"You're saying the banker saw his nephew the other day? And that this man is really cured? That's rather incredible. How was that meeting between the two of them?"

Vidal frowned. "I don't understand why you're asking all these questions. Please understand that I cannot provide you with any further information about my patients. I've already said far too much."

"Doctor. I find your experiments quite exciting. A genuine case of someone being completely healed of a mental ailment is so rare! You can only convince me of the merits of placing a patient with you. Now, did you attend this interview?"

"Yes. I was there. Everything went well, but . . ."

"But?"

"But Cousin returned the following day. He had something important to tell us. He seemed absent. Excited. Euphoric, even. If I hadn't known him, I would have said he was . . ."

"In love?"

"Yes. That's exactly right. In love."

For heaven's sake, thought Lola. *He was crazy about Anna! Or maybe . . .*

"Did he say with whom he was in love?"

"No. He wasn't actually in love. The truth was quite different. A change of destiny, I believe. It sometimes happens in our society, where secrets explode like bombs. He was making a new will, you see. There was a new heir. It so happens that in his youth he had experienced a great and frustrated passion."

Lola recalled the portrait of the lady who looked so much like Anna. That's how Anna had obtained it! It was Cousin who'd given it to her. Might Emina have been this great love of his? Had it been a secret? Why had he given the photograph to Anna?

"Did he have a daughter?" she asked, her voice now changed.

He looked at her with astonishment. "Yes . . . Indeed. He mentioned a young girl he'd found. The fruit of his first love. He believed she'd been lost forever. The woman to whom he had given his heart was married. And then she fell with child. What was he to do about it? It would have been a disgrace to everyone involved. He never wanted to see the child. She was given away to two peasants who had a farm."

Lola continued. "I see. Cousin's great love had this baby. Their baby. And he made it disappear, as people so often do. She was a child of shame handed over with a bundle of money to a couple who called themselves her parents and raised her as their own. But then, her real mother died soon after. He'd deliberately erased this child from his life, but when he saw her again, the spitting image of his lost love . . ."

"Exactly. Those were his own words."

"And what did Cousin offer his nephew in exchange for disinheriting him?"

"He told him he would not be completely forgotten in his legacy. However, his wish was that this man would not squander his fortune, so he gave him some land with an income—just enough to live nicely out in the Allier region. He also stipulated that the land could not be sold or rented out. He didn't want to enable his nephew to get out of the deal and head off to Paris, you see? If he wanted more, it was up to him to earn an honest living."

Isn't that a gift and a half? Lola thought with amusement.

"But then, what about the agreements Cousin had with you? This new happiness, a second life . . . it changes everything, does it not? Would he continue to fund your institution? You've cured his nephew, after all."

"I asked him as much. I asked about the home, about our agreement, but Cousin was clear. Nothing would change his mind on the matter. He wished to continue his support. He dismissed any concerns I had."

His voice was not assured. *He's lying,* Lola thought.

"If I follow, when Cousin left the other night, he talked only of his new happiness and his new arrangements. But the nephew must have been upset. And you yourself were no less so, I imagine. Am I wrong? After all, there was nothing to guarantee your future. And unlike the nephew, you are free to do as you please. You're not locked up in here, are you? The next day, you took the steamer to go and see him to clarify a few points. You went to his villa on Avenue du Petit Juas. Am I right? The discussion didn't go quite according to plan. You killed him. Before leaving early the next morning, you took the murder weapon in the middle of the night to the young girl's abode, her identity and address you'd obtained from the banker. Yes, that fits."

"What is this wickedness?" Vidal asked.

Yet there was no real conviction in his words. It was as if he were bending under the weight of such an accusation. Throughout Lola's monologue, he had been pacing around the room. He would go to the door, look down the hallway, come back, and walk over to the window. He observed what was happening outside, but he simply nodded as she spoke.

Ah! No need to utter another word. I can read the truth in his gestures, reflected Lola. *I'm going back to Cannes as soon as possible, and the next people who step on this godforsaken island will be the police!*

Vidal returned to his desk, took a seat, and massaged his temples. He could no longer take this interrogation.

Lola was certain of her victory.

"You have nothing to regret, monsieur. It was only a matter of time. Rumors abound about your establishment. I've already heard talk of embezzlement and the like. Everyone knows that people are locked up here against their will, that you make deals with families and help them to turn inheritances in their favor."

He looked up with a sudden triumphant expression.

Lola thought he was perhaps demonstrating how proud he was to have succeeded so many times in his misdeeds. But then she realized she was the reason behind his glee.

"By a strange coincidence, madame, Cousin also told me about you. He'd had an investigation conducted into the entourage of his daughter, Anahita. To his great despair, he discovered she had been raised by a slut—or do you prefer the term *demoiselle?* And you were being helped by some ridiculous Englishwoman who has been rejected by all good society. What did you hope for her? That she would become some sought-after courtesan? Were you looking for a way to recoup your investment? What tipped him off was that you introduced yourself to him under an assumed name. We know who you really are."

His eyes shifted toward the door for a fraction of a second. Lola turned to follow his gaze, but she didn't have time to grasp what was happening.

For a nurse was holding a chloroform-soaked cloth in front of her face.

31

UNMASKED

Maupassant arrived at Les Pavots midmorning while I was finishing up the accounts with Rosalie.

He was accompanied by his friend, the journalist Joseph Murier, who wanted to meet with Lola to speak of what he'd found.

I offered them tea up in the living room, for torrential rain prevented us from enjoying it under the pergola in the garden. I was hoping that the storm, or at least the sound of our conversation, might wake my mistress.

I told them about my meeting with Lecerf and what I had learned about Brigadier Rodot at the Rat Noir.

"This is such a hot topic! I've been trying to find out more about it for the past few months," cried Murier. "I would very much like to write an article on the subject, in the spirit of Pouget, or even Guyot! Men feel they have a right over women, and they are able to play out all their fantasies with these girls. It's not what I would call being a man."

I could see that Maupassant was distracted.

"How is your brother?" I asked him.

He seemed to come to life as he responded. "I've been having some long conversations with him, and they're far from easy. He has fits of fury and very inconsistent reasoning. As for me, I alternate between painful seizures, migraines, and ocular paralyses, with rare moments of calm. And I can't even begin to tell you of Mother's health. I feel like I'm drowning in bitterness when I see how she has almost bled herself dry for that good-for-nothing . . . while I . . . Oh, it is of little importance. I finally received a letter from Dr. Blanche with some rather excellent advice. He recommends three places for Hervé. There is a good sanatorium in Toulouse that is private but quite expensive. There is also an asylum in Montpellier, but he failed to provide me with further details. I must come to a decision, however."

"What about the third option?"

"Ville-Évrard near Chelles. But I think it's too far away. Perhaps I should just take him to Paris."

"It is a heavy responsibility, indeed," said Murier.

"Yes, but I can escape it no longer. I lie to my mother and my sister-in-law about his condition. Only my father knows, but he says he's too old to manage it. I am very concerned that his illness is hereditary. It worries me a great deal." As he looked upon our dismayed expressions, he shook his head and laughed with false hilarity. "Don't worry, the world won't end tomorrow! Of that, I'm sure. And I feel strong and capable, whatever some journalists might think. And here at Les Pavots? How are you all? It seems Lola went snooping around in the newspaper archives. I hear she left a message for Joseph. Isn't that right, old man?"

"Yes. She wanted information on the de Caravel family. Or rather on a certain Aba-Melech de Caravel. I looked into it. It's all rather exciting! I found a strange correlation between Cousin and this de Caravel family. Buttura helped me, too, I might add. Our doctor friend knows a great many of the secrets in this good city. Is Lola here? I'd like to tell her everything. Did you all go to bed late last night?"

"On the contrary," I said. "We put out the fires early. The three of us were too upset, you see. Lola was crying. She'd just returned from the cemetery. I admit I added rather a lot of sherry to my passion-flower tea, which made me fall asleep with ease. I don't know whether or not

Lola had a visitor later on. Perhaps that young Ferdinand fellow came to see her in the night—although I know she wasn't expecting him."

Murier jumped when he heard the name. "Ferdinand?" he asked, looking worried.

"He came the other day," I said, turning to Maupassant. "He fought a duel for her. Well, almost, because the duel didn't actually take place, in the end."

"A duel," Murier echoed gloomily.

"I'm surprised she hasn't yet joined us. I'll go see if she's awake," I declared.

But I didn't have time to exit the room when I saw Rosalie scurrying down the hallway. She babbled in a panicked voice.

"I took her coffee to her earlier, but she wasn't there. I assumed she was somewhere in the house, but . . ."

"But?"

"She's gone! She never leaves without telling me! She must have gone before I woke, and I was up at the break of dawn."

"Again?" exclaimed Maupassant.

"What do you mean 'again'?" asked Murier.

"All the young ladies like to run away from this house," said Maupassant.

"Don't talk about our misfortune that way," said Rosalie, rushing into Lola's room for one last check. "*Gracious!* She left a note in the middle of her bed," she shouted.

She returned and handed it to me. I read aloud, "'I can't wait any longer, I can't sleep. Don't worry about me. I'll see you soon.'"

I glanced over at Murier, who looked deeply troubled.

"Why do you look like that? Do you know anything about this?"

"Ferdinand," he said to himself before looking at us. "He has something to do with this. Ferdinand de Bret, isn't it?"

"Paul Antoine introduced him to us as a baron," I said.

"Ah! Well, did he also tell you that Ferdinand de Bret was Henri Cousin's nephew?"

"What?" Maupassant and I shouted out in chorus.

The kettle started whistling in the kitchen, and before Rosalie ran downstairs to see to it, she cried out, "What a mess! I hope she doesn't end up behind bars too. She'll be a suspect. Mark my words."

"Yes, Ferdinand de Bret is the banker's nephew," Murier continued. "A sad reputation has followed him since his years at military school. His case was even presented to Dr. Blanche, who took him into his care on a trial basis but refused to keep him on as a patient. We don't know the reasons behind his decision."

"Paul Antoine told us he had met Ferdinand at a dinner at Blanche's home. He spoke very enthusiastically of the evening because there were so many artists around the table. He found a kindred spirit in Ferdinand—perhaps because they were the youngest among the assembly. Ferdinand doesn't have the same tastes as Paul Antoine, in any case. One would safely assume, in fact, that he has fallen madly in love with Lola. But what are the symptoms of his illness?" I asked.

"He was involved in some dark business. A murder. He had amassed a gambling debt with one of his classmates from the military school, and he couldn't honor it. His young creditor had publicly humiliated him by claiming the debt at a dinner party. And Ferdinand is quite the irritable man, it would seem."

"Irritable?" I was surprised. "Are we sure we're talking about the same gentleman? He seems as sweet as a lamb. Perhaps a little silly in his demonstrations of love. I would say he has an unfailing docility. Lola has him eating out of her palm."

"He likes duels," said Maupassant. "He provoked a man who disrespected Lola."

"You think it's a habit of his?" I asked.

"Indeed. This friend of his to whom he owed money was found with his throat cut in Paris. Ferdinand was suspected, in light of his previous altercations, but the investigation was ultimately unsuccessful."

"Maybe it wasn't Ferdinand, after all?" said Maupassant, leaving the benefit of the doubt to the young man.

"Perhaps. Nevertheless, his uncle had him incarcerated in Vidal's sanatorium. That is why Cousin was partially financing the place. He didn't want anyone to know. Ferdinand was his heir, you see."

"Ferdinand a murderer? I can't believe it!" I shook my head. "And what did you find out about the de Caravel family and Cousin?" I asked.

"More precisely, I'll tell you what I found out about Madame de Caravel and Cousin," the journalist said. "When I heard Anna talking about a notary, I thought I'd ask Buttura. He knows all the secrets of this city. And he owes me a favor. He knows he can count on me for discretion if necessary."

"Don't tell us they had an affair," said Maupassant. "Cousin was all austerity and rigidity, was he not?"

"Well . . ."

"They had a child, didn't they?" I exclaimed.

"Yes. A girl. Emina was married, and her elderly husband was often absent. Too often to be able to claim the child as his own."

"Anahita," I whispered. "That's where the exotic name comes from."

"Yes. Anahita is a pre-Christian goddess of fertility worshipped among Armenians. Emina gave her daughter birth, but she could go no further than that. The pregnancy was lived in absolute secrecy, the birth was performed in secret by Dr. Buttura himself. The child's placement was the subject of some very dark negotiations, I believe. Emina was distraught. Her death was the sad conclusion."

"Did Buttura speak to Cousin before his murder?"

"Yes, Cousin was bewildered when he saw Anna. Her resemblance to Emina confused him. He wanted the doctor to confirm that it was her at all costs."

"Dr. Buttura has known all this from the beginning," I said. "He knew when we took Anna out of the orphanage that she was not the daughter of the Martins."

"Yes, they were given a farm as well as a baby. They declared themselves as her parents. But the farm burned down. They died, and the entire property perished with them. Anna was placed at the Sacré-Cœur. She was a pauper. An adjoining property that had also belonged to the Martins was sold, and the money was used to pay for the first years of her board. Buttura told Cousin the whole story."

"So what Anna says is true," I said. "He didn't covet her. However, he wanted her to leave Lola to go live with him."

"That's right. He told Buttura that he was going to change his will. If she came to live with him, she would be his only heir. Cousin also informed Buttura that he had written to his notary to that effect. But Cousin was still worried that Anna had been educated in an immoral atmosphere and that she lacked essential virtues."

"Because of how we appear in this house," I muttered furiously.

Maupassant nodded with a hint of shame. "I'm afraid so. Appearance is everything."

Our eyes met. He didn't want to say anything more in front of Murier, but he must have guessed that Lola had told me everything about his children, as indeed she had, and that I knew of his double life.

Murier continued, "Buttura told Cousin that it was better for the girl to have learned to read, write, embroider, and play the piano rather than work herself to the bone for the orphanage and sleep in a vermin-infested dormitory at the risk of dying of cholera, as had happened to her companions four years ago. I investigated those deaths, but I never found an explanation for the epidemic. No clues at all."

Maupassant and I exchanged another look, longer than the first one. Fortunately, Murier didn't notice.

He went on. "Cousin was convinced that all that had to be done was to persuade Anna to live with him. He felt old, his life was meaningless, his nephew had greatly disappointed him, and his only love had died. To find Emina again in the guise of Anahita was such a joy. Life had granted him an unexpected gift."

32

PRISONER

When Lola came to later in the day, it took her some time to remember what had happened and how she had gotten where she was. She felt as though her head had been hammered by a lead bar. She looked around. She was tied up with a chain leash locked to her foot with a steel bracelet. It was welded onto the bars of the headboard of the bed upon which she was lying. She was wearing only her underclothes. Her dress and boots had been removed. This angered her immensely.

Everything came back to her. How stupid she was! How could she have thought she could accuse Vidal without him reacting?

He must have anticipated what was going to happen for some time. Lola's back had been turned away from the open door. The male nurse had attacked her from behind and put her to sleep with his poison-soaked cloth. It was a cowardly act. She remembered struggling, but the surprise had worked as intended. The battle had been unequal, to say the least.

She was able to stand and hobble a little of the way toward the barred window, dragging the chain behind her. The storm outside was now raging. She watched the sea hitting the rocks next to the small pier below. Her room was located on the third floor of the large west tower. It overlooked the rugged coastline and the island opposite. She could see nothing of the property itself. She could not detect a single movement of patients or staff. But with such weather, there wasn't likely to be many people outside the building.

So this is my fate, she thought. *I went from the building where patients seem to live side by side in harmony to the great Gothic tower where people are locked up. Perhaps this is where he keeps his most challenging cases. I am now removed from the world.*

She returned to her bed and listened. Unable to see anything, she tried to focus on what she could hear. This part of the sanatorium was much less comfortable than what she had witnessed earlier. She could detect a great many noises that she tried to understand. There was an overall excitement.

The sound of metal objects being scraped across floors, doors opening and closing. There were also voices. Orders being barked, screams, moans.

Is this an institution where people are helped or a place of torture? She was starting to get scared. *Courage is not my strong suit.* She tried to laugh to herself.

She hoped, above all else, that no physical harm would come to her. She could cope with chloroform attacks, bad food, fleas, lice, lack of water, even the cold. But not physical torture.

I won't be able to do it, she told herself. *I am far too weak in the face of pain. I have to find the courage to escape. Miss Fletcher would appreciate that paradox!*

She suddenly heard a scream that chilled her to the bone. She started shouting so that her own voice drowned out the terror of what she heard.

"Open the door! I want to get out! Help!"

She thought she'd be waiting for hours before someone came to see her, but only a few minutes later, she heard footsteps in the hallway, a rustling, and then a bunch of keys being shaken. The door opened, and two male nurses entered.

They were tall and strong and didn't seem to be the type of people one would confront, but they had a direct and almost kind look about them.

"Well, well! What's going on here? What do you want?"

Lola thought their apparent kindness was a trap, and she had no intention of getting caught up in it. So she kept repeating that she didn't understand what she was doing there.

"I believe you behaved in a way that made little sense, madame. Wanting to end your life? It's not acceptable. You're very unwell. But please, don't worry. We have excellent care methods, and in no time at all, you will feel better and be on your way home. You just have to trust us."

So that was the official thesis: She'd wanted to die. She had to be protected from herself.

This was impossible. It would mean anything that was done for her would be for her own "good," including locking her up, depriving her, inflicting electromagnetic treatments on her . . .

"I'm not insane! That's not true!"

"No one is claiming you are. And that's not a word we use here. You're just going through a difficult time. You have to be reasonable and try to calm down. We have enough to worry about today with all this silliness."

"Silliness? Why? What else is happening?"

"The watchman here. He passed on today. We found his body washed up on the beach."

"Not Aristide? Oh no! No!"

"Did you know him?"

"I did! Very well. Since I was a child! How did this happen?"

"He must have fallen in the water and hit his head on the rocks."

Lola would have liked to give in to the sudden grief that seized her, but the horror of the situation caused her to scream.

"It's him!" she shouted. "The doctor! Don't you understand that he's a murderer? Poor Aristide! I don't want to die. Let me out of here! I came to see him about a sick friend, and he locked me up in here!"

The two men exchanged glances. They had clearly heard otherwise. For what person of unsound mind would admit as much? Was there not a particular madness that was recognized by the fact that the diagnosed patient said he or she was not mad?

When one of the nurses started talking to her again in a soothing tone, Lola lost patience and hurled herself forward in an attempt to grab the key ring.

She screamed as loudly and as wildly as she could. The two men could not control her. Lola fought tooth and nail: kicking, hitting, biting. But the nurses were strong, and there were two of them. They pushed Lola back down onto the bed and rushed out the door without locking it. Lola deduced from this that they were planning to return soon. In any case, she was tied to her bed and wouldn't have been able to reach the exit.

She slipped onto the floor and sat with her back against the wall. Lola was delighted to have managed to strike one of the men in the eye and the other in the jaw—although, her knuckles now hurt. *What I just did was rather unbecoming. But it made me feel better.*

The two nurses returned a few minutes later, accompanied by two others. She was forcibly given a drink that tasted like the laudanum she used to calm her anxiety attacks. She felt the restraint being removed from her ankle, and then she was taken away, simply lifted off the ground.

"You will hear from me. I have friends who are journalists and writers. Everyone will know what you're doing here. This is abuse. You will be dragged before the courts," she argued weakly.

The men laughed.

"That's right. And you're quite sane, you say? Don't worry. We know that. We are here to help you behave in a safer manner toward yourself and others. That is all. The law requires us to do so," one of them said.

"What are you going to do to me? Where are you taking me?"

"We'll start with a bath to relax you. It will be cold, of course, but very pleasant. You'll see. It calms the soul. This will be followed by some electric therapy. This you must accept. We need your cooperation. The bath will help us to obtain that. I hope we won't have to tie you up again."

Lola made the task as difficult as she could for them, but they managed to drag her to the hydrotherapy room. The administered substance started to take effect. She felt herself weaken further. When they arrived in front of a padded door, she no longer had enough strength to do anything about it. She wriggled in a miserable attempt to escape—but to no avail.

The room looked like the bathhouses available by the pool on the Croisette. The tubs were lined up next to each other, six in two rows. The walls were made of large exposed stones, gray and chalky. Or it might have been mold due to the damp atmosphere.

Two of the baths were occupied, but there was something odd about them, something Lola had never seen before—they were covered with fitted wood and a steel ring for the patient's head. Only the heads of the two bathers, both women, could be seen. Lola thought they resembled strange coffins, from which the dead person's head protruded.

No steam came out of the baths. Lola shivered. She then noticed the quivering lips of one of the patients. There were large metal containers placed on a furnace that looked to be used for heating water and taps located at the bottom of the vats. Upon closer inspection, the woman closest to Lola appeared to be resigned to what was happening to her. Her eyes were vacant.

In a corner sat two female nurses at a small table with a register. They drank tea and ate biscuits. They looked at Lola indifferently and didn't seem in any hurry to put her in a bath, which made her feel better.

"My nose is itching! It itches! It itches!" shouted the other woman in the bathtub.

A nurse stood and rushed to relieve the woman. Then she leaned over to the first one and asked if she wanted some hot water. The woman, who was clearly shaking from the cold, refused.

"The doctor said it must be cold," she muttered.

"Cold doesn't have to mean glacial," said the nurse. "You've been here for more than five hours. I think it's time to add a little hot water."

Five hours! Lola thought. *What utter misery!*

Without waiting for further comment, the nurse grabbed a jug and filled it with hot water from one of the taps and emptied it through the hole in the board.

The two men had let go of Lola and disappeared while she'd been watching this scene unfold. Through the mist of her drug-addled brain, she still had enough common sense to understand she must refuse this treatment, especially as there was not a jot wrong with her.

She said in the most impassive voice she could muster, "I am not sick. I am very calm, and I don't understand why I have been prescribed this bath."

The other nurse put down her cup of tea and approached her gently. "We've been expecting you. It's just a matter of preparing you for the electricity. You may be calm at this moment, but you had some difficulties earlier, correct? Please don't fret. All this is for your own good. You want to be well again, don't you?"

"I'm not ill, I tell you. This is not right."

The nurse appeared attentive and compassionate as she said, "Of course, of course. We know that. We've read your file here. It says, 'Secret,' on it."

Her tone was so sweet that it made Lola worry even more. This woman was speaking to her as one would to a child.

Why did I come here on my own like this? And what a notion to have accused Vidal like that! What's this "secret" business all about?

"How long will the bath last? I have to get back to the mainland."

This time the nurse had trouble hiding her mirth, and she exchanged a look with her colleague, who turned her head so that Lola wouldn't see her smirk.

"Why are you laughing?" Lola demanded angrily. "I'm telling you the truth. If I'm not back soon, people will start to worry."

"I'm not laughing, madame. It's just that, because of the storm, there's no steamer today. Come on. Just behave and wait a little while you're here. Would you like some tea as I prepare your bath?"

Lola had the strangest feeling. All her physical reactions felt limited . . . as if they were disappearing . . . How would she be able to get out of this? She imagined how she could take the water and attack the nurses, hit them, tie them up, grab their keys, and run away. But her muscles had become as soft as rubber. She reached out her hand to the nurse who had led her to the table and was now serving tea.

The woman then went to fill the bathtub. The water looked cold. She sprinkled the surface with a white powder. A sulfuric smell filled the room, stinging Lola's nostrils. From time to time, the nurse would touch the water with her fingertips and pour in a jug of hot water.

Lola tried to resist again when they started pushing her toward the tub.

"I don't want to be put in there!" she still had the strength to scream.

A further struggle ensued. But finally, devastated and resigned to her fate, just like her unfortunate companions, Lola found herself immersed in water which, although not icy, was nevertheless exceedingly cold. They placed the board on top of her. Her ordeal had begun.

In a small voice, she asked again, "How long is this going to last?"

"That, madame, depends on you."

"Even in my worst nightmares, I could never have imagined this," Lola whispered.

"You are an ungrateful woman," said one of the nurses. "You don't realize that this is a first-class institution. Everything here has been set up for your well-being and comfort."

Lola was beginning to lose all discernment, and it was without irony when she said, "Oh, really?"

"Yes, and you're lucky the doctor is coming to see to you personally, to take care of you properly."

"That is lucky."

"Exactly. Perhaps you would prefer an institution where, instead of baths, there are belts or straitjackets? I've even heard of people like you being chained to walls, their arms above their heads. You know that, don't you?"

"People like who?"

"Patients! You're a patient—you're unfit. Infirm."

Devastated by this last remark, Lola gave up. She let her mind wander and take refuge high in a cloudless sky, flying and observing the scene from a long, long way above.

She had acquired this dissociation technique early in her adolescence, when she had had to share her bed with men who repulsed and frightened her.

But nothing she had experienced thus far in her life could compare to this living hell. Those doors that had simply been shut on her. The corridors, the rooms, this indeterminable detention. The feeling that she would never leave the island again. A suffocation, a sensation of being a nothing . . . a nobody.

Her technique of escape through the mind proved useful in preserving some strength.

It was at this moment that Vidal entered the room.

The nurses greeted him with smiles and deference. The patients were equally impressed by his presence. Lola was surprised that they had the energy to even notice him with all the substances they must have been forced to ingest.

Without even glancing at those present, he headed for Lola's bathtub. He leaned toward her, showing a wolfish grin.

"This will take as long as it takes," he said, "for we must ensure that you are able to listen to reason. We're here to protect you from yourself. Now, repeat after me: *I repent my faults. I will desist in my misconduct. I will abide by the rules of subordination.*"

Vidal's face was so close to Lola's that he appeared blurry. She no longer resisted. She tried to open her mouth to repeat his words, but she could not utter a single syllable.

As Vidal's expression turned to fury, she lost consciousness.

33

STORM

Back at Les Pavots, the questions were flowing. We were wondering why Ferdinand de Bret had made this sudden appearance in our lives, or, rather, in Lola's, mere hours prior to his uncle's murder. Was there a connection? This couldn't be another mere coincidence.

As for me, I had my suspicions. Ferdinand had killed his uncle for the inheritance. I had once read that homicides with inheritance as a motive were the third most common form of murder, after crimes of passion and robberies gone wrong. And what was a crime of passion, anyway? It was often a man killing a woman in a fit of jealousy, not passion.

Murier had an article to deliver to his boss and so left us quickly, requesting we keep him informed of any news. For the time being, he didn't have enough to write a piece for the newspaper, as there were too many unanswered questions.

"I'm going to see if Lola is at her parents' house. She needs to know what we've learned," I said. "I'm worried that she left so early."

"I will accompany you," said Maupassant.

The storm continued to rage. Taking Gaza would have been madness. Water was flowing down the street in the direction of the station, and the path by its side had become a torrent. I handed Maupassant a huge umbrella and grabbed one, too, after slipping on a waxed coat.

We could barely talk over the sound of the rain drumming on the roofs and bouncing off the pavement below our feet. My skirt, although above ankle length, was soaked in just a few minutes. The same could be said for Maupassant's trousers. I had to shout above the din.

I explained that I wanted to stop by the Pantiero to see Mario.

When we arrived, the Pantiero was empty, of course, but we noticed that the small café on the port was sheltering all the fishermen and sailors, their noses glued to the windows. With a fatalistic eye, they watched as the storm pushed their boats to and fro. They must have been wondering what damage they would find when the sky finally relented and stopped directing its anger at our little town.

I recognized Mario's face and realized I hadn't seen him smile once since Anna had been arrested. When we entered the café and located Mario, he told us that he had taken Lola over to the islands in the early hours.

"She had a message for you. She said not to worry and that she'd be back later today."

I felt ill. Maupassant, who had not spoken until then, said suddenly, "What about this Ferdinand? If I understand correctly, he lives over there with Vidal?"

Mario stared at us in turn, a look of confusion in his eyes as we explained everything.

"He did it, then!" the young man yelled. "I'll kill him! He's the reason Anna's locked away!"

I was convinced of this, too, and sensed that Maupassant had also been thinking the same thing for a while. He rarely drew peremptory conclusions without analyzing the pros and cons at length, always considering people's innocence before their guilt. It was this ability that allowed him to see a situation from the standpoint of all parties involved.

"Ferdinand's appearance in Lola's life could hardly be a coincidence, could it?" said Maupassant. "He is the banker's nephew, and he then discovers that Anna is his cousin—a cousin he didn't know existed and who is now his rival? Then the banker is murdered and Ferdinand enters the scene, making eyes at Lola."

"*Good heavens!* She's at his mercy! But why did she go over to that place, anyway?" I sighed.

"It's my fault!" said Mario. "I shouldn't have taken her across!"

"Stop with the whining, both of you," exclaimed Maupassant. "Let's be a little more productive. What can we do now that we have reached this point? We need something concrete."

"Nothing can be done," replied Mario, maintaining his gloomy visage, "as long as this storm continues."

"But Lola is in grave danger if Ferdinand really is the murderer!" I cried.

"Let's keep a cool head," said Maupassant.

"That's easy enough to say!" I shouted.

Maupassant continued with his train of thought. "She is in just as much danger if the culprit is the doctor. And that's her own fault. She left without warning us. Oh, she is unbearable when she thinks herself above the law!"

"No, that's quite different," I insisted. "She suspects him and thus doesn't trust him, which means she'll be careful around him. But Ferdinand is a friend to her."

"There's no way of traveling to the islands at the moment," Mario insisted. "We have to wait."

I couldn't bear it. I wanted to swim to the island despite the tempest. I felt sick at the thought of sitting back and not acting.

"I'm going to see Anna," I said. As Maupassant and I set out again, I explained, "I'll tell her I know everything. This secret must be weighing on her. I imagine she promised Cousin she wouldn't breathe a word of it. Poor girl. She had two torturous choices: to help her father through the autumn days of his life—a father who had come from out of nowhere—or to stay with Lola, who had generously taken her in when she needed it most."

"It seems she had made her choice," said Maupassant. "Otherwise, she wouldn't have come home that night, would she?"

"If that was her choice, why was she so angry with Lola?"

"Anger is a positive sign. It's always better than silence. She said what she thought, but the tide has passed."

The guard at the front of the town hall let us in without leaving the building. It would seem he didn't wish to get wet. If Brigadier Rodot was in his office, we didn't see him.

The same guard accompanied us to Anna's cell. She was sitting on the ground, shaking, with her back against the fold-down bench that she used as a bed. On a small table, there were the leftovers of the food I had brought the day before.

I immediately noticed that her dress was torn at the shoulder. She was holding the sleeve with one hand, and her gaze was fixed.

I spoke gently as I was ushered into the room. "Anna? I am here, my child."

She then saw me and fell into my arms, crying.

"Miss Fletcher, take me with you. I don't want to stay here. I want to go home with you and Lola. It's awful. I didn't kill him."

"I know everything, Anna. You don't have to keep your secret anymore. We know you're his daughter. Did he give you that portrait of your mother, Emina? And then you hid it in my basket?"

She nodded, and I noticed immense relief in her eyes.

"Yes," she whispered. "I wanted to talk to you about it, but I didn't dare. I thought fate would decide for me. One day you would find this secret hidden among the lace."

As Maupassant approached, his jaw hardened. "Who did this to you, Anna? Why is your dress torn?"

Anna bowed her head and blushed. He took her face in his hands.

"You must tell me, Anna. Was it Rodot?"

Had that depraved man tried to violate her? Had he forced her into some sort of degrading act? Had Lola's worst fears come to be? Anna kept her head down, and as I observed her, I felt like my heart was breaking.

The guard came to take us away, shouting that the visit was over. He was flanked by two gendarmes, who marched into Anna's cell just as we left. I looked down the corridor and noticed that Rodot had come out of his lair. When he saw us, he displayed a fleeting expression of triumph. What exactly was he pleased about? My stomach turned as I felt an overwhelming sensation of wanting to throw myself at him to rid him of that smile.

I could hear Anna sobbing.

We turned back to see her being dragged out of her cell, her wrists in handcuffs. What a sorry sight she was.

We stood there, powerless. She must have been petrified.

We followed as she was hauled outside and pushed into a caged box pulled by two old mares who were trembling in the rain and wind.

"Where is she being taken?" I cried.

"The investigating judge wants to see her in Grasse," Rodot snapped before returning inside.

Maupassant stormed back into the town hall.

"Wait for me back at the café," he said before entering through the main door. "I'm going to find Valantin."

34

A Smoothly Conducted Investigation

Valantin was in an excited state when Maupassant entered his office on the second floor. He had been watching the scene below from the window.

"Is that you, Maupassant? I am very pleased to see that this case is finally moving toward its inevitable conclusion. The investigating judge will receive her, ask her a few questions, and, thanks to my thorough investigation, her fate will be quickly sealed. He's read my report. I don't like to leave a crime unsolved. You know me."

"Even if it means making miscarriages of justice?"

Valantin laughed. "Your loyalty is honorable, but an educated man such as yourself—a so-called *naturalist*," he articulated with a hint of condescension, "cannot deny the truth."

"What 'truth'?" growled Maupassant. "The one you bend to your desire?"

His tone shocked Valantin, who demanded an explanation.

Immediately, Maupassant brought himself back under control, knowing he would have a better chance of being heard. He explained our recent suspicions about Ferdinand de Bret. He also explained how Lola suspected Vidal, and that, whatever the case may be, we believed Lola to be in danger on the island.

"That girl isn't quite right," said Valantin. "I will not go risking the lives of my men in this storm to help her. Moreover, she's not in any danger. Your theories are far-fetched, to say the least."

Maupassant, desperate to convince him, then told him of Brigadier Rodot's abusive behavior toward women in the prison as well as those who worked in certain ill-famed establishments within the city.

"That man is corrupt. Why maintain him in your ranks?"

"Yes, I know," said Valantin nonchalantly. "He has developed several bad habits. But it's my fault. When I arrived in Cannes, I asked that some of the officers go underground to try to clean up those dens of iniquity a little, or at least keep them under control. Rodot volunteered, and he's been playing a dangerous double game ever since."

"Well, it's risky. For you too. You've allowed it to go on!"

"Come on, Maupassant, don't be a child. Do you think it's easy to get information about that element of society, about the very people who endanger the lives of our honest citizens? You have to know how to take these kinds of risks when you occupy my position. Cannes is host to royalty from all over Europe. I can't have them meeting crooks on our streets. And I can't have them coming here to seek those sorts of thrills either. Rodot is a good soldier for me. He's zealous."

"I don't doubt it. Your cynicism repels me, though."

"I'll pretend I didn't hear that. I know you're of an impulsive nature."

"That's just it, I'm not. I always choose my words most carefully."

Valantin took a conciliatory tone. "Rodot makes these thugs believe he can protect them from extortion attempts or intimidation in exchange for favors from the ladies. It's not such a huge issue, is it, now? As a result, they believe they are dealing with an agent as corrupt as they are, and he reports every single detail to me."

"He may sometimes go beyond his role without your knowledge," said Maupassant. "Do you think letting him abuse an innocent child in prison allows you to better control your city?"

Valantin looked at Maupassant thoughtfully. "The Martin girl? He's gone too far in that case. I'll speak with him."

The smile that accompanied Valantin's words caused Maupassant to cry out in despair, "Look, Valantin, I don't know what you're up to, but what I've seen here today is outrageous. And since you don't want to hear anything of what I've reported, I'll go save Lola myself, and I'll do my best to bring you back Cousin's killer. When this is all said and done, my journalist friend Murier will be more than happy to make a fool of you. I'm also going to have a few words with Mayor Gazagnaire about all this."

"Oh, do it, Maupassant, do it," sighed Valantin as he returned to his paperwork.

Maupassant marched out of the room, slamming the door behind him.

35

ELECTRICAL MACHINES

Lola was horrified at how long she'd been on the island. The storm had increased in intensity, and she had spent a good part of the afternoon in her cold bath.

Some nurses she hadn't encountered before had eventually taken her out of the water and dried her with a rough linen cloth. She was then put in a woolen nightgown lined with cotton flannel, and her boots were returned to her. She gave them a grateful look, still numb from the chemicals she had ingested. She felt as though she had not a single reflex.

She was taken to a heated room filled with wires, cables, and odd-looking devices on tabletops. She knew what happened in this room, but no patients were currently undergoing treatment. In one corner, there was a sitting area. A young girl, no older than Anna, was in one of the chairs, jerking and rocking. Lola could see she was with child. She seemed so lost, so deep in sorrow. She raised her head and stared at Lola.

"I have no use for those looks you give me, madame," she articulated with difficulty. "I know it's because of you that I'm here. You set up this sorry business to steal my fiancé."

Lola was just about to protest her innocence in this conspiracy when she was offered a cup of steaming tea with a slice of bread. She realized then just how hungry she was. She took a couple of sips and bites before curling up and falling asleep in her chair.

Someone was shaking her arm. The grip was hard. She woke with a start and tried to free herself. But it was not to be. She had returned to her living nightmare and was now lucid enough to realize this.

A face distorted with anxiety was bent over her. It took her a few moments to recognize who it was.

"Lady Sarah! What in the name of God are you doing here?"

"Don't play your games with me. I know it was you who betrayed me to my husband!"

"Not at all! Has blaming me for everything become a sport around here? Why should I be responsible for your fate? And hers too!"

She looked around her, pointing. There was no nursing staff there, and the young girl with the swollen belly had disappeared too. They were alone.

"If it wasn't you," Lady Sarah continued, "how did he know I would eliminate the only evidence proving I was irresponsible, financially speaking?"

"Even if he knew, he can't prove a thing without the contract, can he?"

"So you didn't sell those papers to him?"

"Of course not! You hired me. I'm not in the habit of betraying my clients. I have a reputation to maintain. And you paid me more than enough!" Lola was now on her feet and examining the room. "By the way, I need the second part of that payment. I know I won't be entitled to it until you destroy the contract, but I'll need it. And you'll have to give me back the paper I signed too."

"Why didn't you come to find me? You must have known I was brought here. Gabriella saw me."

"I certainly did not."

"I see."

"But was it not voluntary on your part to come here?"

"Of course not!"

"Well, I can give you your file whenever you want." As she spoke, Lola walked over to the two heavy doors. Of course, they were locked.

"If I ever leave here, I'll take them gladly," Lady Sarah replied bitterly.

"The same goes for me. I think I'll be here some time yet," replied Lola in the same tone.

Lola turned to Lady Sarah and observed an electrical device beside her.

Lady Sarah placed her head on her hands with some difficulty. It was only then that Lola noticed that Lady Sarah was wearing a wide leather belt over her pretty dress. Two rings around her wrists were attached to the belt.

She stared at the older woman with both horror and compassion.

"I don't need your pity," Lady Sarah said with a laugh. "I'll get out of this situation. I'm going to write to my father and explain what's happening to me here. My husband has tricked him, but if he reads my letter, he will understand what is at stake. I am his beloved daughter, after all. I'm all he has. What I want to know is what you are doing here." After uttering these words, a wild laugh followed that sent a chill down Lola's spine. Was Lady Sarah really losing her mind?

"I came here this morning to confront Vidal. He is Cousin's killer."

"And what business is that of yours? Why don't you just let people murder whomever they want in peace? He deserved it, didn't he? Who will miss him?"

There is something seriously wrong here, thought Lola.

"Oh yes," Lady Sarah continued. "Your little protégée! That's right! Word gets around. Are you trying to exonerate her? What about our dear Miss Fletcher? Is she not looking for you yet?"

"Haven't you seen the weather out there? There is no way of traveling between the mainland and this island." Lola approached Lady Sarah. "So stop with your nonsense, or I'll come to believe that you are no longer of sound mind. Instead of fighting, we should be supporting one another. If I can get out of here, I could be useful to you. I could find you a lawyer, at the very least."

"You are right. How can I help you?"

"Have you heard anything since you've been here? Something that might allow us to escape?"

"There's a young man here who holds you in high esteem. He's a resident in one of the *easier* wings, and he's on better terms than I am with the good doctor. He'll be out soon. He's cured, I hear."

"Really? In high esteem, you say. It's quite possible. I know a lot of prominent gentlemen. Who is it?"

"Actually, he seems very much in love with you. He defended you this morning when I was in consultation in Vidal's office. He stormed in and ordered Vidal to release you, or at least to free you from the tower."

"I thought it was a 'secret' that I was being treated. But why are we in here together? Don't they know we are acquainted?"

"They may not. They don't necessarily know everything."

"And this young man—how did he find out about my presence here?"

"That, I know. It's the nurses who talk. They have been discussing your case and that you were taken in for hydrotherapy. He overheard them, and he was so angered. The doctor told him you were dangerous and that you had something to do with Cousin's death."

"What nerve!"

"The young man told him you had nothing to do with it. 'You know that, Vidal!' he said. He was rather threatening, in fact."

"Ah! You see! I'm right! I'm not the only one who suspects the doctor, apparently!"

"Vidal seemed uncomfortable and asked the young fellow if he'd talked to Aristide this morning."

"The watchman," said Lola.

Lady Sarah frowned. "You amaze me. You already know the staff by their names? How do you know who Aristide is? I had no idea whom they were talking about. You are truly unbelievable! You've only just arrived!"

"It's mere coincidence," replied Lola. "Aristide opened up the gates for me early this morning. But he's been found dead since, down by the rocks. It so happens that I've known him since I was a child."

A silence set in. Lola was wondering who her unexpected defender might be and whether there could be a relationship between poor Aristide's and Cousin's deaths. She continued to examine the devices, looking for ways to immobilize them. She tore out some of the wiring and cables.

"What are you doing? Are you out of your mind?"

"Yes, that's just it," said Lola with an ironic tone. "I find it strange that we have been left together unattended. When two women like us are left to fend for themselves in a room full of machinery such as this, it would be a mistake to be surprised by the result."

"Well, they will know that I had nothing to do with it, since my hands are tied," said Lady Sarah.

"I thank you for your courage and your spirit of solidarity," said Lola.

These words stung Lady Sarah so much that she stood and started kicking the chairs, tables, and appliances, completing the work started by Lola.

"It's not very wise, what you're doing. I didn't want them to realize the damage straight away. If the devices were not working, they might think it was a technical failure, which would keep them preoccupied and perhaps give us the opportunity to escape."

"A technical failure? You've ripped those wires—look at them!"

"A rat could have done it. They're always gnawing at them."

The sound of footsteps caused them to freeze. A key turned in the lock, and two male nurses entered. The noise of the furniture being overturned must have reached them despite the padding on the doors.

At the sight of such disarray, their faces contorted with rage. *Of course*, Lola thought. *The doctor will know they left us unattended. They fear for their livelihoods.*

The men grabbed them and dragged them into the corridor. Lola felt as if their strength had increased tenfold alongside their anger. That's when Lola heard the screams. There was a deafening commotion coming from the bottom of the tower.

"What's going on?" asked Lola.

"It's a mutiny we have on our hands here," said one of the nurses. "This place is never the quietest, but this is the worst I've known it. Somebody obviously couldn't find anything better to do than go around opening up the cells. That's why we had to leave you. One of you was tied up and the other asleep! And now you're starting too!"

"That's right," said Lola. "You never know what to expect with the insane."

The man looked at her suspiciously. He was clearly wondering if she was mocking him. She looked at him as innocently as she could. "And it's always the women who are the worst," she said.

Lady Sarah and the other nurse were walking ahead of Lola. Suddenly, Lady Sarah stopped and threw herself to the ground before kicking the legs of her guardian. He lost his balance and fell down next to her.

He shouted in surprise, "Ah! Little trollop! She's bitten me! Auguste! Come and help me, boy! Get her! She's got the devil in her, that one."

Auguste, who had been holding Lola back, threw himself into the melee by kicking Lady Sarah while she was down at his heel. Lola could see that this was something he'd done more than once. She was lost somewhere between the desire to defend Lady Sarah and the need to escape. But when she saw Lady Sarah's triumphant gaze, she realized

Lady Sarah had planned everything so that Lola could get away. She started to run. Once she was out of this hell, she would find a way to get some help to Lady Sarah. This she swore to herself.

She quickly found the spiral staircase, made of huge carved stones, and raced down them as if she were flying. She happened upon a corridor that she guessed led to the courtyard outside.

She went to open a door. Damnation! It was locked.

She heard footsteps and took refuge in the first open room she found. There was laundry everywhere. She put on a wide, long apron and tied it at the back, praying it would hide her nightgown. She would have needed a shirt and striped skirt to make it look like she was wearing a real uniform, but there was no trace of anything like that here. She twisted her hair into a severe bun on her neck before putting on a white headdress.

She left the room and walked partway back down the corridor. Just then, two nurses came from the left and opened a big door leading back to the main part of the building. She followed them calmly, and no one asked her any questions.

She had almost made it. There would be a way out now that she had left the tower behind.

She sighed, feeling the heaviness in her chest starting to lift.

Her next task was to find the key to the exterior gate that poor Aristide had opened for her.

She had only spent one day in this place, but it felt like she had been there for months. The mundane conversation she'd had with the doctor that morning now seemed like a distant memory. Since then, she had been drugged, tied up in a cell reserved for those who had lost their minds, and undergone hydrotherapeutic treatment or, at least, what was referred to as a treatment in this place. But she knew it could have been worse. She had almost been treated with electricity, and the effects from that could have been permanent.

She walked calmly, giving controlled and benevolent smiles to all those she passed. Four patients who were playing cards in a living room called out to her to ask if mealtime was approaching and if they were invited to dine at the doctor's table that night. Fearing agitation, she reassured them, telling them that dinner would indeed be soon and that all of them would join the doctor. The game continued while a serving girl asked them if they preferred orange juice or tea. *Goodness, the service is good here,* she thought. *I understand now why the board is so expensive.*

Her apron and headdress enabled her to gradually move closer toward Vidal's office, where she had seen a closet with keys. Once the key was in her pocket, she would leave and find refuge in a fisherman's cottage. Or maybe even the fort. Someone would be willing to take her in for a few hours until the storm subsided.

Vidal's door was closed. She stopped, looked right and left, glued her ear to the wood, and, upon hearing nothing, slowly turned the handle. She entered quickly and closed it behind her. As she made her way farther into the room, she saw Vidal's feet protruding from under his desk. He was on the floor in much the same position as the one in which Cousin had been found.

36

BACK AT THE FISHERMEN'S CAFÉ

Soaked to the bone, I joined Mario back at the fishermen's café. He was no longer subdued, for he was desperately trying to convince his boss to let him go to the islands to save his sister. But Gaglio, although a good man, didn't want to hear of it. His boat was his livelihood, and he had no intention of allowing it to be destroyed anytime soon.

Gaglio was one of the few people who wasn't looking out the window at the storm. He was instead playing cribbage with two friends. I recognized Lola's father, Beppo Giglio, as one of them. When he saw me, he banged his canes together and jumped up on his one leg.

"Come!" he said to me.

He forced me to sit by the stove, moving a fellow customer out of the way so that I could take the chair closest to the heat.

"You will catch your death if you don't warm up!" Beppo cried.

"I'm afraid it might be too late."

He shouted out to the man behind the bar to bring over a grog. I was shaking.

"Very hot! Plenty of honey!"

I sneezed several times, my nose running. Added to that was the fact that my throat was itching and I was coughing violently. Those around me may well have believed I was developing a serious case of pneumonia. But it was to be expected in such conditions as these.

As I had not brought a handkerchief, Mario, who had joined us, handed me his. I feared the worst, but I had forgotten that his mother was a conscientious laundry woman. The handkerchief, although cut from a simple cotton canvas without embroidery, was impeccably ironed and even perfumed with lavender.

"The other day," I said to Beppo, sniffing loudly, "you were saying something about Lola, but you didn't finish." The words came out of my mouth without my being able to contain them and despite the troubling feeling of disloyalty I felt.

"Are you talking about money? She always wants more money. She will never be satisfied."

"No," I said sadly. "It's not money that's her problem. It's her place in the world."

"Yes, that's right. And the guilt she still bears. It's a bad mix. Not knowing where you belong and feeling guilty at the same time. It's all because of my leg."

"She's not responsible for your accident, is she?"

"No, but she thinks she is. This is the fault of the war, though, and I don't even blame the Prussians! Everyone has to pick a side, right? That's just the way it is. When I went to Normandy in 1870, she gave me her dragon egg and told me it would protect me, like I had told her it would always protect her. Well, I came back like this, and she's never forgiven herself. She thinks the magic didn't work somehow and that it's her fault."

He hit his stump.

"I'd changed too. My character. She thinks I'm angry with her, but I came back alive! How many comrades I saw sitting out in the fields in freezing temperatures, exhausted, never to get up again. When the desire to end it all overwhelmed me, my finger would brush against the stone in my pocket. That's how I held on. That's how I got home. It was thanks to her."

"But have you told her that, Monsieur Giglio?"

He stood and moved away from me, grumbling. "Never. That's not for a father to say. She should understand it."

I sat there thinking, taking small sips of my hot brew, when Maupassant, also soaked, came in to join us.

"I did everything I could to convince Valantin to take a boat out to Vidal's place."

"And did you succeed?"

"I don't know. I don't even know if they have a boat, in fact."

"What about Rodot? Did you say anything to him?"

"Let's just say I threatened to speak to my journalist friend if someone wasn't sent over to the island."

"What are you talking about?" Mario interrupted, suddenly worried. "Who is this Rodot? What did he do?"

I continued to talk to Maupassant. "You mean you traded your silence for his action? But it's despicable!"

I was outraged, though I didn't see how he could have done better. Honestly, I had imagined that he would demand Valantin and Rodot be immediately removed from service.

I was angry that I had not reacted differently when the same man, four years earlier, had abused Lola. Did that mean that somewhere in my mind, I found sexual violence toward a woman such as Lola to be less serious? Was that because of what she did for a living?

"Don't believe for a moment that I'll stop there, Miss Fletcher," said Maupassant. "For now, I need to act quickly. I'm leaving tomorrow to take Hervé to Montpellier, but I can't go while Lola's in danger. We'll go in the *Bel-Ami*. I sent a messenger to find my crew, Bernard and Raymond. We can do this ourselves. Bernard won't be happy. He hates choppy waters. But he's a brave soul. It's time to see what he's made of!"

37

AN UNEXPECTED ENCOUNTER

In Vidal's office, just after discovering the doctor's lifeless body, Lola heard a rustle. She turned her head to her right just as a shy voice ventured, "Lola?"

She couldn't believe her eyes. It was Ferdinand crouched behind the door. Her tender little lamb looked so very happy to see her again. He stood and extended his arms out to her. She rushed toward him.

"My beloved, I've been looking all over for you!" he cried.

"Ferdinand, it's so good to see you! I came to thwart Cousin's killer, but I was locked up as though I'd lost my mind."

"Why is Cousin any concern of yours?"

"You know that! My Anna . . . She's being falsely accused. I have to get her out of the clutches of the law."

"Oh, I missed you so!"

He took her in his arms and kissed her. After the terrible day she'd just had, she felt a sense of relief. She needed to let herself fall into his embrace, to rely on someone stronger than herself.

"What did they do to you? Why are you wearing that white hat?"

"Never mind that for now. What about you? What are you doing here?" she asked between caresses.

"I am a patient here, my sweet girl. My uncle wanted me to stay for my nerves."

"What nerves? It's incredible the number of abusive confinements in this place," she said, tearing off her cap.

"It's not abusive at all. It is meant to heal my melancholy. My uncle was a good man. And I am cured now. I'll be going soon, but I hope what I just did doesn't stop me from being allowed to leave."

"What did you do?"

He whispered with a smile, "Will you scold me?"

"Of course not."

Lola turned her head, and her gaze fell for the second time upon Vidal's inert body. She had completely forgotten him in the surprise of seeing Ferdinand.

"Don't tell me you . . . you . . ."

"Oh, my beauty, you don't believe me a murderer, do you? I struck him, but it was for a good cause."

"How so?"

"He refused to tell me where he'd taken you. When I heard you were in the west tower, I ran over there without thinking. I stole some keys, opened all the padded cells, and searched the rooms, but it was in vain. Most of the rooms are empty. And I made a grave error. I didn't close the doors in my wake. The patients who were not secured started screaming and wandering around." He was overcome with emotion. "I was so worried I'd never find you. Where were you?"

"I spent some time in one of the therapy chambers. Then I was taken to the hydrotherapy room, and then to the electrical treatment laboratory."

"Oh, my poor, poor little wonder. What did they do to you? I will kill them for this. How dare they touch you!"

Lola laughed. "You sound just like my brother, Mario. He wants to kill whoever murdered Cousin, because he says he or she is the reason Anna's locked away."

Ferdinand suddenly stood straight.

"I have to find the key to the outer gates. I don't care about the storm," she said, bending down to feel Vidal's pulse. "You did the right thing here. He's out cold, and at least he won't bother us for a while."

Ferdinand, like a puppy, shivered with excitement upon hearing Lola's compliment.

"I came back here so he would tell me where you were, but he refused to utter a word. I was so livid! I couldn't help but hit him. I was just about to head back out to continue my search when I heard your steps in the hallway. I hid because I didn't know who it was."

"I have to get out of here before he awakens."

"A marvelous plan, my dear. We can leave together. Now that I am rich, we can do as we please. We can even go to America, if we so wish, to San Francisco, and I'll buy a theater just for you. You have such a beautiful voice. It will be wonderful to start our lives afresh and get away from all these unfortunate people."

Lola thought he was getting a little carried away and that it was hardly time to make such plans, but she put his words down to fear . . . or love . . . or relief. That being said, he was behaving rather strangely. In certain moments, he was exalted, drawing her to him, covering her with kisses, and at others, a hard expression crossed his eyes, his mouth became bitter-looking, and he would turn away from her.

Although she was concerned about these sudden shifts in his mood, she didn't want to ask what might be bothering him. However, the word *rich* had caught her attention.

"What do you mean when you say 'rich'? Paul Antoine told me you were already rich. Why did you say 'now'?"

"Paul Antoine knows nothing of my financial setbacks these last two years. But that's all behind me. Now my fortune is final and immeasurable."

Lola could not help but believe he was mocking her. But in her constant need to find a protector, she could not help but hope. What if she'd really found the right man this time? What if she finally had a rich, young, and lovingly supportive patron of her own? She could learn to adore such a fellow, couldn't she? This would change her. This would make her situation better.

"And from where does this sudden wealth hail?" she asked, pressing herself into his powerful arms.

"You know that. Cousin is my uncle."

"But your name is . . ." She couldn't recall Ferdinand ever having said his surname in front of her. "What was your name again, Ferdinand?"

"Baron de Bret. My dear mother was Cousin's sister, and she married de Bret. She died in childbirth, and my father succumbed to a duel in my early childhood. I barely knew him. Cousin raised me, if you can call it that. Let's just say he provided for my education."

A hint of bitterness was evident in his voice.

"I am his only family. However, it was too much for him to house me in his private mansion, though that place was far too big for one man!"

Lola realized that her dreams of security were beginning to collapse.

"You're his only family, but the will hasn't yet been read, has it? How can you be sure you're the only heir? Vidal said something about—"

"I know. I destroyed all remaining evidence. He was going to disinherit me in favor of that little harlot."

"What harlot?"

No matter how much she looked at Ferdinand's face, she refused to see the truth for what it was. Her brain, usually so insightful, simply would not deduce fact from fiction. The sordid, frightening reality . . . everything in her was fighting against it.

"This Anahita! I mean, really!" replied Ferdinand. "That horrible girl who did nothing but cause you heartache!"

Lola shook her head to try and awaken her senses. All this was getting very complicated. She couldn't think straight.

"I was just obeying Vidal. He wanted me to do his bidding. After my uncle's visit here to discuss the will, Vidal and I had a long talk. I felt so desperate. All the long waiting and isolation on this island with the hope of one day enjoying his fortune, and now some stranger was going to take everything? I was on the verge of suicide when the good doctor helped me to see matters for what they were, that not all was lost. I could still get into my uncle's good graces. All I had to do was show him that this girl was just a ruffian. A guttersnipe. And of course, to steal the new will and destroy it."

"Don't listen to him. He's lying. He's confused."

It was Vidal, who was now regaining consciousness. Lola looked down at the doctor with dread. He was going to stop them from leaving. He might even kill them.

"Don't look at me like that!" the doctor shouted as he got to his feet. "He speaks nonsense. I had nothing to do with the death of his uncle nor the idea of accusing that poor girl. I kept explaining to him, after Cousin's visit, that it was necessary to accept one's fate with good grace. I even offered to accompany him to Cannes to negotiate with Cousin, to have him draft a more favorable will. But in no way did I encourage him to destroy official documents!"

His tone didn't ring true to Lola's ears.

"So you went to Cannes with him?"

"No, he didn't want me to. I stayed here."

"That's not true," Ferdinand said. "He was there. He didn't leave the island with me, but only so Aristide wouldn't see him. I don't know how he managed it, but he came by other means, and he was there, all right. In fact, he guided me. He told me to take the letter opener and to strike my uncle. But I didn't want to."

"How can you pay attention to the ramblings of a madman?" Vidal asked Lola.

"A 'madman'? But he's cured, is he not?"

"He may have had a relapse," Vidal said as he rubbed his neck. "Assaulting your doctor is not symptomatic of good mental health."

"Too late! I have a valid certificate! You signed it!" Ferdinand cried.

"So Vidal didn't leave the island with Ferdinand, but he still visited Cousin's villa at some point," Lola said to herself quietly, working out her thoughts. She looked at Vidal. "You tried to soften Cousin on the issue of the new will, fearful you would lose his donation. When faced with failure, you killed in cold blood. You placed the clues near the body, which means you must have assaulted Anna on the street and stolen her bracelet. It was you!"

"What an imagination, my dear! I didn't put anything anywhere. I've never even set eyes on the girl. I don't know anything about her except what Cousin told me."

"That evening, before you arrived," Lola continued, "Anna had had an interview with Cousin that upset her. He told her the whole tale and gave her a portrait of her mother. He tried to force her to leave me and to live with him, but he moved much too fast for her. She ran away back home to us. It was then that you came on the scene at the villa. But how did the letter opener find its way to her bedchamber?"

"It doesn't matter!" exclaimed Ferdinand as he pulled her toward him. "My little flower, you worry too much about this little bastard of a child. You forget how she disrespected you. Don't take it out on Vidal. Think of him as the reason we found one another."

"Be quiet!" exclaimed Vidal. "Can't you see that this trollop is not on your side?"

"What did you say?" asked Ferdinand.

He took a statuette from the desk, flew forward, and smashed it into the doctor's forehead. Lola screamed.

"If there's one thing I will not tolerate, my darling, it's people dishonoring you! He'll be out for a while."

The young man then rushed to the closet and grabbed a large set of keys. He opened a drawer, took out a scalpel, and slipped it into a pocket. He tore off Lola's apron and grabbed her gently but firmly by the waist.

"Come along, sweetheart. I know where Aristide kept Vidal's boat. We're going to the Americas. I was a canoeist in my youth. Navigation holds no secrets for me. With a good sail and a cabin, we can go around the world just like Phileas Fogg. Then we'll settle in San Francisco rather than traveling around everywhere."

"It's impossible, Ferdinand! The sea is raging. Let's run to the commander's house instead and wait for this tempest to pass."

Ferdinand hugged her tighter against him and kissed her on the neck.

"Don't think anymore, my love. I'm here. It's all over now. You will finally be able to enjoy your life. I won't let anyone else hurt you."

"You're so right. The most important thing is to get out of here. They are all under the orders of the doctor. There's no way I'm going to be locked up again."

"Follow me," he said. "I just have one matter to deal with first."

He didn't run out toward the exit. Instead, he went as far as the entrance of the corridor leading to the great tower. He entered, continuing to hold Lola close to him.

Despite the fact that he ostensibly held her so she could barely move of her own volition, Lola never felt he wanted to keep her prisoner. She saw only the form of a passionate love that she felt had manifested itself on the day they had met.

When they entered the west tower, Lola felt a true sense of terror radiating within the old Gothic walls. Screams of rage, anger, and triumph greeted them. Nurses chased patients who were dressed in bathrobes or camisoles, or were the ones being chased. The staff had not been able to bring the revolt under control. Ferdinand tipped the confrontation in favor of the residents.

He managed, with the help of his recently acquired weapon and bunch of keys, to lock some of the employees in the laundry room where

Lola had changed earlier. It was just then that her thoughts turned to Lady Sarah. She must have been caught up somewhere in the confusion.

"I have to find someone," she said.

"There's no time for that. How can you think of anything other than our future?"

But she could not abandon Lady Sarah to her fate.

"She's a neighbor of mine. I saw her here earlier, poor thing. I had no clue she was a patient, and I can't leave her unprotected. Just let me talk to her. You'll help me find a way to save her. I beg you."

"We don't have time to look. Think of how many floors there are."

"Let me call out to her. If she's not too far away, she'll come to me, and we'll take her with us."

"Very well. I have other business here too."

Ferdinand wanted to destroy the electrical machines before leaving the tower. Contrary to what he had claimed, Lola imagined he'd had to suffer them.

As they ran through the corridors and up the stairs, he opened all the doors, clearly unable to remember the exact location of the laboratory. Trailing him, Lola shouted Lady Sarah's name. They climbed to the fourth floor and entered a room on the right. They'd found it. Lola and Lady Sarah, of course, had already destroyed much of the equipment. He stopped in front of the mess. The sight had rendered him speechless.

"I did this with my friend," said Lola proudly.

"You're a brave woman!"

A noise came from a corner of the room, startling Ferdinand. He rummaged through the debris and eventually flushed out Lady Sarah, who had been hiding in a closet.

When she saw Lola, she sighed in relief. "Oh, it's you! How fortunate! Why did you come back?"

"I told you I would come for you," said Lola. "I'm leaving this place. This gentleman wants to come with me. We will seek help outside."

"That's not all," Ferdinand said. "We're going to the Americas."

Lady Sarah stared at him and raised an eyebrow. "In this weather?"

"I'm an excellent navigator," replied Ferdinand, offended by her doubts. "And I apologize, but I can't take you. You'll have to manage on your own two feet."

"Could you at least help untie me?"

Ferdinand, acting very much the gentleman, set out to free her from her manacles. He started by trying some of his keys, then, losing patience, grabbed a piece of machinery and smashed the steel circles, causing Lady Sarah to quiver at each blow.

She broke free with a yelp of joy. "At last! Thank you!"

"Come with us! We may just manage this!" said Lola.

They ran back down the stairs, and when they arrived at the door to the room where the staff was incarcerated, Lady Sarah stopped. She could hear the commotion from within. Lola explained to her what they'd done.

"Let me in there," said Lady Sarah. "The police will come to rescue them. They'll think I'm a staff member. Are there uniforms in there?"

"Yes, but the others know you're not one of them. They will immediately report you," said Lola.

"That's true. I don't know what to do. What does it actually take to get out of this place?"

"Legally, you need a certificate signed by the doctor," explained Ferdinand. "That's what I have. But he's somewhat indisposed."

As they walked out back to the main building and into the courtyard, a number of patients followed them. Ferdinand and Lola started to make their way toward the gates, but as they neared them, Lady Sarah stopped and simply stood there, as if unable to move.

"Come, nobody is looking at certificates out here. We will get you to your father," said Lola.

But Lady Sarah remained in the midst of a cluster of delirious patients, which was rapidly increasing in size.

"Good luck," she said to Lola.

As the storm raged around them, Ferdinand urged a small group of patients to hunt down more of the staff and lock them up in the tower.

"Take straitjackets! Put them on by force! Make sure to give them their fill of laudanum!"

An old man, one arm hanging from his jacket, approached them and asked if they had seen his wife, Joséphine. "I have a campaign to manage, and they're holding me back," he muttered.

So it's true that madmen think they're Napoleon, Lola thought. *How strange.*

Dragged away by Ferdinand, she could not continue the conversation.

She was afraid how he would react to her sudden departure. Even though she did not hold Vidal and his methods in high esteem, she was aware that many of those kept in detention here were, in fact, insane, and knowing that the entire building was now in their hands frightened her. They were a danger to themselves and others.

She forced Ferdinand, who was pulling on her arm with impatience, to a standstill. Thoughts of the doctor had brought further questions to her mind.

"Did you actually see Vidal destroy Cousin's new will?"

"Indeed. He burned it in the fireplace. And I then watched him stab Cousin."

Lola spluttered. She had her witness! Ferdinand had seen everything. So it *was* Vidal.

"What about the clues? The letter opener . . . The blood . . . How did they get into Les Pavots?"

"Vidal made me do it. Forgive me, I know you love that girl, although she disrespects you. That's why I came to your house. Vidal knew everything about little Anna. About you too. He wanted me to meet you, to break into your house, and to leave the evidence."

"So he planned it all?"

"Of course. Why do you even doubt it?"

It was imperative now that Lola leave with Ferdinand and persuade him to tell the whole truth once they reached the mainland.

Clutched against him, she felt as though she were suffocating as they set off walking again. She had to switch roles. She needed to be in control here.

"You are so ingenious, my love! I will follow you to the end of the world. But please just allow me to breathe a little. I'm suffocating! Why don't we just hold hands?"

The sweetness in her voice convinced Ferdinand, who came to an abrupt halt and looked at her with emotion.

"How I love you! How happy we will be!"

He kissed her with ardor, and they continued making their way to the gate.

Still holding Lola's hand, he opened the gate and carefully locked it behind them. They were, by now, soaked to the bone.

Lola tried to calculate how to reach the fort on the other side of the island, but Ferdinand was already dragging her to the nearby beach, where a boathouse had been built into the rock.

They were fighting the elements as they moved. The gusts felt much more powerful now that they were outside the walls. Lola struggled against Ferdinand's strong grip.

38

SEASICKNESS

In the end, Maupassant's arguments had borne fruit, and Valantin had decided to come with us to the island.

Before we boarded the *Bel-Ami*, Valantin arrived with two of his henchmen, just in time.

Valantin couldn't bring his usual contingent of officers. He explained how he hoped to see the commander on the island and that with a few soldiers, they would be able to fetch Vidal and take him back to Cannes for questioning.

Despite this change of heart, Valantin had not wanted to interrupt the judicial machine, and the prison van had continued to make its way to Grasse, braving the torrential rains and furious winds to take Anna Martin to the courtrooms.

The girl would be alone at her trial. If we couldn't bring Vidal or Ferdinand back as suspects, who knew what would happen to her?

To our great displeasure, Valantin had brought Rodot along.

Bernard and Raymond, Maupassant's crew, handed me a piece of rope and told me to tie myself to the rail around the deck. I didn't believe myself to be prone to seasickness, but with the accumulation of the storm, my feverish state, and my anxiety, I started to feel the most dreadful stomach cramps. My body couldn't take it anymore.

From this position, I was able to follow all the maneuvers of the two crew members, who were impeded greatly by the aggression of the storm and taking the names of Maupassant and Valantin in vain as they struggled to man the boat.

Maupassant was warming himself on the lower deck with Mario and Valantin.

The two brigadiers preferred to stay outside. They were feeling as sick as I was. Rodot proved as much when he leaned over the guardrail and released the contents of his stomach.

We'd only covered perhaps a quarter of the distance to the island when a violent nausea took hold of me and prevented me from following events.

Throughout the crossing, I stayed bent over the side of the boat, returning to nature what little food I had eaten since that morning. And because the onset of a cold gave no sign of surrender, I felt quite the martyr.

Although I'd been drenched when I'd boarded, there were no words to describe how wet I was by this point. As we neared the first island, the waves surged into a vortex, which we narrowly escaped. Who would have thought that this little stretch of water, ordinarily so quiet, could turn into a nightmare of these proportions? Now I understood better why no boat would go out, why Gaglio had refused to risk his vessel, why fishermen—men with a good deal of common sense—had not wanted to risk their lives! Cannes was not on the Atlantic coastline, yet I finally understood one of the remarks I'd overheard back in the café: *When a storm blows here, the devil awakens.*

Our arrival was far from gentle, although the pier on the north side of the island was well protected. The boat moved as if consumed by a rage, hitting the edge of the pier.

As I tried to put a foot down onto dry land, the boat jolted back and forth, and I failed to find my balance. Maupassant, who was already ashore, leaned over and grabbed me by the waist. With great vigor, he lifted me up as if I were made of nothing but straw. Even though he'd been frail of late, the man still had great strength.

As he placed me down on the boards, he held me a little longer than was necessary, trying to catch my eye. I gave him a miserable and cold look, but it appeared to have no effect.

"Listen, I know you're as strong as an ox," I said before sneezing loudly, "but just calm yourself. You've more than made your point. You can let me go now."

He laughed as we followed Mario, who was already running up the small, muddy incline at the other end of the pier.

"Stay on the *Bel-Ami* and wait for us!" cried Maupassant to his crew.

He had no need to say it twice. The two men secured the boat before rushing into the cabin.

When we reached the first fork in the path, Valantin left to find the commander, ordering his men to accompany us and help where necessary. This order did not please Rodot, who looked at Maupassant with a threatening eye. Mario stayed as far away from Rodot as possible. He wasn't sure what had happened but must have sensed he couldn't trust him.

Nevertheless, the five of us continued toward the south side of the island.

In front of the large gates leading to the mansion, we found ourselves unable to advance any farther. The doors were locked, and no one answered our calls.

"The sound of the storm must be preventing them from hearing us," said Mario.

We could not imagine, of course, that the whole place was now in the hands of the patients and that they had no means of opening the gates. My cold was not likely to improve as we stood under the ever-worsening downpour.

Mario spotted some slightly protruding stones in the wall and began to climb. He was light and agile. Once on the other side, he smashed the wooden bar that held closed a small doorway next to the large double gates. We had another Maupassant on our hands.

Several people ran from the entrance of the building across the garden toward us. To our amazement, they rushed past us, out the doorway, and into the pine forest below.

We ran to the main building and walked through to the entrance hall.

The sight that awaited us left us stunned.

Dozens of people were mingling, and the ambiance was of an astonishing disorder. It took us several minutes to understand that these people were the residents and that there was no trace of a nurse or guardian in sight.

In some of the living areas, the quieter patients played cards. Others were having tea. One was performing a Chopin piece on the piano. However, some were curled up in corners, trembling, their eyes closed, clearly terrified of the chaos.

It was evident that there were certain patients who had never before known this part of the house. And they were the most threatening of characters. They wandered around grimacing and instilling fear in those near them with their incoherent reasoning. They were talking to people that only they could see. It almost seemed as though they were parodying what popular mythology told us of madmen.

The officers who accompanied us, including the infamous Rodot, did not lead the way, and I am sure they would have been more comfortable facing barbaric hordes of Prussians rather than the ghosts of humanity before our eyes.

As we explored further, a plaque on a door indicated that we now stood in front of Vidal's office. We knocked before turning the handle. But there was no way through. It was locked. Of course, it was.

A man's frail voice could be heard from within. "Who is it?"

"Police! Open the door!" Rodot shouted.

The handle turned, and we entered.

Vidal stood there, a stream of blood pouring from his forehead. He seemed relieved to see us. Behind him, in an armchair, with her back half-turned, sat a woman in a pale-blue quilted satin bathrobe, sipping a liqueur as if she were visiting a friend's house. I immediately knew her. My heart skipped a beat.

Lady Sarah.

She turned to us with a welcoming smile.

"Look at the state of your dress, Miss Fletcher! We keep running into each other, do we not? Might fate be playing a wicked trick?"

Maupassant looked between us, appearing displeased. He clicked his heels together like the soldier he hadn't been for these past twenty years.

"Very well! Since no one has taken the pains, I will introduce myself. Guy de Maupassant, writer and friend of Miss Fletcher. I hope your stay here has been of benefit to you. The last time I saw you, I must say you looked in better health. Although, it was from a distance, granted."

"How gallant," she replied ironically. "Have we previously met?"

"Four years ago at a ball at the Cercle Nautique, I believe."

"Really?" she said, pretending to search her memory.

"You had upset our mutual friend somewhat," Maupassant said, nodding at me.

She gave him a dismissive pout. "I don't remember you. Notwithstanding, I may have heard of your name."

Maupassant sighed in exasperation. I knew it was intentional on Lady Sarah's part and that she most certainly knew who Guy de Maupassant was. For who hadn't heard of him?

He turned to Vidal. "What happened?"

Vidal ignored him and addressed me. "Please sit down. I don't know why you're here, and I don't understand what's happening in my establishment. I decided to wait for it all to return to a state of calm."

He then spoke to the officers in a dry tone. "Gentlemen, could you bring some order to the place?"

The agents were so disturbed by the situation that they had forgotten, albeit temporarily, what they had come for—to interrogate Vidal, to find Ferdinand, and to save Lola.

"Go to the west tower," Lady Sarah told them. "You will find a number of nursing staff locked up in the laundry facilities there. You'll need the keys before you go. They can then help you put the patients back in their rooms."

"There is a set in that closet there. I would be happy to accompany you," Vidal whispered, "but it may not be a good idea. It's better if they don't see me for the moment. Plus, I need to protect these ladies and gentlemen until our guests are back *in situ*."

"I'm going with them," said Mario. "I need to find my sister." He took me aside and whispered, "If I find my chance to get that pig Rodot, I'm taking it!"

Before I could say anything to stop him, all three of them left the room.

I heard Mario call out in a mocking tone, "Come on, Brigadier, they're just like any other human being."

His father's alcohol-induced outbursts may have accustomed him to the behaviors caused by mental disorders, as he did not seem at all worried about what lay ahead.

Maupassant, perhaps hoping to come across as sardonic but unable to do so, said to Lady Sarah, "Aren't you going to join the other patients?"

If he wanted to humiliate her by reminding her that she was within these walls as a resident, he didn't manage to do so. She laughed and gave him a detached look, but I still perceived a shadow of relief in her tone.

"I am well again now," she said, waving a discharge certificate that had been signed by the doctor.

"Already? But when were you admitted?"

"Only two days ago. My stay has been short, I know. This is because Dr. Vidal's methods are extraordinary. Miraculous, even. Isn't that right, Doctor?" Vidal looked uncomfortable as she continued. "Or the diagnosis was wrong. It happens sometimes."

Vidal coughed, then sat behind his desk, while I took him to task.

"We've come to collect our friend Lola Deslys. Have you seen her? She left Cannes at dawn."

His discomfort was visible. "No. Madame Deslys, you say?"

He turned the pages of the register, as if searching for the name.

"He's lying," Lady Sarah said calmly. "I first met her in the electrotherapy room. That's right, electrotherapy. This gentleman is ahead of his time, you see. He studied with Duchêne himself. He can afford all kinds of fanciful research, using his patients as test subjects, isn't that right, Vidal?"

"Don't listen to her. She's confused," he replied, glaring at her.

He must have felt safe in his locked office, particularly as the officers had now departed, but he did seem irritated about being caught in a blatant lie.

His words and especially his eyes had an inhibiting effect on Lady Sarah. She opened her mouth and then closed it again, turning toward the window, giving up saying anything more.

"And you know Ferdinand de Bret, don't you?" I asked.

"Of course," said Vidal. "He's Cousin's nephew. Cousin was murdered. I have some information on that matter, as it so happens."

"Save your revelations for the police. Just tell us if you've seen de Bret or Madame Deslys, if you please."

"No. I've seen neither of them. Why?"

"He's still lying," said Lady Sarah. "I saw them both a little while ago. Ferdinand de Bret is going to inherit a fortune, I understand."

I exchanged a worried glance with Maupassant. Lady Sarah noticed this. However, she refrained from voicing her thoughts yet again.

"I think Monsieur de Bret misunderstands his inheritance," said Maupassant. "Monsieur Cousin discovered a daughter he had never met. She was born of an adulterous affair. It appears he passed on all his property to her. Monsieur de Bret is too late, I'm afraid."

"I don't think so, no," said the doctor. "We know about the girl, but it seems Monsieur Cousin did not have time to write a new will. It is therefore the old one that will prevail, and in that one, Monsieur Ferdinand de Bret is the sole heir."

"And what about you and your work here, Dr. Vidal?"

"Precisely. It is provided for in the original will. All was duly registered. Monsieur de Bret must continue to finance this establishment."

Vidal gave Lady Sarah a stern look, as if to warn her not to intervene again, and continued to speak. She didn't even deign to turn her head fully toward him, but her expression was closed, stilted. I, who knew her well, understood she was quite desperate to speak but that something was preventing her from expressing herself. What did she know?

The doctor continued, becoming increasingly confident, seeming to add some refining touches to his story. The way he spoke was befitting of a great orator.

"It so happens that I, too, was in Cannes on the night of the crime. I followed Monsieur de Bret, who had planned, with my agreement, to talk to Cousin. He wanted to plead his case with his uncle, you see. There were some odd goings-on that night, and I'm certain you will be interested in my testimony. I saw Ferdinand enter the villa. I then spotted a young girl dressed in pink just outside. She was disheveled and holding a sharp object that looked to be covered in blood. She seemed to be running away. In fact, it was as if she'd seen a ghost. She simply disappeared into the night.

"I decided to enter the villa and arrived in the library to the sorry sight of Cousin. He was bathed in a pool of blood. Ferdinand, who had been searching the house for Cousin, then came in behind me. I rushed to keep him away from the scene. I pushed him toward the porch. 'Go have fun, young man,' I said. 'For once, you're in town. Why not go to the theater? It's not every day you get my permission!' I laughed when I said this, trying to make him feel at ease. But he replied that he had come to see his uncle. 'Your uncle has gone to the theater,' I told him. And I watched as he walked away. He looked quite sprightly, if I remember."

Lady Sarah shrugged, and the slightest of sighs escaped her lips, but she didn't refute anything the doctor had just said. If she had knowledge of something important, why didn't she say as much? Though, how could she have known anything? She hadn't been there.

"Ah! And that's when Ferdinand met Lola Deslys," said Maupassant.

"But we already know how he met her," I exclaimed. "He visited Les Pavots with Paul Antoine. What really happened that night at Cousin's?"

"I just told you!" cried Vidal, now visibly upset.

If he were to be believed, it meant Anna was the one who'd killed Cousin, her own father—something a people's court would not look kindly upon.

Lady Sarah spoke clearly and slowly as she looked me in the eye. "De Bret is somewhere outside. He wants to take your friend with him to the Americas and marry her, after receiving his inheritance, no doubt. He says he is an excellent navigator."

This shocked me. Ferdinand de Bret and Lola were somewhere out there amid the raging elements?

A scream emanated from the doctor's throat. "You!" he shouted, his features distorted by rage.

He ran at Lady Sarah and grabbed her by the throat. Maupassant pulled at him from behind but struggled to bring him under control.

I searched the room and found a straitjacket in a drawer. Between the three of us, we managed to put it on him.

Maupassant wrote a message for the police explaining that Vidal was a key witness, perhaps even a suspect, and that he had attacked Lady Sarah. He gave her the note.

"You will give this to the officers when they return. Keep an eye on him. Lock yourself in after we leave."

We left the office and went in search of Mario. When we found him, we explained the situation, and the three of us left the place.

I had just started to warm up when I found myself out in the storm again like a drowned rat.

We had to hold on to one another for fear of the wind blowing us off our feet.

"There's a shelter down on the beach. We can look out to sea from there. They will have left the island already!" Mario shouted.

39

A Frail Vessel

While we had been talking with Vidal, trying to clear up the whole story, and Mario had been trying to get back at Brigadier Rodot while looking for his sister, Lola had been trying to drag Ferdinand to speak with the commander of the fort. To her, de Bret was an essential witness and could help her get Vidal under lock and key, thereby saving Anna.

But he held her close to him. He could see she was resisting, and this angered him. He pulled her to the boathouse.

He tried to open the door without letting go of Lola's hand, which was not an easy task, because she was now protesting with all her might.

"This is madness! Come with me to the fort instead. We can speak with the commander. He'll have people there who can help us. We'll be safe. Please, Ferdinand! Stop being so petulant! You can see that it's impossible to navigate in this weather! Let's at least wait until there is a lull."

"We will wait here!" he roared.

He managed to pull away a bar from the door, and they stepped inside to shelter. Ferdinand may have wanted to go to sea more than anything, but he was also evidently enjoying this moment of respite. He took her in his arms.

"To think that you betrayed me," she said in a sad tone. "You forced that meeting with Paul Antoine in order to get into my house!"

"I beg you. Forgive me. I didn't yet know you as I do now! How could I have guessed that fate would put an angel like you in my path? I believed every word Vidal said, and I was simply following his advice to try to get a closer look at the girl who was to disinherit me."

He proudly showed her a scar on his thumb.

"I even deliberately cut myself with the letter opener to stain that insolent girl's dress. I had it with me the entire time at the theater and hid it in her room while your whole house slept. Including her! I don't know what I would have done if she had awoken. But any further thoughts of manipulation left me once I came to know you better. The next day I was supposed to return to the island, but I had to see you again. I had to breathe the same air as you, to spend another night with my most beloved one. You see? And then there was that duel! I went there in the early morning with Paul Antoine as my second. Then the next night, I came to you!"

"I was unwell," murmured Lola. "You took advantage of my weakness."

Lola leaned into his chest. She feigned submission to try to convince him to go to the fort.

The wind caused the door to blow open and clatter against the rocks. The foam from the crashing waves splashed their faces.

"No! I cannot bear your reproaches. One day you will understand. You will forgive me."

He hugged her tightly.

"Perhaps," she said, then startled with a sudden thought. "Oh, my God! The next day . . . the portrait of Emina. You understood it all. It was a possible lead, and you wanted it gone."

"Yes, I'm the one who stole it. I was jealous . . . That abominable girl. All that time you spent looking for clues to save her. I couldn't suffer it. I took it from your purse, and I went to the end of the Croisette and swam back to the island."

"You swam?" she asked in an admiring tone despite herself.

"I did. I had to come back here to think things over. I needed to find a way to receive my inheritance and take you away from all this. I knew Vidal would be angry. I didn't want him to learn of my love for you. Aristide helped me return to my room discreetly. I don't think Vidal noticed I'd even gone."

"But . . . What . . . ?"

"No more questions!"

Ferdinand's enamored expression suddenly turned to rage. He grabbed her by the waist, stepped over the edge of Vidal's boat, and threw her down onto the open bottom. Her forehead hit a bench, and she felt overcome by the violence of the blow.

Before she was able to stand, he grabbed the oars and pushed the boat out of the boathouse and into the waters below. He fought with all his strength against the current.

Lola tried to jump from the boat, but Ferdinand dropped the oars, grabbed a rope, and tied their wrists together.

Driven by what appeared to be superhuman strength, Ferdinand continued to row furiously. Once they were a few dozen meters from the shore, he threw the keys deep into the water.

"What the hell is wrong with you all?" Ferdinand shouted out toward the raging waves, as if addressing hostile pagan gods.

"Ferdinand? What's come over you?"

He repeated her words. *"Ferdinand? What's come over you?"*

He took a slim piece of card from inside his jacket. Emina's portrait. In a theatrical gesture, he brandished it to those furious gods of his before tearing it to pieces and throwing them out into the sea. The shredded fragments of the likeness of the young woman with the most tragic of destinies floated for a moment on the surface before Lola lost sight of them.

It was at this moment that it all became clear: Lola finally recognized Ferdinand as the dangerous madman he was.

"But then . . . but then . . . ," she stammered, her emotions overwhelming her.

"Yes! Do you truly believe I'd give up my inheritance because of your stupid loyalty to that silly little girl? Say your prayers. These are your very final moments, my love. You're the only one who knows the truth."

"And . . . Vidal?"

"Vidal won't say a word. He has too much to lose! I promised him I would help him, just as my uncle had, and I doubt Cousin would have continued sending money once I'd left. Vidal was very worried about losing that support."

"That's why I suspected him. What a fool I am!"

"If he talks, I also have a lot to say of him."

Lola felt absolutely defeated as she wondered, *Did his uncle have him locked up for good reason? Is he out of his mind? His logic is not that of a simpleton. He reasons well enough. But if he's sane, it would mean he murders to his advantage, with calculation and coldness. And he pretended to love me. Did his uncle know of his violent nature? Or did he have him locked up because he was mismanaging his fortune? Did he hope that Vidal's methods would put Ferdinand back on the right path? Where does madness begin and end? Can you be a killer and still be sane? Isn't it always madness to take a life?*

She suddenly thought of Aristide. "Aristide . . . You also . . ."

"Oh no! You're not going to continue with this, are you?"

"What did Aristide have to do with this? He didn't do anything to you!"

"He accompanied me to Cannes that day. I knew the lout would talk, that he would betray me. But that was the doctor's doing."

"What do you mean?"

"He allowed Aristide to come with me, you see."

"But you were seen by everyone in Cannes! Everyone knows you were there that night. Even me. Aristide or no Aristide."

"That's right! But the fewer witnesses, the better! And you know, my darling, you mustn't make the mistake of believing an individual who looks like a good man, is a little stupid, and speaks with a cheap accent can't be harmful all the same."

"My darling?" questioned Lola.

"Exactly. Likewise, do not imagine that because I have to eliminate you, I love you any less. You're the love of my life, Lola! I will never forget you!"

Lola held her hands to her ears.

Her lovely Ferdinand. One of the finest actors she'd ever known. Not only was he a lunatic, but he was dangerous. A homicidal maniac of the worst kind—someone who killed by calculation.

The conversation had been conducted in fits and starts, while water poured over them and the sea continued to move violently. Lola had to scream to be heard, and Ferdinand spat his words out to the heavens above, as if taking God as his witness.

They had arrived almost in the middle of the channel between the two islands when Mario spotted them from the shore.

The frail boat appeared and disappeared, bobbing above and below the horizon, sometimes driven into deep troughs and sometimes rising up on the foaming crests of the waves. To Mario, the figures on the vessel looked as fragile as insects on a twig.

"Lola can't swim," he said. "We have to catch them before they head out into the open. If they move any farther offshore, we'll lose them."

"Go get a fisherman from the north of the island," said Maupassant. "Have him lend you a boat."

"It's too far away, and none of them will want to help us in this weather," said Mario.

"Go and get the *Bel-Ami*, then!" he shouted.

"It will be too late," I said. "By the time we cross the island and make our way back over here, they will be out of reach."

Maupassant frowned. "You're right, and Raymond and Bernard will not sail her for us. They can't swim either."

"I know what to do!" Mario shouted. "Miss Fletcher taught me well. I'm going to swim to them."

Before Mario could take off his shoes, Maupassant grabbed him by his arms and told him to look for ropes and buoys so he could help pull them back in. Maupassant was not going to risk having such an act of heroism taken away from him by a child!

Mario didn't want to do as he was told. Maupassant towered over him and shouted, "You're too young to die! And although I don't think I'm that old, I've had enough adventures should the reaper come for me today."

As he was talking, he held Mario's arm with one hand while taking off his shoes with the other.

I felt giddy with anticipation. What was the purpose of all the swimming trophies I'd won in my youth if not to try to save Lola today?

Without thinking, I started to undress, because swimming with my heavy petticoats and oilskin coat would be a guaranteed way to sink. They were already soaked, but I threw my clothes and boots into the shelter, ran along the jetty in front of the building in my light petticoat and shirt, shivering from top to toe, and dived into the water.

Maupassant followed, leaving Mario no choice but to stay on shore and watch out for our return, for we would be sure to need help.

Our movements, although difficult in such violent turbulence, led us chaotically toward them.

Fortunately, Ferdinand was a poor sailor, although he would never have said as much. He was rowing in a very disorderly manner, and the breakers were positioned against him, preventing him from moving as fast as he would have liked. The current was now pushing the boat inland.

Each wave threatened to smash up their pitiful rowing boat, while we fought against the movements of a sea determined to engulf us. There were moments when I thought I had finally reached them and others where I couldn't see a trace of their vessel.

When Ferdinand saw us heading toward him, he began to yell in our direction, but his words were lost in the crash of the waves and deafening thunderclaps above.

Lola, her face dripping with either seawater or tears, crouched beside him, saying nothing. She looked at us with anguish. When we thought that one of us might grab the side of the boat, the current would come up from under the vessel and push us away.

Suddenly Lola screamed, "Careful, careful! He's got a knife!"

I managed to make out a sharp object in Ferdinand's grasp. He looked reproachfully at Lola, which made me fear the worst. I had managed to grab the ledge. Ferdinand leaned in toward me with a scream of rage. He started striking out at the edge of the boat with his weapon, and with the good fortune that often accompanies scoundrels, he managed to catch my hand. Blood spurted and started running down my arm as I screamed in pain and let go.

"If one of you tries to approach again, I'll kill her!"

"He's going to kill me, anyway!" cried Lola.

He then grabbed Lola and took her in his arms. He whispered something into her ear as he held his knife close to her face.

Coughing and spitting, I managed to throw one foot over the edge of the boat and pull myself up. Maupassant swam up behind me and lifted me the rest of the way. I fell inside, feeling weak and leaving traces of blood in my wake.

I feared for my life as I caught Ferdinand's eye. There was something wild about the way he looked at me.

He let go of Lola, took the rope that connected them, and used his knife to cut it. Despite how difficult this must have been, he accomplished the task with incredible speed. He then pulled Lola up to her feet and threw her into the water before jumping in after her.

I rushed over to where Lola had been sitting just seconds earlier.

It all happened far too quickly for me to have been able to prevent it. I tried to convince myself that had he wanted to stab Lola or me, his knife would have made easy work of it. But then I realized that, in fact, he might want to drown her, but I couldn't grasp his motives.

Was he trying to make her death look like an accident? This may well have been his original intention, but it would have been difficult for him to counter our testimony now.

As I tried to reach out to Lola with one of the oars, Maupassant swam around the boat with a vigorous stroke. Lola appeared and disappeared on the surface of the water. She was fighting for her life. Maupassant dived into the waves several times and eventually came back to the surface, holding her in his arms. He threw her over the edge of the boat as if she weighed no more than a parcel before pulling himself up beside her.

I grabbed Lola's petticoats and managed to pull her fully inside, and Maupassant threw himself back and landed heavily behind us.

For a moment, it felt as though we were safe.

However, despite the terror Ferdinand had caused, none of us had it in us to let a man die before our eyes. I tried to call out to him as he treaded water a short distance away.

But the movement of the boat was too much for me. I squatted and bent my head over the side to vomit. Lola sat next to me, holding on to the bench with every ounce of strength she had. She looked catatonic. She had just escaped death, and she knew it.

"Come back! You're going to drown!" Maupassant shouted to Ferdinand.

He held out an oar so that he could grab it, but Ferdinand turned from us and started to swim away at a fast pace. He seemed to be heading toward the shore of Saint-Honorat.

Had he misjudged the weight of his clothes? He would be dragged to the bottom of the ocean in no time at all. Or was it premeditated? He turned to us and screamed, "Wait for me, Lola! I'll come back for you once I have my fortune!"

His head sank under the surface for several seconds. He came back up, gasping for breath, spitting, a sudden panic in his eyes. He repeated this pattern again, twice, and then did not reappear. Lola had turned her back on him. Was it beyond her strength to see him die? Or, on the contrary, did his inevitable end leave her indifferent?

Maupassant, an agnostic like myself, clearly had no pious thoughts as the dramatic scene unfolded. He made no sign of the cross as he watched him go under. I felt saddened.

But Lola was already thinking ahead.

"Can we make it back to the island?" she whimpered.

She knew we were not out of danger. We still had to endure more rough seas. But we had an experienced sailor with us, and the current was taking us where we wanted to go.

Maupassant skillfully navigated the boat back toward the small jetty in front of Vidal's mansion.

But no matter how hard he tried, he couldn't steer the vessel through the last stretch of water to reach the shelter.

From the mainland, Mario made desperate gestures. He was screaming, but we couldn't hear a word. On the third attempt, we understood that he was telling us to go around the island and back toward the *Bel-Ami*.

Maupassant was thinking about his next course of action just as we felt a rock hit the hull. We heard a sinister crack. Lola screamed. Of course, we knew we had to get out of the boat, but the reefs were so sharp and the waves so chaotic that we, too, could drown or be thrown against the rocks.

As the vessel propelled us closer to dry land, Maupassant firmly grabbed Lola, certainly believing, and rightly so, that I did not need his help. We all jumped.

Hurt, bruised, and bloodied, we managed to throw ourselves onto the wooden jetty.

No sooner had Lola hit the ground than she scrambled to her feet and clamored, "Alive! We're alive!"

40

A Night at the Barracks

I retrieved my clothes from where I'd left them and dressed stealthily. My hand was bleeding heavily. I was in shock with the sheer misery of the situation I now found myself in.

Maupassant picked up his jacket from the ground and fished out a special ointment from his pocket. He was the king of bits of string and miracle remedies. He had a gift when it came to finding just what you needed at the bottom of one of his many pockets.

He tore a piece of my petticoat and smeared it with his ointment before wrapping it around my hand.

We then walked with haste toward Vidal's sanatorium as the rain continued to pound down. On the way, Lola told us everything she had learned from Ferdinand, and we shared with her news of the situation that had come to us via Murier.

A group of soldiers came to meet us and escorted us through the courtyard.

The residents had been returned to their respective rooms, duly locked in, and the staff had regained control.

The soldiers, now placed at the disposal of Valantin and supervised by the commander, had intervened and managed the unrest superbly.

I could not help but think of all those poor lost souls confined within such cold walls against their will.

In the first lounge we entered, Lady Sarah was having tea, chatting with a woman whom she introduced to Maupassant as Duchesse Marguerite d'Estorg. She looked at me from the corner of her eye and turned her head as if she hadn't seen me. I remembered that this lady had, last winter, launched a trend that involved disguising oneself as a man at masked balls. Then suddenly we hadn't heard from her. So this was where she'd been hiding.

We were taken to the doctor's office. Lady Sarah followed us. Rodot was guarding the door. Lola stiffened as she neared him. He made a despicable sound at the back of his throat as he watched her approach, as if he were going to spit.

The commander welcomed us into the doctor's office with eagerness. As a matter of fact, it was especially to Lola that he gave this warm welcome. I imagined she already knew him, but they acted as though they were meeting for the first time.

He sent one of his men down to the kitchens to prepare some hot chocolate and stoked the cinders in the fireplace. A nurse brought us towels, and we wrapped ourselves in them. We started to feel better, despite our shivers. Another nurse properly bandaged my hand, which was no longer bleeding. Was this the effect of Maupassant's miracle ointment?

The doctor had had his straitjacket removed. Outraged by the treatment he had received, he was subjected to a brief interrogation by Valantin.

He failed to understand much of Vidal's version of the situation, and for good reason, since the doctor provided nothing but false accounts and various accusations with the hope of exonerating himself, no doubt.

He spoke vehemently of Anna, offering invented details to try to have her convicted of Cousin's murder. But as we started discussing Aristide's death, it became increasingly difficult to blame Anna.

When he learned, upon hearing Maupassant's account, that Ferdinand de Bret had drowned, he changed his story and started accusing the banker's nephew instead.

Even if it meant giving up the inheritance, Vidal evidently preferred to save his skin. However, he had misjudged the degree of his involvement in the eyes of the authorities and the importance of our testimonies, and he was summarily arrested. When Rodot entered the room to handcuff him, Lola shuddered.

She wanted to get back to Cannes at all costs, worried upon discovering that Anna was alone in front of the judges in Grasse. But the wind hadn't yet died down.

We had to wait for the storm to pass before we could return to the mainland.

Lola detested the thought of spending the night in the mansion, so traumatized was she by her experience there. She preferred to accept the commander's invitation to sleep at the barracks, where there were rooms reserved for visiting civilians.

And so we all followed her, relieved, too, not to have to remain in such a place.

Lola mocked the men present as she spoke to the room. "For you gentlemen, perhaps staying the night here wouldn't be such a frightful experience. Every insane man is considered a genius, is he not? Yet if a woman considers herself one, she is declared insane!"

Lady Sarah approved with enthusiasm. A senior nurse had agreed that she could leave. Thus, she enlisted the services of a chambermaid who would accompany her. They both followed us to the fort.

Vidal stayed all night in his apartments, guarded by Rodot and his colleague.

Part of the guard also remained on the premises.

When we arrived at the fort, we were assigned rooms. I shared mine with Lola. The thought of us being in the same space eased my pain. We were brought cadet uniforms as dry clothing. I was delighted. The more masculine the better, as far as I'm concerned.

And the fact that our trials and tribulations had ended like something out of an Offenbach farce also tickled me.

The commander was thrilled to have guests. It was a jolly gathering at the dining table that evening. Maupassant went to reassure his crew and later insisted on sleeping in the cabin of his dear *Bel-Ami* to keep them company despite the noise caused by the storm, which was still just as powerful.

During the meal, Lola cheered us all by singing. Yet some of our party were still desperately grieved as we imagined Anna in Grasse.

Despite how cold I still felt and with my growing fever, injured hand, and dreadful fatigue, I managed to stay up for a few more hours. I retired to our room before anyone else, and I couldn't tell if Lola had joined me there later or if she had slept in the commander's room, because when I woke the next morning, she was already up and dressed.

We were given our clothes back dry.

During the night, the storm had vanished just as quickly as it had come.

The blinding sun shone brightly over the damage the wind and rain had left behind.

Vidal, handcuffed, was taken away by the police on the first steamer, and Lady Sarah and her new chambermaid went along with them. The four of us followed on the *Bel-Ami*.

Mario was livid that he hadn't managed to carry out his act of revenge on Rodot. He told us in great detail of every missed opportunity.

I managed to calm him down by explaining that he should now turn his thoughts to the future.

François Tassart, out of his mind with concern, was waiting for his master on the docks. Maupassant was to take his brother, Hervé, to Montpellier, and François wanted to accompany him.

Commissioner Valantin and his men took Vidal directly to Grasse. We walked over to watch him being placed in a police vehicle. Prior to leaving, Rodot informed us that we were not allowed to see Anna.

"Hush now! I'm going, anyway!" said Lola.

Lady Sarah was nowhere to be seen.

We spent some time back at the house, washing, changing, and making ourselves look presentable. I then coupled Gaza to our carriage.

Pierre Gaglio, Mario's boss, had been very angry when he'd seen us arrive on the shores of Cannes and had told the young man he was to return to work in haste.

But Murier, who met us just as we were leaving Les Pavots, was happy to escort us. He couldn't take his eyes off Lola. Rosalie wanted to be part of the expedition, too, of course, and she joined them in the back of the car.

As we were about to set off, I suddenly felt very ill. I had hidden from everyone the truth about my state of fatigue, but the fever was catching up with me now.

Lola forced me to return to the house and go to bed. Rosalie made me an herbal tea and gave me a bottle of Mariani wine to help, should I start to feel lonely.

"Who will drive?" I lamented.

"No one is indispensable," Lola said, "but I will miss you! I'd much rather your health were fully restored. I'll have Gustave called."

Gustave was her former coachman. She had been forced to let him go due to financial instability, but he had found a position at Delpiano, a local cab company. However, since the firm had fallen into bankruptcy, he had been unemployed.

"I think he'll be happy to come home and work for us," she said.

Later, as I heard the carriage move away from the house, I fell into a restful sleep.

They had to wait some time before the investigating judge would hear them. It seems that Commissioner Valantin had not been fooled by Vidal. He was to be held in custody pending his trial. The charges were defined as extortion, misappropriation of private documents, and impeding the course of justice. Murier had a great deal about which to write. Complicity in murder, however, was not even mentioned.

.Our little Anna Martin was released, and when everyone returned to Les Pavots, I was dead to the world and didn't hear a peep.

Epilogue

I don't know what Rosalie had put in my tea, but after sweating the entire night, I woke the next day as fresh as a daisy and full of renewed energy. I rushed into Anna's room.

The happiness I felt when I saw her sleeping peacefully in her pink quilted bed was beyond all description.

However, as the days unfolded, we came to understand that our Anna was in shock. She jumped at the slightest noise and couldn't stand the voices of men. Except Mario's, for he came to see her every time his boss gave him even a moment off.

Sherry spent long hours near her, following her every move.

I advised her to get a lawyer should she wish to request Cousin's inheritance, being his only daughter. I explained that she was now a very rich heiress.

This would have been easy enough with the will, but it had been destroyed. All that remained was Cousin's letter to his notary, who said that he was going to change the will, but he did not say in whose favor.

By bringing the case to court, Anna could easily prove that she was Cousin's illegitimate daughter, especially with Buttura's testimony, but she knew that this would cause a scandal.

With everything she had just been through, she didn't feel strong enough to take on such a fight. It didn't matter to her that the state would recover the immense fortune. She never wanted to hear of it again.

There was also no trial for Cousin's murder since Ferdinand, now considered officially to have been the assailant, was declared deceased. The case was closed, and little by little, the turmoil it had caused us all began to drift from our memories.

I expected to hear about Lady Sarah's trial against her husband and father, but I never got news of it. Lola had returned the contract to her. They had met at Madame Alexandra's. Lola would later tell me that she had no desire to receive further payment of any kind for her service, not after what they had gone through together in the asylum. Since then, no one knew what had become of my former mistress and lover. She was no longer in Cannes.

In order to attempt to forget these dark events and bring joy back into our hearts—especially Anna's—we organized a dinner at home one Sunday.

We cleared the furniture from the second floor to set up a large table worthy of the Grand Hôtel. Rosalie ordered the entire feast from the Faisan Doré, and we were given the best of everything they had: ortolans, foie gras, crayfish, and belle Hélène pears, not to mention the famous peach melba ices!

In the middle of the preparations, Basile, the messenger boy, appeared as if by magic. He was smiling, as he'd obviously taken a detour to Rosalie's kitchen and gorged himself on cakes. He gave a note to Lola, which she read and promptly threw out the window.

"Is there an answer?" asked Basile.

"If you're asked for one, you can tell him that he can chase all he wants, but not to hold his breath."

The child laughed at the idea but then looked troubled.

"Will you remember that?" she asked.

"I could never say it!" he said. "He's a high-ranking man! He'd have me whipped!"

She searched through a drawer on her chest and handed him a large five-franc coin. He whispered with admiration.

"Goodness! I like coming here! You're my favorite customer now, lady!"

Rejoicing, he ran back downstairs.

When I had a moment, I went outside to pick up the crumpled paper from the lawn. It was a note from Eugène's father, Edmond de Bréville. The cur hadn't forgotten the promise he'd made to Lola that he'd send her a message with a choice of times and dates. I giggled as I imagined his reaction to her response.

I went into the kitchen to help Rosalie. Anna was with her, smeared with flour. She was learning to make brioche with candied fruit.

Little Basile was there, too, watching with great attention.

"Basile," Anna said, "you will tell your sister that I will visit her within the week to thank her. Without her, I wonder if I would still be alive today."

She handed the child a little bit of the dough she had flattened out and asked him to cut it with diamonds to make biscuits. He took a penknife out of his pocket and began his task with great seriousness, sticking out his tongue as he did so.

I exclaimed, "I think we have a future chef on our hands here!"

The compliment gave him cause to blush. He pretended to grumble, but I could sense the emotional effect of my words.

There was something magical happening in that kitchen. It was as though he'd found his calling.

When Basile later left the house, I asked Anna to explain what she'd said to him.

"You never told us under what circumstances Basile's sister found you that night."

She whispered, "I was hidden in a cellar, and the door was ajar. It was on Impasse de la Bergerie. Thérésine came in looking for something and saw me crouched in a corner. She took me into her home, gave me food, and allowed me to sleep there for a few hours. She told me that she worked in a laundry and that she knew Lola. I ran away in the early morning. I didn't want her to get in any trouble."

As evening came, only our closest friends remained at the house. Mario was sitting next to Anna. But she quickly disappeared back into the kitchen with Rosalie. He followed her, preferring their company to ours. Paul Antoine had also joined us. He blamed himself for having introduced Ferdinand to Lola.

"And I thought I had you financially secure for life! How much I have yet to learn of this world."

Lola, who never allowed herself to feel downtrodden for long, had met a certain Marquis de Fumerol at Madame Alexandra's. She had been hanging on to his coattails ever since. The marquis had clearly fallen in love—as they always did—and never left her side.

And he always brought some of the finest wines when he visited, so I was also somewhat pleased by his constant presence.

Maupassant had just returned from his travels.

"I drove Hervé to Montpellier," he told us. "He's in an asylum there. It was full of the most sordid and awful people. What we witnessed in Vidal's appalling establishment should have prepared me! But it was dreadful beyond comprehension."

He looked desperate.

"I will return for him tomorrow. I can't leave him there. I can't sleep. I have decided that we will take the train to Paris on Tuesday, and I'll have him treated at Ville-Évrard. The place comes highly recommended to me by Dr. Blanche. He'll be better off there. Let us hope that he will regain his health soon enough."

"I will come to wave you off at the station," said Lola, looking suddenly sullen upon hearing of Maupassant's imminent departure.

"No need, *Belle Amie*," he said. "There will be my mother, my sister-in-law, the baby, the nanny. I won't be able to pay you any attention."

"It is of no matter, Guy. Don't worry. I'll stay on the bridge. It will be enough. I like to come and wave when you leave."

"And collect me when I return."

"Yes, I'm one of your most avid readers," she said and then laughed.

"If anyone ever made a reader out of you, they'd be a success, indeed, my dear!" he cried.

This exchange made me feel so cross on her behalf that I spilled my glass of Romanée-Conti 1865, which, in turn, caused a scandalized exclamation to fall from the marquis's lips.

"Oh no, Miss Fletcher! Don't blaspheme like that in front of me!"

Paul Antoine then told us that he had no inclination for his usual merry-go-round of a social life these days. "My father is in the worst of trouble. He had a stroke and is paralyzed on one side. The doctor has predicted a few more months, a year at most of life for him. It was a harsh winter in Cannes this year. I admit that his turn has come as a shock to me. I'm going to have to attempt to show some interest in the family business. I need to help my mother a little more."

"So, you will inherit?" asked Maupassant, always interested in any detail of which he might make use in a story.

"She showed me my father's will. There are conditions to my inheritance," he explained. "I'm trapped. If I am to inherit all the property, workshops, income from his factories and flower plantations, I must marry within two years of my father's death and then produce an heir within the year. Can you believe it? Me? Marry? How will I do that? What an old goat he is! There's no way out of it. But I'm still so saddened to see him in such a sickly state."

There was a silence, and I cast a discreet glance at Lola. It was as if I could hear the workings of her brain. She knew I was looking at her as she lowered her eyes and straightened her back slightly. To give herself some countenance, she leaned over and grabbed Sherry, whom she gently placed on her lap.

Nothing had escaped Anna, who had quietly returned, nor indeed Maupassant. The girl raised her eyebrows.

I turned to Paul Antoine and asked in an innocent tone, "You'll have to make a good marriage, I suppose. Someone of fortune and rank?"

He stared at me maliciously. "The will does not specify anything of the kind. Only the word *woman* is used."

I decided a change of subject might be in order. Lola placed the cat on the floor and stood to position a roll on her phonograph. The marquis followed her and embraced her tenderly.

Murier stared at them and then quickly looked away. I noticed envy in his eyes, followed by what I assumed to be resignation. Or regret. I felt a furious empathy for him. We were both rivals in a love we would never come to know.

A nasal voice came out of the amplifier, and we all sang together. As we laughed, I spotted something, and I saw it had not escaped Murier's keen eye either—an exchange of glances between Paul Antoine and Lola. Paul Antoine's was mischievous. Lola's was filled with questions, expectation . . . and caution too.

No. Surely, they wouldn't . . .

A Note from the Author

For those who'd like to delve a little deeper into the story, I want to let you in on some of the details I uncovered during my research. You can also visit my blog, where you'll find ample information on the history of Cannes. Why not take some time and enjoy a walk through the Cannes of old?

Let me start by talking about the locations I used in the book, starting with Lola Deslys's villa, Les Pavots.

I wanted her to live in a house that was neither too sumptuous nor too expensive. Of course, it had to have existed at the time the story is set, so that I could be inspired by it. I needed to fully contemplate her home, to imagine Gabriella, Lola, and Maupassant passing through its gate and leaning over the balcony.

For a long time, I wandered aimlessly around Cannes, creating potential routes that Lola might take: How would she get to the theater, the hotel, the old town to see her mother, Maupassant, and so on? This is how I came to understand that the train station would be an essential and strategic position for Lola. From the station came and went rich and influential men, and so it was vital that she could see the arrival of trains and understand when and where all the winterers, as announced in the local newspaper, would be staying.

This worked out perfectly, for the district just above Cannes station was developed around 1883 thanks to an unprecedented real estate operation: the construction of Boulevard de la Foncière, now Boulevard Carnot (it was renamed upon President Sadi Carnot's assassination in 1894).

Houses, buildings, streets, and boulevards were built at incredible speed, and it fast became a new, fashionable, and lively district—exactly where Lola would have liked Eugène to have her house built.

The house that inspired me still exists, now stuck between other, newer buildings at the corner of Avenue Saint-Nicolas and Rue Marius Aune. It has all the characteristics of the period cottage houses that were built in Cannes during the last quarter of the nineteenth century. In fact, Maupassant's very last place of residence in Cannes, in 1892, the Chalet de l'Isère, was built in the same style. It, too, still exists and is currently a charming little hotel that stands at 42 Avenue de Grasse.

The size of Les Pavots seemed perfect to me, for it would allow Lola to spread her wings there. It had an ideal view of the station and was next to the Hôtel Central, a very recently built palace at the time, now the Lycée Bristol. This palace was given to the city and later became a school in 1934.

The real estate boom on Boulevard Carnot rapidly turned into a Lehman Brothers–style disaster, and not a soul saw it coming. It was this scandal that guided me when plotting *The Shattered Portrait*. The character of Henri Cousin was inspired by the real banker Henri Germain, founder of Crédit Lyonnais and instigator of the Boulevard de la Foncière project.

The second theme of the novel—the fashion of "homes" for the insane, a result of the 1838 law imposing that every French department is required to have a public establishment specially designed to receive and treat the insane—led me to make use of another emblematic location in Cannes, "Le Grand Jardin."

This property, situated on one of the two Lérins Islands, Île Sainte-Marguerite, to the south, just opposite Île Saint-Honorat, has always been something of a mystery for the people of Cannes, for it stands invisible to them, surrounded by large walls built at the request of Cardinal de Richelieu. It is the only private property on Île Sainte-Marguerite. It is planted with rare species of flora and had always been used as a resort. It has belonged successively to kings, including Louis XIV, various dukes and counts, governors, a famous nineteenth-century actress, a sculptor, a real estate developer, and members of the bourgeoisie. Owned by an Indian billionaire since 2008, it was put up for sale again in July 2018.

It's the perfect place to imagine an asylum, and so I took the plunge. As for how it would function, visiting the house of Dr. Blanche and listening to the testimony of Albert Londres helped me enormously.

Many nineteenth-century artists with syphilis went mad. It was not known at the time that the disease inevitably led to such an end. The big question then was whether genius necessarily implied madness or whether it was the other way around.

The Maupassant family paid a high price for this sexually transmitted disease, since Maupassant's younger brother, Hervé, died in the asylum for the insane in Lyon-Bron and Maupassant's own life came to an end in the famous Dr. Blanche's house because of it.

Part of the novel's action also takes place on Maupassant's sailboat. In 1888, the year in which *The Shattered Portrait* is set, Maupassant is the owner of a sailboat, the *Bel-Ami*, which he sometimes anchored in Antibes and sometimes in Cannes. Originally, the *Flamberge*, a thin, eleven-meter-long small yacht known as a "cutter," measuring nine tons, belonged to his writer friend Paul Saunière, who had once been Dumas's secretary. Flamberge was the name of the best-selling bookstore in a novel by Saunière.

Saunière donated it to the Cercle Nautique de Nice, which used her for several regattas before selling her to a ruined gambler, the Count of Lagrange. The count soon grew tired of her and abandoned her for a while at the Ardouin shipyard in Antibes. She went by the name of

Audacieux (*The Bold*) when Maupassant finally found her, purchased her, and renamed her the *Bel-Ami*.

He bought her for eighteen hundred francs. Her hull was tapered and her sail wide. Eight people could fit on board even though there were only four berths for passengers. Two experienced sailors formed the crew, Bernard and Raymond. They were recommended by Muterse, Maupassant's friend and fellow lover of the sea.

Maupassant was filled with pride every time he climbed on board. The teak deck, the solid rigging, the copper bar—he paid for everything thanks to money from his novel *Bel-Ami*. This magnificent sailboat really was the symbol of his literary success, his childhood dream come true.

As you stroll along the old port in Cannes, you can allow your mind to wander, as I did, thinking of the time when the *Bel-Ami* was moored there, and picturing the Norman silhouette of the writer, jumping with an agile step up onto the bridge. Sometimes, I like to think that I'm not merely imagining this scene, but that he's still here, among us.

Maupassant loved Cannes and the Mediterranean: the colors, the smells, the flowers. It was on its shores that he lived his final moments of freedom.

> "I float in a winged home that is rocked and cradled; pretty as a bird, tiny as a nest, softer than a hammock, wandering over the waters at the caprice of the wind, independent and free!"
>
> —*Guy de Maupassant, Sur l'eau*

Acknowledgments

Writing a novel doesn't start the day you sit down at your computer to type out the first chapter. It is the result of a long process, and throughout this journey, the people you meet are of vital importance.

That is why I would, first of all, like to thank Maggy Wollner, with whom I facilitated writing workshops on Cannes during the belle époque.

For this, the second volume of the trilogy, I again spent long hours at the Cannes municipal archives. I would like to thank Josephine Saïa, who guided my historical research on Cannes, as well as all the people in the archives. They all welcomed me with a smile and guided me through the jungle of municipal decrees, real estate funds, and local newspapers of the time. The association (Friends of Cannes Archives) was also very helpful. Thanks to Jacqueline Leconte and Liliane Scotti and also to the friends of Victor Tuby's mill.

My beta readers have given so much of their time. Thanks to Julien Biri, Lionel Cavalli, Catherine de Palma, Danielle Boulois, Amanda Castello, Xavier Théoleyre, Hélène Babouot, and Brigitte Aubert, who each provided their unique perspectives and feelings.

I warmly thank Claude Marro, historian, former professor of history at the Stanislas Institute, vice president of the Scientific and Literary Society of Cannes, who not only provided access to the annals of the society (of which Maupassant himself had been a member), but who took the time to review the first draft of the novel to note any anachronisms in terms of the history of Cannes.

Similarly, Noëlle Benhamou, a specialist in nineteenth-century literature and, particularly, Maupassant (she created the Maupassantiana website), was kind enough to reread the novel to check whether everything about Maupassant was right and whether everything I had invented might have been likely.

It is Laurent Bettoni to whom I owe great thanks. After his proofreading, I was able to rework certain parts of the novel. I thank him wholeheartedly.

I am lucky to have met Gabriella Page-Fort and Jeffrey Belle. Without them, this novel would not exist; and my gratitude is infinite. I thank my editor, Sara Bellver Mares, for the French version, for it is a pleasure to be supported by her.

About the Author

Alice Quinn lives on the French Riviera, surrounded by her family and cats. After achieving great success with the Rosie Maldonne mystery series, featuring *Queen of the Masquerade, Queen of the Hide Out,* and *Queen of the Trailer Park*—which was a #1 bestseller in France—she changed her register and plunged with delight into historical intrigue in Cannes in the belle époque, an era full of intriguing contrasts. *The Shattered Portrait* is the second novel in her Belle Époque Mystery trilogy. For more information about the author, visit her at www.alice-quinn.com.